******

# The Historical Experiment
## by A. Biasio
### *Published by Biasio Press*
#####

ISBN: 979-8-230-86666-4
Published by Biasio Press


Published by Biasio Press

In the heart of present-day London, amidst the bustling streets and timeless landmarks, a quiet civil servant finds her life irreversibly upended. Without warning, she is abducted and thrust into the shadowy confines of a classified government project—one shrouded in secrecy and ambition. The initiative, ominously referred to as **The Historical Experiment**, is an unprecedented endeavour: it seeks to assemble individuals of European origin from various eras, all brought together to explore the limits of human adaptability and resilience across time.

The program's true intent, however, is far from altruistic. At its core lies a calculated strategy to shape the future of society by mastering how individuals from disparate time periods can acclimate—or fail—to contemporary life. For the protagonist, her assignment is both unique and unsettling. She has been chosen as the "litmus test," a critical player in the government's grand vision. Her task is deceptively simple yet fraught with challenges: to integrate, guide, and ultimately facilitate the assimilation of a single subject entrusted to her care.

But this is no ordinary subject. Codenamed **"Bering,"** her charge is Braham Beckett, an enigmatic army officer whose lineage traces back to a storied chapter of history. Beckett is a descendant of the intrepid pioneers who, in 1747, joined Vitus Bering's ill-fated Alaskan expedition—a journey etched in the annals of exploration as a tale of ambition, endurance, and tragedy. Pulled from his own era, Braham carries with him the rugged pragmatism and indomitable spirit of his ancestors, but also the scars of a time where survival demanded both ingenuity and sacrifice.

As these two lives collide, the experiment spirals into an intricate web of alliances, conflicts, and revelations. The protagonist must navigate not only the challenges of acclimating Braham to a world that is both alien and overwhelming to him but also the growing unease about her role in a project steeped in moral ambiguity. What begins as a government-sanctioned study into human adaptability evolves into a deeper exploration of identity, belonging, and the very nature of humanity itself.

Together, they must face the question: Can the past truly coexist with the present, or will the experiment prove that some boundaries were never meant to be crossed?

## Chapter 1: A glimpse into ordinary

Eleanor blinked against the harsh light, disoriented and groggy. Her head throbbed, and her wrists ached from the tight restraints. She tried to move, but her body felt heavy and sluggish. Panic gnawed at her as she realized she had no idea where she was or how she had gotten there.

A metallic voice echoed in the confined space. "Welcome, Eleanor," it said, devoid of emotion. "You are now part of Project Chronos."

Fear turned to confusion. Project Chronos? What was that? She tried to remember the events leading up to her abduction, but her mind was a blank. The last thing she recalled was leaving work and heading home.

Suddenly, the restraints released, and Eleanor was free to move. She cautiously sat up and looked around. The room was stark and minimalist, devoid of any personal touches. A single, narrow bed occupied most of the space, and a small table with a chair sat in one corner.

A door at the far end of the room slid open, revealing a corridor bathed in an eerie blue glow. A figure stepped out, their face obscured by deep shadows. "Come," the figure said, their voice echoing in the silent hallway. "It's time to meet the others."

Eleanor hesitated, her heart pounding in her chest. She had no choice but to follow. As she walked down the corridor, a sense of dread washed over her. She knew that her life was about to change forever.

Eleanor Pritchard was a creature of habit. Every morning, her alarm would buzz at precisely 7:15, jolting her from the comfort of her small, rented flat in South London. She'd follow the same routine: a quick shower, a hastily prepared breakfast of cereal and fruit, and a commute on the crowded Underground to the Ministry of Culture.

Her job as a junior policy analyst was, by her own admission, "incredibly dull." Days were spent poring over endless reports, drafting memos, and attending meetings that seemed to go on forever. Eleanor often found herself daydreaming about escaping the monotony of her life, perhaps traveling to a far-off land or pursuing a hobby she'd always been too afraid to try.

But Eleanor was a pragmatic woman. She knew that her steady government job, while uninspiring, provided a sense of security that she valued. And so, she continued to dutifully fulfill her duties, even as a part of her longed for something more.

Little did she know that her ordinary life was about to be turned upside down. A storm was brewing, one that would sweep her away from the familiar and into a world of mystery and danger.The civil servant's abduction marks the beginning of a thrilling journey through time and culture, as she becomes an unwitting participant in a government experiment that challenges the boundaries of human adaptation. As she grapples with her new reality, she finds herself forming an unlikely alliance with Braham Beckett, whose ancestral connection to the ill-fated Bering expedition adds a layer of historical intrigue to their shared predicament. Together, they must navigate the complexities of their roles within the project while uncovering the true motives behind the government's ambitious and potentially dangerous undertaking.

One morning had changed Eleanor's destiny and routine: she had arrived late at the subway, having to stand the entire journey with her hands clinging to the support bars. She longed to savor a hot coffee and a donut at her office, but fate had other plans for her that day.
Eleanor rushed through the bustling streets of South London, her thoughts consumed with the typical worries of being late. She finally reached the Ministry of Culture, only to bump into someone in her haste. Papers flew everywhere, and she heard a deep voice apologize, "I'm so sorry. Are you okay?"
She looked up and met the eyes of Brandon, a tall, handsome man with dark skin and captivating black eyes that seemed to reflect the depths of the universe. His genuine concern made her heart flutter. "I'm fine, really," she said, trying to gather the scattered documents.
Brandon crouched down to help her, his presence calming her nerves. "I'm Brandon, by the way," he introduced himself with a warm smile. "You look like you could use a coffee. How about we grab one together?"

Eleanor couldn't help but smile back, her stress momentarily forgotten. "I'd like that," she replied.

As they walked to the nearest café, Eleanor found herself inexplicably drawn to Brandon. She loved the smell of his skin, the warmth of his smile, and the kindness in his eyes. Over coffee and donuts, they talked about everything—from their jobs to their dreams, and Eleanor felt a connection she hadn't experienced in a long time.

Brandon shared his own story, revealing that he worked at a nonprofit organization aimed at preserving cultural heritage. His passion for his work was infectious, and Eleanor found herself captivated by his dedication. As they chatted, she felt her usual routine slipping away, replaced by the possibility of something new and exciting.

Little did she know that this chance meeting would be the start of a significant change in her life, one that would intertwine her fate with Brandon's in ways she could never have imagined. As they exchanged contact information and bid each other goodbye, Eleanor felt a sense of anticipation and hope for the future.

Her life was about to be turned upside down, but for the first time, she welcomed the change with open arms. Brandon had unknowingly become a catalyst for her transformation, and together, they would face the mysteries and challenges that lay ahead.

Eleanor discovered an unexpected and exhilarating world of love and passion with Brandon. Their relationship grew deeper, filled with spontaneous adventures and intimate moments that made her feel more alive than she had ever felt before. The smell of his skin, the intensity of his gaze, and the warmth of his presence became a sanctuary from her otherwise mundane existence.

But as their connection intensified, Eleanor began to notice unsettling changes in her life. What started as a subtle feeling of being watched turned into a persistent sense of paranoia. She would catch glimpses of shadowy figures out of the corner of her eye and hear whispers that seemed to follow her.

At first, she dismissed it as nerves—an overactive imagination fueled by the excitement of her new romance. But the feeling grew stronger, and soon, Eleanor couldn't shake the sense that she was in danger.

One evening, as she and Brandon relaxed on the couch, she confided in him. "Brandon, I think something's wrong. I've been feeling like I'm being watched. I know it sounds crazy, but I can't shake the feeling."

Brandon's brow furrowed with concern. "Have you noticed anything specific? Anyone following you?"

Eleanor shook her head. "Not exactly, but I think it might be related to something at work. There were some documents I reviewed a few weeks ago—sensitive information about an ongoing investigation. Ever since then, things have felt off."

Brandon listened intently, his protective instincts kicking in. "We'll figure this out, Eleanor. You're not alone in this."

As the days passed, Eleanor's unease grew. She began to see signs that her fears were not unfounded. One evening, as she walked home from work, a black car followed her at a slow pace. When she turned to confront it, the car sped away. Her heart raced, and she quickened her pace, eager to get home to the safety of Brandon's arms.

Eleanor's suspicions were confirmed when she received an anonymous note slipped under her door. The message was clear and chilling: "Stop digging where you don't belong."

Panicked, she showed the note to Brandon. "What am I going to do? I don't even know who to trust anymore."

Brandon's expression hardened. "We need to find out what they want. We can't let them intimidate you."

Together, they began to piece together the clues. Eleanor realized that her discovery of sensitive information at work had put her in the crosshairs of powerful and dangerous individuals. Her life was at risk, not because of her relationship with Brandon, but because she had stumbled upon a truth that others wanted to keep hidden.

Determined to protect her, Brandon reached out to his network of contacts, using his resources at the nonprofit organization to uncover more information. As they dug deeper, they uncovered a web of corruption and deceit that stretched far beyond what Eleanor had initially suspected.

Their journey was fraught with danger, but Eleanor found strength in her love for Brandon and the support he provided. Together, they navigated the treacherous waters, determined to expose the truth and protect each other from the shadows that threatened their lives.

Eleanor's life had indeed been turned upside down, but she faced the challenges with newfound courage. The storm that had swept her away from her ordinary existence now became a crucible in which her true strength and resilience were forged. And through it all, Brandon remained her anchor, guiding her through the darkness and into the light.

## Chapter 2: The Vanishing Act

Eleanor and Brandon had settled into a comfortable routine. Their weekly escapes became a sanctuary, a reprieve from the world's chaos. They would explore the city, discover new cafes, and share laughter over simple pleasures. Their bond grew stronger with each passing day, and Eleanor felt a sense of contentment she hadn't known before.
Yet, despite the happiness she found in Brandon's presence, the feeling of being watched never left her. It was always there, lurking at the edge of her consciousness, like a dark cloud on a sunny day. The sense of unease only intensified when she began to notice a peculiar figure shadowing her movements.
Every time Eleanor stepped outside her usual routine, she would catch a glimpse of him—an old man with a strange disfigurement on his face and a long black jacket. His presence was unsettling, and no matter where she went, he seemed to be there, watching her with an intensity that made her skin crawl.
One evening, as Eleanor and Brandon were leaving their favourite café, she spotted the old man standing across the street. His eyes bore into hers, and a shiver ran down her spine. She gripped Brandon's arm tighter. "Brandon, he's there again," she whispered, her voice tinged with fear.
Brandon followed her gaze, his expression turning serious. "We need to find out who he is and why he's following you," he said resolutely. "Let's not go home just yet. We need to shake him off."
They walked briskly, taking random turns and doubling back on their route in an attempt to lose the old man. But no matter what they did, he seemed to always reappear, like a ghost haunting their steps. Finally, they ducked into a small alleyway and hid behind a dumpster, holding their breath as the old man walked past, oblivious to their presence.
"We can't keep doing this," Eleanor said, her voice trembling. "I feel like I'm going insane."
Brandon hugged her tightly. "We're going to figure this out. You're not alone in this."

The next day at work, Eleanor found it difficult to concentrate. Her mind kept drifting back to the old man and the strange note she had received. Her paranoia was growing, and she knew she had to get to the bottom of it.

That evening, she decided to dig through her old files, searching for any clue that might explain the unwanted attention. As she sifted through countless documents, a particular set of files caught her eye. They were records from an investigation she had reviewed a few months ago, containing sensitive information about a clandestine government project known only as "The Shadow Initiative."

Her heart raced as she read through the details. The project involved covert operations, surveillance, and the use of advanced technology to manipulate political outcomes. The more she read, the clearer it became that she had stumbled upon something far more dangerous than she could have ever imagined.

Suddenly, there was a knock at her door. Startled, Eleanor quickly hid the files and opened the door to find Brandon standing there, concern etched on his face. "I think we need to talk," he said.

Eleanor let him in and explained what she had found. Brandon listened intently, his expression growing graver by the minute. "This explains a lot," he said. "We need to be very careful. If they know you've seen these documents, they'll stop at nothing to silence you."

As they discussed their next steps, neither of them noticed the shadowy figure standing outside, watching them through the window. The old man with the disfigured face had found them once again, and his presence was a chilling reminder that they were in far more danger than they realized.

Eleanor's ordinary life had been shattered, and she was now entangled in a web of conspiracy and peril. With Brandon by her side, she would have to navigate this treacherous path, uncover the truth behind The Shadow Initiative, and protect herself from the shadowy organization that was determined to keep their secrets hidden at any cost.

Only the cold hand of Brandon could give Eleanor back her security, her full presence, her sincerity.

One day, as Eleanor was returning from the subway, she tripped on a raised sidewalk and fell heavily to the ground. Her clothes were covered in dirt, and she felt a sting on her knees. Frustrated and embarrassed, she decided to go back to her apartment to change since it was only four blocks away.

Eleanor called the office to inform them of her delay and then headed back home. As she approached her apartment gate, she felt a strange sense of unease. Pushing the thought aside, she stepped through the gate, only to notice a huge black Mercedes van parked conspicuously nearby. Before she could react, she felt a sudden, sharp blow to the back of her head. The world spun around her, and she fell forward, the last thing she heard before darkness consumed her was the sound of someone swearing. "Oh no," she thought, but then she heard nothing more.

When Eleanor regained consciousness, she found herself in a dimly lit room, her hands and feet bound to a chair. Panic surged through her, but she forced herself to stay calm. Her mind raced as she tried to recall what had happened.

The door to the room creaked open, and the old man with the disfigured face and long black jacket stepped inside, accompanied by a burly man who seemed to be his muscle. The old man approached her, his eyes cold and calculating.

"Ah, Eleanor," he said, his voice dripping with condescension. "You've become quite the nuisance, poking your nose where it doesn't belong."

Eleanor's heart pounded in her chest. "What do you want from me?" she demanded, trying to sound braver than she felt.

The old man smiled, a chilling sight. "Information, of course. You stumbled upon something you shouldn't have, and now we need to make sure you don't cause any more trouble."

Eleanor's mind raced. She had to stay strong, had to find a way out of this. But just as her thoughts began to spiral, the door burst open, and Brandon charged in, his face set in grim determination.

With swift, precise movements, Brandon disarmed the burly man and incapacitated him. The old man, taken by surprise, stumbled back, giving Brandon the chance to untie Eleanor.

"Are you okay?" Brandon asked, his voice filled with concern.

Eleanor nodded, tears of relief streaming down her face. "I am now," she whispered, clutching onto him.

Brandon guided her out of the room and through a labyrinth of corridors, their footsteps echoing in the silence. They made their way to an emergency exit and burst out into the night air, gasping for breath.

As they escaped into the shadows, Eleanor knew that her life would never be the same again. But with Brandon by her side, she felt a renewed sense of strength and determination. Together, they would uncover the truth behind The Shadow Initiative and bring those responsible to justice, no matter the cost.

As Brandon and Eleanor sprinted through the shadowy streets, their relief at escaping quickly evaporated when a group of men armed with Kalashnikovs emerged from the darkness, blocking their path. The men were clearly military, their stern expressions and disciplined stances leaving no doubt about their intent.

One of the soldiers, a tall man with a scar running down his cheek, stepped forward. His accent was thick and unmistakably Russian. "Stop right there," he commanded. Brandon and Eleanor froze, their breaths coming in quick, shallow bursts.

"Who are you?" Brandon demanded, trying to keep his voice steady despite the fear coursing through him.

The Russian soldier looked at them with cold, calculating eyes. "That does not matter. What matters is what you have seen," he said, his tone leaving no room for argument. "You must understand, you cannot trust anyone. Not your government, not your friends, no one."

Eleanor's heart pounded in her chest. "What do you mean?" she asked, her voice barely above a whisper.

The soldier's gaze hardened. "There are forces at play here that you cannot comprehend. You have stumbled upon something very dangerous. For your own safety, you must forget everything you have seen and stay away from this."

Brandon stepped forward, his protective instincts flaring. "And if we don't?" he challenged.

The soldier's expression remained unyielding. "Then you will find yourselves in grave danger. This is not a game. If you value your lives, you will heed my warning."

The group of soldiers began to close in, their weapons at the ready. Brandon and Eleanor exchanged a quick, fearful glance. They knew they were outmatched and outgunned. Reluctantly, they raised their hands in surrender.

"Fine, we'll go," Brandon said, his voice tense with frustration. "But we won't forget this."

The Russian soldier nodded, his eyes never leaving theirs. "Remember, trust no one." With that, he signalled his men to stand down, and they slowly retreated into the shadows, leaving Brandon and Eleanor standing in the empty street, shaken and bewildered.

As they made their way back to safety, Eleanor couldn't shake the soldier's words from her mind. The world around her had become a web of secrets and lies, and she didn't know who she could trust. But one thing was certain—she and Brandon would have to navigate this treacherous path together, no matter the cost.

Eleanor and Brandon sat in the dimly lit prison cell, their hands and feet bound tightly. The cold, damp air added to their sense of despair. Through the small barred window, they could hear the Russian soldiers talking about their victims, their voices echoing through the corridors. Eleanor's mind raced as she tried to make sense of their situation. She glanced at Brandon, who was deep in thought, his expression mirroring her own sadness and frustration. "How far away from the city do you think we are?" she whispered, her voice barely audible.
Brandon shook his head, his eyes scanning the room for any clues. "I don't know, but we need to figure it out. If we can understand where we are, we might have a chance to escape."
Eleanor nodded, her mind working to piece together the fragments of information they had. The building was old, with thick stone walls and narrow hallways. The air was heavy with the scent of mildew and decay, suggesting that it hadn't been used for legitimate purposes in a long time. "We were in the van for at least an hour," Eleanor recalled. "But they could have taken a roundabout route to confuse us."
Brandon's eyes narrowed as he considered their options. "We need to listen carefully to what the soldiers are saying. They might slip up and give us a clue about our location."
As they sat in the cell, straining to hear the conversations outside, Eleanor couldn't help but feel a glimmer of hope. Despite the dire circumstances, she knew that with Brandon by her side, they had a fighting chance. They just needed to stay strong, stay vigilant, and find a way to turn the tables on their captors.

Eleanor and Brandon clung to each passing day, their bodies weakening with every meager meal slid between the bars. The food was hardly enough to sustain them—a watery gruel and stale bread that left their stomachs aching for more. The hours bled into each other, a monotonous rhythm of hunger, fatigue, and whispered strategies for escape. Their captors rarely spoke directly to them, but the muffled conversations and occasional bouts of laughter from the soldiers outside only deepened their sense of isolation.
One night, as they lay on the cold stone floor, Eleanor's eyes fluttered open to an unusual glow filtering through the barred window. At first,

she thought it was the moonlight, but the hue was off—a soft, eerie blue. She nudged Brandon awake, her heart racing.

"Do you see that?" she whispered, pointing to the faint glow beyond the window.

Brandon sat up, his eyes narrowing as he followed her gaze. The light pulsed rhythmically, casting strange shadows across the walls. Then, faint footsteps echoed through the corridor, unlike the heavy boots of their captors. These were lighter, almost ethereal.

"What the hell is that?" Brandon muttered, his voice barely above a breath.

Eleanor crawled closer to the bars, her pulse quickening. "I don't know… but it's coming closer."

As the glow intensified, strange figures emerged from the shadows. Their forms were hard to define, shifting and shimmering as though made of liquid light. The air grew thick with an unearthly hum, resonating in their bones. Eleanor's instinct was to recoil, but she couldn't tear her eyes away from the otherworldly beings.

The figures stopped in front of their cell, their glowing forms filling the space with a surreal brilliance. A wave of calm and dread washed over Eleanor simultaneously. One of the beings extended a hand—or what resembled a hand—toward them, and for a moment, the cold air felt warm, almost comforting.

Then, everything shifted.

The hum grew louder, a symphony of strange tones that vibrated through their very core. Eleanor and Brandon clutched their heads, a sharp pain searing through their temples. The room spun violently, and the glow consumed their vision until there was nothing but blinding blue.

Eleanor's final thought before succumbing to the darkness was a fleeting one: *This is it. This is either salvation… or the end.*

When they awoke, the world was different.

## Chapter 3: A New Dawn

Eleanor's eyes fluttered open to a disorienting, vibrating hum. Her vision blurred before slowly sharpening to reveal the cramped interior of a van—a Chrysler, gray and unremarkable. She was completely restrained, her arms and legs bound tightly to the seat. The cold metal of the restraints bit into her skin, sending a wave of panic coursing through her veins. She struggled against them, but they didn't budge. The faint scent of motor oil and damp fabric filled the air, mingling with her mounting fear.

Through the van's windshield, Eleanor caught sight of a surreal landscape, one that seemed ripped straight out of a dream—or a nightmare. In the distance, nestled in the depths of a colossal canyon, was a strange structure unlike anything she had ever seen. A series of massive, interconnected domes spread out like pearls on a string, their white surfaces gleaming against the rugged, earthy tones of the canyon walls. Smoke—or perhaps steam—billowed from chimneys jutting out of the domes, curling into the crisp air and adding an eerie veil to the scene.

She blinked, her mind struggling to process the alien beauty of the sight. The buildings glowed faintly under the pale daylight, their pristine surfaces untouched by time or decay. The arrangement of the domes was intricate, almost too precise to be human-made. They were connected by thin, lattice-like walkways suspended high above the canyon floor. The overall effect was both mesmerizing and unsettling, as though the structures didn't belong to this world.

"What… is this place?" she whispered to herself, her voice hoarse.

Her captors weren't visible. The driver's seat and passenger seat ahead were empty, the van idling in eerie silence. Eleanor's gaze darted to the side window, but the view offered no further clues—only more of the canyon and its impossibly alien neighbourhood.

The smoke rising from the chimneys danced lazily, but there was something unnatural about it. It seemed alive, curling and spiralling in deliberate patterns before dispersing into the air. The more she stared at the scene, the more the sense of mystery deepened. This was no ordinary canyon, and this structure wasn't the work of any human architect she knew.

She heard a faint hiss behind her, followed by the sound of movement. Her pulse quickened as footsteps approached the van. She craned her neck as best she could, trying to catch a glimpse of who—or what—was coming. The rear doors creaked open, and the bright light of the canyon flooded the van's interior. Squinting against the glare, Eleanor's heart skipped a beat.

Two figures stood silhouetted against the light. Their forms were humanoid but taller, leaner, and somehow... wrong. Their skin glistened like polished marble, and their eyes—large, dark, and reflective—studied her with an unsettling intensity. They wore flowing white garments that seemed to shimmer and ripple like liquid under the light. One of them stepped forward, inclining its head as if studying her. Its voice, when it came, was soft and melodic, yet completely alien. It spoke in a language she couldn't understand, its syllables resonating like a song trapped between a whisper and a chime. The other being moved to the side of the van, producing a device that emitted a faint hum.

"Where am I?" Eleanor demanded, finding her voice despite the fear constricting her throat. "What do you want with me?"

The first figure tilted its head further, as if considering her words. Then, it reached out a hand—slender, with too many joints—and touched her forehead gently. The moment its fingers made contact, Eleanor's mind was flooded with images: the domes, a pulsing light within their core, machines that seemed to grow and breathe, and countless figures like these beings moving through the halls of the alien city.

Eleanor gasped as a final image burned into her mind: Brandon, unconscious, being carried toward the largest dome at the centre of the canyon.

Before she could scream or resist, the figure withdrew its hand, and the world around her dissolved into white light once more.

Eleanor groaned as she regained consciousness, her head pounding and her limbs heavy. The sensation of cold metal against her skin jolted her fully awake, and she realized she was strapped to a chair—no, a medical chair, with restraints pinning her arms, legs, and torso in place. Her heart raced as she struggled against the bindings, but they held firm.

She scanned her surroundings. The room was stark white, illuminated by an intense, sterile light that seemed to come from everywhere and nowhere at once. Directly in front of her stood several figures clad in strange uniforms—white suits that shimmered faintly under the light. Their faces were obscured by helmets that glowed softly, and through the translucent material of the helmets, Eleanor could barely make out vague, shifting features—lips that didn't seem quite right, as if they were still learning how to form.

The figures spoke among themselves in a slow, deliberate tone. Their voices were melodic yet disjointed, with an uncanny rhythm that sent shivers down her spine. She strained to make out the words, but the language was unlike anything she had ever heard. It was filled with elongated syllables and sharp, sudden clicks that seemed to resonate in the air.

Her gaze shifted to the opposite side of the room, where Brandon was restrained in a similar chair. His head was slumped forward, and his breathing was slow and laboured. Panic bubbled in her chest.

"Brandon!" she called out, her voice hoarse and trembling.

One of the figures turned toward her, the faint outline of its lips shifting into what might have been a smile—or a grimace. It stepped closer, its movements fluid yet eerily precise. Eleanor froze as the figure leaned in, its face inches from hers. Through the hazy helmet, she saw the lips move, forming sounds that resembled speech but were unintelligible. The voice, though soft, carried an unsettling weight, like a whisper amplified in her mind.

Another figure approached, holding a device that pulsed with blue light. The two figures exchanged words, their tones growing more deliberate. Eleanor caught fragments of their conversation—words that seemed to ripple in her mind rather than her ears.

"...assimilation... group... incomplete..."

One of them gestured toward her and then toward Brandon. The others nodded slowly; their movements synchronized. The leader of the group turned back to her, its helmet glowing brighter. A voice, clearer now, echoed in her head.

"You... will join."

"Join what?" Eleanor snapped, her fear fuelling a sudden burst of defiance. "What are you doing to us?"

The figure tilted its head, as though considering her question. It raised a long, jointed hand and tapped the side of its helmet. A series of images flooded Eleanor's mind: rows of humans seated in similar chairs, their faces blank and lifeless; towering domes filled with machinery and light; a glowing core deep within the largest dome, pulsing like a heart.

Then came the words again, spoken directly into her mind: "You... will be... part of the whole. Improved. United."

"No!" Eleanor shouted, pulling against her restraints with renewed vigor. Her voice cracked as she turned her head toward Brandon. "Brandon, wake up! Please, wake up!"

The figures turned their attention to Brandon, who was beginning to stir. His eyes fluttered open, and confusion flashed across his face before morphing into fear as he took in his surroundings.

"What's... happening?" he mumbled, his voice weak.

"They're trying to do something to us," Eleanor said, her voice urgent. "They want to... 'unite' us with some group."

Brandon's eyes locked onto hers, a flicker of determination cutting through his fear. "We're not letting that happen," he said, his voice low but firm.

The figures around them continued their discussion, their voices growing louder and more agitated. One of them pointed at Brandon, and another adjusted its glowing device. Their vague lips moved uncertainly, as if debating their next move, but their body language betrayed no hesitation. Eleanor's chest tightened as the realization sank in: whatever they were planning, it wasn't going to end well.

The leader stepped forward again, raising the device and pointing it toward Eleanor's head. A faint hum filled the air, growing louder with each passing second. Eleanor's pulse thundered in her ears.

And then, in an act of sheer desperation, she screamed, "You'll never break us!"

Brandon followed suit, shouting, "We're stronger than you think!"

The sound of their voices seemed to startle the figures, who paused mid-action. The leader hesitated, its glowing helmet flickering momentarily. For the first time, Eleanor thought she saw uncertainty in their movements—uncertainty that might be their only chance.

Eleanor's world dissolved into a suffocating blackness. The last thing she remembered was the sharp, precise pain of something piercing her skin near her jaw, followed by the sensation of a presence—an unfamiliar face, barely illuminated by a faint glow in the surrounding darkness, its expression unreadable. She tried to scream, to resist, but her body betrayed her, falling limp as her consciousness slipped away.

When she awoke, her body felt strangely weightless, as though the very air around her was pressing her down and lifting her up at the same time. She blinked against the soft, diffused light filtering into the dome-like room. The ceiling arched high above her, patterned with intricate, glowing designs that pulsed faintly, resembling constellations in an alien sky.

Eleanor sat up slowly, her body weak and trembling. She realized she was lying on a simple cot, its frame a metallic silver that reflected the light from above. Around her, dozens of other cots stretched in neat rows, each occupied by a person. She scanned the room anxiously. Everyone else was either asleep or lying still, their faces pale and slack, like statues caught mid-thought.

Her hand flew to her jaw, where she remembered feeling the sharp pain. There was no blood, no visible wound, but a slight ache lingered beneath the skin. She touched the area tentatively and felt a faint, metallic bump beneath the surface, small enough to go unnoticed but foreign enough to send a shiver down her spine.

Eleanor swung her legs over the edge of the cot and stood, her knees buckling slightly. For the first time in what felt like an eternity, she was unrestrained. No chains, no bindings—she was free. But the freedom felt hollow, its edges tinged with unease. She glanced at the others surrounding her. They were an odd group, their appearances varied but all somehow... wrong.

A tall man with sharp, angular features and unnaturally bright blue eyes sat cross-legged a few cots away, staring straight ahead as if lost in thought. Beside him, a woman with wild, silver-streaked hair muttered to herself, her hands twitching in small, precise movements that seemed almost mechanical. Near the edge of the dome, a child no older than ten sat silently, her wide eyes reflecting the glowing patterns above as she hugged her knees to her chest. Each face bore an expression of quiet desolation, as though they, too, were grappling with a reality they couldn't fully comprehend.

Eleanor took a cautious step forward, her bare feet brushing against the smooth, cool floor. The air inside the dome was still, almost unnervingly so, and carried a faint scent of ozone. The walls, like the ceiling, seemed to pulse faintly, as though the entire structure was alive.

"Where am I?" she whispered, her voice cracking in the oppressive silence.

The silver-haired woman turned her head sharply, her pale, almost translucent eyes locking onto Eleanor's. She tilted her head, studying her like one might examine a curious object.

"You're awake," the woman said, her voice low and rough, as though she hadn't spoken in years. She gestured vaguely to the room around them. "This is where they bring us. After they take... whatever they need."

Eleanor's stomach churned. "What do you mean? What did they take?"

The woman shrugged, her movements slow and deliberate. "Pieces of us. Memories. Maybe more. You'll feel it, eventually. The emptiness."

A cold dread settled over Eleanor. She glanced at the others again, this time noticing the subtle, almost imperceptible changes in their features—unnatural symmetry, overly bright eyes, and an eerie calm that seemed to cling to them like a second skin.

"Who are they?" Eleanor asked, her voice barely above a whisper.

The woman laughed, a hollow sound that echoed in the dome. "They don't have names. Not like us. But they call this place *The Nursery*. For building... something new. Something better."

Eleanor's throat tightened. "And us? What are we supposed to be?"

The man with the bright blue eyes spoke for the first time, his voice cold and monotone. "We are the foundation. The raw material for their perfection."

Eleanor's legs wobbled, and she sank back onto the cot, her mind racing. She thought of Brandon, her heart aching with a mix of worry and desperation.

"Where's Brandon?" she demanded, looking between the strangers. "He was with me—another man. Dark hair, brown eyes. Where is he?"

The silver-haired woman's expression softened, but only slightly. "If he's not here, he's somewhere else. Maybe in the domes. Or maybe..." She trailed off, her gaze dropping to the floor.

"Maybe what?" Eleanor pressed, her voice rising.

The man turned to her, his unblinking eyes piercing. "Maybe he's already become part of the whole."

Before Eleanor could respond, the dome filled with a soft hum, and the glowing patterns on the walls brightened. The air seemed to shift, growing heavier, charged with an energy that made her skin prickle. The others sat up straighter, their movements synchronized as though responding to an unspoken command.

And then, as the hum grew louder, the only thought racing through Eleanor's mind was clear and urgent: *I need to find Brandon—and I need to get us out of here.*

But there was no trace of Brandon.

The afternoon dragged on, yet time felt fluid, slipping through Eleanor's fingers as she tried to piece together what had happened. The others in the room seemed to awaken fully as the hours passed, shaking off their initial stupor. Slowly, they began to interact, their movements and words uncoordinated at first but growing more purposeful with time.

Before long, the atmosphere in the circular room changed. It became charged with an almost frenetic energy as the group started to assemble in the centre of the dome. Eleanor, still seated on her cot near the edge of the room, watched warily. In less than half an hour, the quiet murmurs had transformed into a deafening cacophony of voices, each member speaking with rapid urgency. The acoustics of the dome amplified their chatter, making it almost unbearable.

Eleanor stood cautiously; her legs still shaky. She approached the group, hesitant but curious, drawn in by the sheer intensity of their interaction. There were twelve of them, each unique in appearance but eerily similar in demeanour. Despite the seeming chaos of their conversations, there was a strange coherence to it all. The group seemed to operate as a single organism, their voices overlapping yet harmonizing, their movements distinct but synchronized.

The silver-haired woman from earlier turned to Eleanor, her pale eyes narrowing slightly. "You're not connected yet," she said bluntly, her voice cutting through the noise.

"Connected?" Eleanor asked, frowning. "What do you mean?"

The woman gestured to the group. "It's like a web. Once you're in, you'll feel it. The thoughts, the patterns... it's how they've made us. No chains, no locks, but this—" she tapped the side of her head—"it's stronger than steel."

Eleanor's stomach churned. She had noticed something odd about the group's behaviour, a subtle but undeniable unity in their actions. They finished each other's sentences, anticipated each other's movements, and reacted as though guided by an invisible thread. It was unsettling.

She took a step back, her instincts screaming at her to keep her distance. "I don't want to be connected," she said firmly.

The silver-haired woman smirked, though there was no warmth in it. "You don't have a choice, darling. You've already been marked. You felt it, didn't you? That spike in your face? It's not just a mark—it's the key. They're letting you adjust before they bring you fully into the fold."

Eleanor's hand flew to her jaw, her fingers brushing the faint bump beneath her skin. She felt her breath quicken, her heart pounding in her chest. "How do I stop it?" she demanded, her voice trembling.

The group's chatter suddenly quieted, as if they had all heard her question. Twelve pairs of eyes turned toward her, their expressions unreadable but intensely focused. For a moment, the room was suffocatingly silent, the weight of their collective gaze pressing down on her.

Then, the man with the bright blue eyes spoke, his voice calm but chilling. "You don't stop it. You can't. Once you're marked, you're part of the process. The only question is how much of you will remain when it's done."

Eleanor's blood ran cold. She stumbled back, her mind racing. *I need to find Brandon. I need to get out of here before it's too late.*

The silver-haired woman watched her carefully, her expression softening just slightly. "If you're going to fight it, you'll need help," she said. "The kind they won't let you have."

Eleanor narrowed her eyes. "What kind of help?"

The woman hesitated, glancing at the group before leaning in closer to whisper. "There's someone. Outside the domes. A survivor who escaped the connection. If you want answers—if you want to find your friend—you'll have to find him."

Eleanor's heart leapt at the possibility. "How do I get out of here?" she asked urgently.

The woman's lips twitched into a grim smile. "That's the hard part. They'll know the moment you try. But if you're fast enough, you might make it to the tunnels before they stop you."

Eleanor looked toward the group, now fully immersed in their synchronized chatter once more. The walls of the dome seemed to pulse, as if alive, as if listening.

"I'll find a way," she whispered, more to herself than to anyone else. *I have to.*

## Chapter 4: The man from the past

The fog rolled in thick waves over the suburban streets of London, muffling the sounds of the city and casting a gray pall over the world. It was the kind of day that pressed its weight on the soul, urging most to retreat indoors, seeking warmth and familiarity. But Braham Beckett wasn't most people.

Seated in the storefront of a modest bar tucked between a second-hand bookstore and a pawnshop, Braham sipped slowly from a cup of coffee that was far too hot to drink comfortably. He didn't seem to mind. The warmth of the porcelain mug against his palm was steadying, grounding him as he sorted through the whirlwind of thoughts swirling in his mind. The bar itself was unremarkable—dimly lit with mismatched furniture and the faint scent of spilled ale and damp wood lingering in the air. The patrons were few, scattered in booths or hunched over the bar, their faces drawn with the same quiet melancholy that matched the weather. Braham sat near the window, his back to the wall and his eyes on the street beyond. The glass was fogged at the edges, blurring the figures that passed by, but Braham's gaze remained sharp, his awareness heightened. He wasn't here by chance. He rarely went anywhere without purpose.

His appearance was as deliberate as his presence. A wool coat hung neatly over his lean frame; its collar turned up against the chill. His dark hair, peppered with the faintest hint of gray, was slicked back in a way that seemed effortless. A scar, faint but unmistakable, cut a thin line across his left eyebrow—a relic of another life, another world. His eyes were sharp, a stormy gray-blue that seemed to pierce through the fog and into the thoughts of anyone who dared meet them.

Braham Beckett—codenamed "Bering" by the shadowy network he once called home—had been many things in his life. A soldier, a spy, a man of science. But none of those titles quite captured the essence of the man. He was an enigma, a relic of a world that had moved on but couldn't quite forget him.

His past was a mosaic of contradictions. Born to a family of academics in Cambridge, he'd shown early promise in engineering and cryptography, earning accolades and scholarships that could have set him on a path of quiet brilliance. Instead, he'd taken a darker route, drawn to the thrill of intelligence work. The Cold War had been his proving ground, his mind and body sharpened in the crucible of espionage. He became known for his ability to navigate impossible situations, his knack for decoding not just messages but people.

But the world had changed, and so had Braham. The fall of the Berlin Wall had marked the end of an era, but for Braham, it was only the beginning of his disillusionment. Governments shifted alliances like chess pieces, and the moral certainties of his youth dissolved into a murky swamp of pragmatism and betrayal. He'd left the game before it could consume him entirely—or so he liked to tell himself.

Now, years later, he found himself once again drawn into the shadows, though not by choice. Something was stirring on the edges of human understanding, a threat that made even the most cynical intelligence veterans take notice. Whispers of experiments gone wrong, of people disappearing, and of strange technologies that defied explanation had reached Braham's ears through channels he thought long dormant.

The sound of the bar's door creaking open snapped Braham from his thoughts. He didn't look up immediately, instead taking another measured sip of his coffee. He felt the shift in the air, the faint tension that came with the arrival of someone out of place.

A figure approached his table—a man in his early thirties, clean-shaven with a neatly pressed trench coat and the unmistakable posture of someone who had spent time in military service. The man hesitated for a moment before pulling out the chair opposite Braham.

"Bering," the man said quietly, using the codename like a key to unlock the conversation.

Braham set his mug down and leaned back, studying the newcomer with a practiced gaze. "You're late," he said, his tone casual but edged with authority.

"Traffic," the man replied, though his slight unease betrayed that it wasn't the truth. "I didn't think you'd actually agree to meet."

"I'm full of surprises," Braham said dryly. "Let's skip the pleasantries. Why am I here?"

The man glanced around nervously before lowering his voice. "We need your help. There's a situation—something... unprecedented. People disappearing. Facilities being built off the books. And..." He hesitated, as if the words themselves were dangerous. "There's talk of non-human involvement."

Braham raised an eyebrow, his expression unreadable. "Non-human," he repeated, his voice flat. "You've been watching too much late-night television."

The man leaned forward; his voice urgent. "It's real, Bering. And it's happening now. We've intercepted data from a site in Siberia—anomalies, technology we can't explain, and people... being changed. Transformed into something else."

For the first time, Braham's expression shifted, a flicker of interest crossing his face. He leaned forward, resting his elbows on the table. "And what does this have to do with me?"

The man hesitated before sliding a thin dossier across the table. "You have a reputation. You've dealt with... unconventional threats before. You're one of the few who might be able to make sense of this."

Braham opened the dossier and scanned its contents. The images inside were grainy but unsettling—blueprints of structures with strange, organic designs; photos of people with unnatural modifications; and a map with several locations circled, including one in a remote canyon. His jaw tightened. "And if I say no?"

The man's gaze hardened. "Then you're leaving a lot of people to die. This isn't just a threat to a single nation. It's global."

Braham closed the dossier and tapped it against the table thoughtfully. He didn't trust this man, didn't trust whoever had sent him. But the images in the file... they struck a chord, a memory of something he'd encountered once before, long ago. Something he'd hoped never to face again.

He drained the last of his coffee and stood, sliding the dossier under his coat. "You've got my attention," he said. "But don't mistake that for trust. Let's see where this rabbit hole leads."

The man nodded, relief washing over his face. "I'll be in touch."

As Braham stepped out into the foggy street, he felt the weight of the dossier under his arm and the familiar pull of the unknown. Whatever this was, it wasn't going to be simple—or safe. But then, safety had never been his strong suit.

Braham adjusted his coat against the damp chill of the street, his mind racing. The man's urgency had been palpable, but Braham needed more than grainy photos and vague warnings. He needed proof, something concrete to separate fact from conspiracy. As he walked, his boots echoing on the wet pavement, his thoughts circled back to the dossier now tucked securely under his arm.

The possibility that this was some elaborate hoax gnawed at him, but there was another, darker possibility that unsettled him even more. He stopped under the awning of a closed shop; the faint glow of a streetlamp casting shadows over his face. Pulling the dossier out, he flipped it open again, scanning the contents with a more critical eye. The photos of the supposed victims drew his focus: hollowed-out expressions, strange scarring on their bodies, and, in some cases, disfigurements that bordered on the unnatural. It wasn't just the anomalies that struck him—it was the sheer number of people listed. Pages upon pages of names, locations, and vague summaries of their last known activities.

If even half of these disappearances were real, it was enough to alarm anyone. But for Braham, it wasn't the victims that drew his attention—it was the methodology. This wasn't the work of an amateur group or rogue organization. The precision, the resources required to orchestrate something of this magnitude—it screamed of a larger, more brutal entity at play.

*A pharmaceutical corporation,* he thought grimly. His gut told him this wasn't about aliens or myths; it was about power and greed. He'd seen it before—companies pushing the boundaries of human ethics to chase technological frontiers. They hid behind shell corporations, off-the-books research facilities, and the malleable laws of remote countries. And when something went wrong, the victims disappeared, buried beneath layers of denial and bureaucracy.

Braham's jaw tightened as the pieces began to fall into place.

He was interrupted by the man from the bar, who had followed him silently out into the foggy street. "You're still not convinced," the man said, his voice low but steady.

Braham snapped the dossier shut and turned to face him. "What you've given me isn't enough. Photos and maps? They could be staged. Names? I've seen fabricated lists before. If you want me involved, I need proof—tangible proof that this isn't just paranoia dressed up as a mission."

The man hesitated, his eyes darting to the dossier Braham held. "The people are real. I swear it."

"Swearing isn't good enough," Braham shot back. "I want to see records. Hospital logs. Police reports. Evidence that someone is actively covering this up. And if you've got footage, unedited, I want to see that too." He took a step closer, his voice dropping to a dangerous tone.

"And don't bother feeding me half-truths. If I find out you're lying, this conversation is over."

The man's expression shifted, a flicker of unease crossing his face. "It's not that simple," he began, but Braham cut him off.

"It never is," Braham said coolly. "That's the point. You think this is some shadowy conspiracy with otherworldly implications? Maybe it is. But my money's on human hands pulling the strings. Big money. Big power. And if I'm right, you're dealing with an organization that's willing to sacrifice lives to push their agenda." He tapped the dossier for emphasis. "These people didn't just vanish. Someone took them. Someone with resources—and no conscience."

The man swallowed hard, his confidence faltering under Braham's piercing gaze. "We've been tracking a lead," he admitted finally. "There's a facility. Remote, heavily secured. Siberia."

Braham raised an eyebrow. "Siberia? Convenient. Let me guess—off the grid, no legal oversight, and the perfect place to hide a few hundred bodies if things go sideways."

The man nodded reluctantly. "That's why we need you. You've dealt with operations like this before. You know how they think, how they work."

Braham studied him for a long moment, his expression unreadable. Finally, he sighed and looked away, his thoughts churning. "If this is as big as you're suggesting, you've already underestimated the stakes. This isn't just some rogue experiment. It's systemic." He turned back, his eyes narrowing. "And if I'm right, you've got no idea what you're up against."

The man said nothing, his silence confirming Braham's suspicion. Braham slid the dossier back under his coat and started walking. "Get me those files," he called over his shoulder. "Medical records, victim histories, anything you've got on this Siberian facility. And make it quick. If you're not careful, you might disappear too."

The man didn't follow. He stood in the misty street, watching Braham disappear into the fog, his heart pounding.

Braham, for his part, was already planning his next move. His gut told him this was bigger than even the man had realized. And if that was true, it wasn't just the victims he needed to worry about. It was everyone.

Braham stopped in his tracks as his interlocutor, now visibly more composed and serious, called after him. The tone of the man's voice had changed—less pleading, more resolute. It was the kind of shift Braham recognized from his days dealing with informants: the moment when desperation gave way to hard truth.

"CSM FarmCure," the man said, his words carrying weight.

Braham turned slowly, his brow furrowing. The name was familiar—too familiar. He didn't need a dossier to know about CSM FarmCure. It was one of the largest pharmaceutical conglomerates in the world, with a reputation for aggressive innovation and an equally aggressive legal team to bury any controversy that came their way. They were the kind of corporation that didn't just operate in gray areas—they thrived in them.

"Go on," Braham said, his voice steady but edged with suspicion.

The man stepped closer, lowering his voice as though the fog itself might be listening. "Their headquarters is in Zurich—state-of-the-art, heavily fortified. But that's just for show. Their real operations, the ones that matter, are scattered across remote locations. Facilities in South America, Eastern Europe, Siberia." He paused, his eyes locking with Braham's. "Lately, those facilities have been receiving cargoes—large shipments with no declared contents. Origin unknown."

Braham raised an eyebrow. "You're saying a pharmaceutical company is moving unregistered shipments to secret facilities guarded by militias? Sounds like more than aspirin production."

The man nodded grimly. "They're not just guarded. These places are protected like military bases. Armed personnel, restricted airspace, and no official government oversight. And then there's the timing—these shipments started arriving just weeks before the disappearances you see in that dossier."

Braham crossed his arms, processing the information. "And you think CSM FarmCure is behind this? What exactly are they doing in those facilities?"

The man hesitated, his lips pressing into a thin line. "We don't know the full extent. But there's chatter—encrypted communications we've intercepted. Phrases like 'adaptive trials,' 'biological integration,' and... something about 'genomic re-engineering.'" His voice dropped even lower. "They're pushing the boundaries of human biology. If the rumours are true, they've developed technology that makes CRISPR look like child's play."

"Genomic re-engineering," Braham repeated, his expression darkening. He didn't need a degree in molecular biology to understand the implications. "You're talking about altering people. Not just curing diseases, but fundamentally changing what it means to be human."

The man nodded. "And there are whispers of something worse—field trials. Testing on live subjects. The kind of experiments that no government would ever authorize."

Braham exhaled sharply, the weight of the situation settling over him. He'd seen corporations push the limits of morality before, but this... this was something else. If CSM FarmCure was using their resources to carry out experiments on unwilling subjects, it wasn't just unethical—it was monstrous.

"You've got guts coming to me with this," Braham said finally, his tone softer but no less serious. "If they're as powerful as you say, you're risking your neck just talking about it."

The man gave a small, bitter smile. "I know the risks. But someone has to expose them. We can't let them keep playing God."

Braham nodded slowly, his mind already turning over the possibilities. This wasn't just a mission—it was a war against an entity with more money, power, and influence than most governments. He would need to tread carefully, but he also knew he couldn't walk away. Not from this.

"All right," Braham said, his voice firm. "Get me everything you've got on these shipments and their destinations. If there's a crack in their armor, I'll find it."

The man looked relieved, though the tension in his shoulders remained. "I'll be in touch. But you should know—they're watching. People who dig too deep into CSM FarmCure tend to disappear. Be careful."

Braham smirked faintly. "Disappearing isn't as easy as it sounds. Trust me."

As the man melted back into the fog, Braham stood alone on the damp street, his thoughts racing. He knew this wasn't just another job. It was bigger, darker, and more dangerous than anything he'd faced in years. But beneath the layers of doubt and caution, a familiar fire stirred in his chest.

It wasn't just about the victims anymore. It was about stopping whatever nightmare CSM FarmCure was trying to unleash.


Braham leaned back slightly in his chair, the dim light of the laptop screen casting a pale glow on his face as he scrolled through his findings. The bar's Wi-Fi was surprisingly stable, allowing him to access databases and forums with ease. His fingers moved quickly across the keyboard, pulling up a map of known CSM FarmCure locations. Switzerland, Germany, Singapore, Brazil... all prominent hubs for cutting-edge research.

But as Braham's eyes traced the dots marking their facilities, he couldn't shake the feeling that the real action was happening somewhere far from prying eyes. *These places are too public,* he thought, rubbing his chin. *Too regulated.*

His thoughts drifted as he began speaking softly to himself, a habit he'd picked up over years of working solo. "Not in the UK," he muttered. "Too many government restrictions. Europe's tighter with laws, even with loopholes. South America's easier to bribe, but it's messy. Too much noise. Where would they go if they wanted silence? Isolation?"

He opened a new tab and started searching for territories with minimal government oversight. His mind ticked off the criteria as he typed: remote locations, weak governance, and climates that could support infrastructure without drawing attention. He quickly skimmed reports on countries with loose regulations on private land ownership and foreign investment.

"Central Asia," he murmured, his eyes narrowing as the map loaded. "Kazakhstan? Maybe. Open spaces, and the government's open to big investments. But too many oil barons to stay unnoticed." He shook his head and scrolled further. "Siberia, though... now that makes sense. Harsh conditions, low population, and plenty of land to buy under the radar."

A quick search confirmed his suspicion: several large swaths of land in Siberia had been purchased in recent years under shell companies with vague names. No specifics, but enough to raise a red flag. One of the articles mentioned an unnamed buyer who had poured millions into a compound described as "an experimental agricultural facility." Braham scoffed. "Agricultural, my arse. That screams cover story."

He tapped the table lightly as he considered the implications. If CSM FarmCure was truly operating there, the location would be a logistical nightmare for anyone trying to investigate. Miles of frozen tundra, unreliable transportation, and extreme weather would keep most people far away. It was the perfect hiding spot for something they didn't want the world to see.

But Braham wasn't most people. His hand hovered over the keyboard before pulling up one final search: **unusual cargo shipments Siberia 2024**.

The results weren't immediate, but after a few clicks, he found a thread on an obscure forum frequented by investigative journalists and whistleblowers. One post in particular caught his attention: *"Heavy shipments through Arkhangelsk port destined for Novosibirsk. Contents: unlisted. Military-grade containers observed."*

His pulse quickened. He knew the ports in Arkhangelsk were notorious for their lax inspections. If CSM FarmCure was shipping something to Siberia, it would make sense to route it through there.

Braham leaned back and rubbed his temples, the pieces of the puzzle falling into place. He didn't need to know every detail to see the bigger picture. The cargo, the remote facilities, the disappearances—it all pointed to one thing: CSM FarmCure was operating outside the bounds of morality, maybe even humanity itself.

He closed the laptop and slipped it back into his vintage bag, taking a sip of his now lukewarm coffee. His jaw clenched as he stared out the window into the foggy street, his reflection faint against the glass. "If they think Siberia will keep them safe," he said under his breath, "they've underestimated how far I'm willing to go."

Sliding a few bills onto the table, Braham stood and slung the bag over his shoulder. He'd need more than a laptop and a hunch to take this further. It was time to dig deeper—and if he was right, Siberia would soon become the stage for something far bigger than anyone could anticipate.

# Chapter 5: A journey through time

Braham sat in the slightly worn lounge chair of the airport waiting room, his vintage bag resting by his feet. The faint hum of announcements and the shuffling of travellers filled the air, but his attention was locked on the photographs displayed on his phone. He swiped through them one by one, his frown deepening with each image. Grainy shots of unidentified containers, blurry figures in hazmat suits, and shadowy outlines of what appeared to be domes in the Siberian wilderness.

The photos were unsettling enough on their own, but it was the accompanying notes that pushed them into the realm of outright conspiracy. Phrases like *"biological testing protocols"* and *"genetic drift trials"* were scrawled in messy handwriting on the margins, paired with coordinates that pointed to places miles away from any recognized civilization. The more Braham studied them, the more the theory seemed plausible, no matter how absurd it sounded at first.

His thoughts were interrupted by a buzzing in his pocket. Pulling out his phone, he read a message from Jimmy, his contact:

**"Running late. Flight's delayed anyway. Be there in 15."**

Braham sighed, slipping the phone back into his pocket. Jimmy was late, but so was the flight—it was a wash. He glanced at the departure screen overhead:

**Moscow → Novosibirsk. Delayed 45 minutes.**

The extra time wasn't necessarily a bad thing. Braham needed a moment to process the weight of what Jimmy had handed him so far. While Jimmy's intel had been reliable, it also hinted at the involvement of locals near their Siberian destination. According to the notes, there were individuals in a remote village who had either witnessed or participated in the strange operations tied to CSM FarmCure. If they could be convinced to talk, they might offer the proof Braham needed.

*Locals hiding something,* Braham mused as he flipped through the photographs again. He lingered on one that showed what looked like a small village, half-buried in snow, with a solitary smoke trail curling from one of the chimneys. The caption beneath it read:

**"Access point confirmed. Agents in area. Contacts unreliable."**

Unreliable or not, it was all they had. If the people in the village were protecting CSM FarmCure's operation, it wouldn't be out of loyalty—it would be out of fear. No one faced down an organization of that scale without significant incentive—or coercion.

Braham stretched his legs and leaned back in the chair, his gaze drifting toward the large glass windows overlooking the tarmac. The sky was gray and heavy, the kind of weather that mirrored his thoughts. He'd been in tight spots before, but this was different. He wasn't chasing a single criminal or tracking a lone lead. This was bigger, systemic. And the deeper he dug, the more it felt like he was stepping into a labyrinth designed to swallow anyone who dared enter.

The sound of footsteps pulled him from his thoughts. He looked up to see Jimmy approaching, his coat flapping slightly as he hurried across the lounge. The man dropped into the seat beside Braham with a sigh, brushing snow from his shoulders.

"Sorry about that," Jimmy said, his breath visible in the cold air. "Traffic was a nightmare. You'd think they'd clear the roads better in a place like this."

Braham gave a slight nod, his eyes still scanning the photographs on his phone. "The flight's late too, so you're not the only one dragging your feet."

Jimmy chuckled nervously but quickly grew serious when he noticed the photograph Braham was studying. "That's the village," he said, tapping the screen. "It's remote, and the people there keep to themselves. We've got a few contacts, but they're cautious. They've seen what happens to people who ask too many questions."

"Have they now?" Braham said, his tone flat. "What about these 'agents' your notes mentioned?"

Jimmy hesitated, his gaze darting around the room. "They're... well, they're not ours. Locals claim to have seen outsiders in the area—armed, not military, but definitely trained. Could be private contractors hired by CSM FarmCure to keep an eye on things."

Braham raised an eyebrow. "Hired muscle in a village like that? Subtle."

Jimmy shrugged. "They don't have to be subtle. The place is isolated, no one's coming to check on them. They can do whatever they want."

Braham leaned forward, resting his elbows on his knees as he mulled over the information. "And you're sure this is the only access point? If they've got this much security, there's got to be another way in."

Jimmy shook his head. "Not unless you want to trek through miles of frozen wilderness with no guarantee you'll find anything. The village is our best bet. It's close enough to the facility, and if we play it right, the locals might give us something useful."

Braham nodded slowly, his mind already running through potential approaches. "Fine. But if we're going in blind, we're going in prepared. No surprises."

Jimmy gave a grim smile. "With this kind of operation, surprises are the only guarantee."

Braham said nothing, his eyes fixed on the fogged-up window. The plane might be delayed, but the clock was still ticking. Every second they waited brought them closer to whatever CSM FarmCure was hiding—and the danger it posed to anyone who tried to stop them.

The plane's engines hummed steadily as it ascended, leaving behind the gray, foggy skies of London. Braham sat next to Jimmy, their eyes scanning the interior of the cabin. Despite the journey's length, they had little conversation, both lost in their own thoughts. The air was stiflingly hot, an uncomfortable contrast to the freezing temperatures of Siberia that awaited them. After a few minutes of enduring the heat, both men simultaneously removed their thick outer jackets, revealing their lighter gear underneath.

Their movement, though casual, drew the attention of a few nearby passengers. Braham couldn't help but notice a pair of eyes on them. Military caps. They were worn by two men seated toward the front of the cabin, their posture rigid, their expressions unreadable.

Braham's gaze lingered on them briefly, a slight frown forming. They were too well-dressed, too disciplined, to be mere travellers. They had the air of professionals—men who had been trained for operations far beyond a regular flight to Siberia.

*Military or mercenaries,* Braham thought, his eyes narrowing. *Doesn't matter. They're here for something, or someone. And I bet they don't like unexpected company.*

Jimmy, sensing the shift in Braham's attention, leaned slightly forward and followed his gaze. He didn't say anything at first, but Braham saw his hand subtly inch toward his bag. He was checking for his sidearm. The plane wasn't crowded, but the presence of these men—along with the uncertainty of their mission—was enough to raise Braham's instincts to the surface.

"You think they're with us?" Jimmy muttered under his breath; his voice low enough not to attract attention.

Braham shook his head slightly, keeping his eyes on the soldiers. "Doubt it. We're not exactly the 'meet and greet' type, and they're not wearing civilian gear. They're here for a reason, but it's not good."

Jimmy smirked, though it didn't reach his eyes. "You're always such an optimist, Braham."

"Someone has to be," Braham replied dryly, adjusting his seat as he considered his next move. "We should keep our heads down. Don't make eye contact unless we have to. If they're military, they won't be too keen on us being... *out of place*."

As the flight continued, the plane's steady hum failed to mask the low murmur of voices ahead. Every few minutes, the military men exchanged words in a language Braham didn't recognize—Russian, perhaps? It didn't matter. He had spent enough time in international hotspots to know that body language spoke louder than words, and these men were anything but relaxed. They were on alert.

Jimmy noticed Braham's unease. "I'll check the flight plan when we get closer," he whispered. "If we're heading straight into Novosibirsk, it's either a detour or a coordinated drop-off. Either way, we can't afford to look like we're in a hurry."

Braham nodded but kept his focus forward, trying to make sense of the situation. These soldiers, or whatever they were, were likely tied to CSM FarmCure. The secrecy surrounding their operation, the remote location, and now the strange presence on the plane all pointed toward one thing: they weren't just headed to Siberia for a simple mission. There was something larger, something more dangerous brewing beneath the surface, and Braham was right in the middle of it.

The flight progressed uneventfully for the next hour, the tension palpable, but the silence between Braham and Jimmy was filled with a shared understanding: no one was safe. Not with CSM FarmCure involved. Not with military-looking personnel on board. And certainly not with whatever plans had been set in motion long before they'd even stepped onto the plane.

Eventually, the overhead announcement cut through the tension, signalling their descent into Novosibirsk. The air had cooled again, but the military men in front remained stoic, their eyes trained on the cabin. Braham knew they weren't there by accident, and he had a sinking feeling that their mission—whatever it was—was directly linked to him and Jimmy.

As the plane began its final approach, Braham turned to Jimmy. "Stay alert," he said, his voice firm. "Whatever happens, we need to get eyes on that village. CSM FarmCure won't stop at anything to keep their secrets. Not now."

Jimmy nodded, his fingers lightly brushing his jacket where his sidearm rested. "Got it. But if this turns into something bigger, we'll need to be ready for anything."

Braham didn't answer. He didn't have to. The look in his eyes was enough—he had already decided. As the wheels of the plane touched down on the snowy runway of Novosibirsk, Braham felt the weight of the mission ahead. This was only the beginning, and it was already darker than he'd imagined.

The flight had passed in a strange mix of tense quiet and forced relaxation. Braham and Jimmy sat back and watched a film on the plane's small screens, the soft glow of the display helping to pass the time. The meal was standard—a cold, slightly warmed format dish that had little flavour, but at least it filled the stomach. They washed it down with a few glasses of wine, which helped dull their sharp senses, even if only for a brief moment.

Despite the calm facade, both men were keenly aware of their surroundings. The atmosphere was thick with the sensation that something was coming, something they hadn't quite figured out yet. They exchanged few words, focusing instead on the faces around them—the two military men still sat near the front, eyes ever-watchful, never relaxing.

As the plane descended toward Novosibirsk
, the looming city appeared beneath a blanket of light fog, a far cry from the starkness of Siberia that awaited them. They knew they couldn't let their guard down—not here, not now. The mission was only just beginning, and the true test would come when they reached their final destination.

Once they disembarked, the cold air of Moscow greeted them like a slap in the face. Despite the late hour, the airport buzzed with activity as people rushed to their gates or hurried out to the cold streets.

But there was no time for sightseeing. Braham and Jimmy stepped into the terminal, their eyes scanning the crowd. They were expecting someone. They didn't have to wait long.

In the corner of the arrivals hall, two men stood by a small kiosk, their eyes locked on the newcomers the moment they stepped through the door. Both men were dressed in heavy coats, the kind suited for the brutal cold of Siberia. Their appearance was unremarkable, nothing that would raise suspicion to the casual observer, but to Braham's trained eye, there was a certain stillness to them—a deliberate composure, as if they had been waiting for this moment for longer than expected.

Jimmy nudged Braham subtly, giving him a look. "Those the guys?" he whispered.

Braham nodded slightly, his hand brushing against the strap of his bag as he adjusted his stance. "I think so. Let's move."

They walked toward the two men, who didn't make a move until Braham and Jimmy were almost upon them. Then, one of them, the taller of the two, gave a small nod of acknowledgment.

"Mr. Beckett. Mr. Jimmy," the man said, his Russian accent thick but not unpleasant. His voice was calm, measured. "We have been waiting for you."

Braham gave a curt nod, eyes narrowing as he scanned the man's face. The second man, shorter and more solidly built, said nothing but his presence was just as imposing. He looked to be more of a bodyguard than a talker.

"Everything's set?" Braham asked, keeping his tone neutral.

"Yes," the first man replied. "We will take you directly to Novosibirsk. No delays. No suspicions. It's a long journey, but we will be discreet."

Discreet. Braham didn't entirely buy it, but he knew better than to question it. His eyes flicked to Jimmy, who gave him a brief nod of agreement. No point in asking too many questions right now. The men were just doing their job, and their job was to get them out of Moscow and toward their destination without drawing attention. Anything more than that would have to wait until they were safely on the road.

"Lead the way," Braham said, his voice calm but firm.

The taller man gestured toward the exit. "Follow us. We'll keep to the shadows."

Without further discussion, the group made their way toward the airport's exit, where a sleek, black van awaited them. It was unmarked, no logos or identifying features, blending perfectly into the background of the busy airport.

As they climbed into the vehicle, the cold air bit at Braham's skin, and he pulled his jacket tighter around him. The city of Moscow felt distant now, a mere waypoint on a much larger journey. His focus had already shifted to what lay ahead: Novosibirsk and whatever secrets it held.

The van started moving smoothly, gliding through the streets of Moscow before they hit the open road. The landscape shifted from the city's sprawling buildings to stretches of barren countryside, the night falling darker as the miles passed by.

As the vehicle sped on, the silence in the van was palpable. It wasn't uncomfortable, but there was a distinct tension, a sense of expectation hanging in the air. Braham's mind was already running through the possible scenarios in his head, the questions he needed answers to, and the risks he'd be taking once they reached their destination.
Jimmy seemed to sense the same thing, leaning slightly toward Braham. "What do you think? Do you trust them?"
Braham didn't answer immediately. He wasn't sure. There were too many unknowns, too many questions left to ask. But he knew one thing for certain—this wasn't just a trip to Siberia. This was the beginning of something much larger, and he had no intention of letting anyone pull the strings without him knowing exactly what was going on.
"We'll know soon enough," Braham said, his voice steady. "Let's just stick to the plan."
The road ahead was long, but it was just the beginning. They weren't just heading to Novosibirsk—they were heading straight into the heart of whatever CSM FarmCure had been hiding. And Braham was determined to uncover it, no matter the cost.
The travel took about 2 hours, they arrived in a small village situated between mountains and snow.
The snow was white tall half meter but streets were in good conditions. Their destinations was a great house outside of the city, quite dishabituated from outside, with two enormous blocks linked by a glass veranda sopraelevated. Braham approached the imposing structure with a mix of anticipation and trepidation, his eyes scanning the weathered exterior for any signs of life. As he drew closer, he noticed intricate carvings adorning the wooden beams of the veranda, hinting at the building's former grandeur. The silence that enveloped the property was broken only by the crunch of snow beneath his feet, adding to the eerie atmosphere that seemed to permeate the air.

The Siberian boys, contacted by an old acquaintance of Braham's, let them into the enormous house and immediately put them at ease; they lit a large stone hearth in the hall where enormous tapestries depicting hunting scenes were displayed; they took some deer meat and immersed it in a liquid solution containing aromatic herbs and garlic. All the bags were taken in the other side of the buildings were Braham and Jimmy after an hour could have a shower and relax with a cup of coffee.
The room was large with chemin, one wall was completely made of ancient stone and the head of a boar was on display above a huge stone

architrave where the fire crackled slowly, warming the room vigorously, the two principal beds was made in wood with a reclining leather headboard.

The suspended chandelier was composed of an old metal band obtained from a barrel where a dozen light bulbs illuminated the room hidden by wrought iron profiles and a strange paper shape that gave particular reflections to the light.

The figure was then adorned with wrought iron tips which gave the whole thing an older, almost medieval feel.

The furnishings of the room were the completed with a round table and four wood chairs, one sitting room with a small tv, an old rounded copper tube.

The meeting was at 8pm for a dinner of venison and cooked vegetables; the dinner was set to be a sumptuous affair, with the rich aroma of roasting venison already wafting through the air. The guests, a mix of local dignitaries and visiting scholars, began to arrive, their excited chatter filling the room as they marvelled at the rustic yet elegant decor. As the host welcomed each newcomer, the chef and his assistants bustled about in the adjacent kitchen, putting the finishing touches on the hearty meal that would soon grace the ancient wooden table. The flickering candlelight cast dancing shadows on the stone walls, enhancing the medieval atmosphere and creating an intimate ambiance. As the guests settled into their seats, the host raised a goblet of rich red wine, proposing a toast to the evening's gathering and the shared pursuit of knowledge. The clinking of glasses and the scraping of chairs against the worn wooden floor mingled with the crackling of the fire in the hearth, setting the stage for an evening of intellectual discourse and culinary delight. The aroma of savory dishes wafted through the air, tantalizing the guests' senses and heightening their anticipation for the feast to come. As the first course was served, conversations began to flow more freely, with scholars from different disciplines finding common ground and sparking lively debates. The host, ever attentive, moved from group to group, introducing guests to one another and gently steering discussions towards the evening's central theme of interdisciplinary collaboration.

The party was given in their honour, and the guests were dripping with happiness and emotion for the two foreigners, until the final dessert, the alcohol and the the red Thea.

After half past midnight the diners began to abandon the party, filling the alleys of the village in the cold north wind where the full moon illuminated the white snow and ice.

  Braham observed well that people always referred to an old "sherpa" of the village, he must have been a hunter/butcher expert in game and known by everyone in the area. He immediately asked who he was and how to hire him for their mission.

Some dishes intrigued Braham a lot, such as beef tongue with fern and salad with stewed venison, so he wanted to meet the chef, who came from the city of Kondruvonka, and stayed to discuss until the end of the party.

# Chapter 6: The cage of mystery

As the group's speculation spiralled into wild theories, Eleanor remained silent at the bar table. The polished surface reflected the faint outlines of the dome's intricate lattice above, its geometric precision at odds with the chaotic landscape outside. Her mind, however, was far from the excitement of her peers.
Eleanor's memories of her arrival were fractured—she recalled a sharp, sudden vertigo, a blinding flash, and then an oppressive nothingness that consumed an entire day. When she awoke inside the dome, disoriented and wary, her analytical mind took over. She had inspected every detail of the structure, from the engineered precision of the joints to the curious vents embedded in the wooden floorboards that now radiated heat. It was clear to her that nothing about this place was accidental. The fully stocked kitchen, conspicuously devoid of alcohol, only deepened her unease. Who had provisioned it? For what purpose? And why such strict control over their options? As the others debated the dome's origins—scientific experiment or alien intervention—Eleanor's thoughts turned inward, questioning the intent of their unseen captors.
Her scepticism grew with each detail she observed. The food, though abundant, seemed engineered, with identical portions of meticulously labelled items. Even the heating vents emitted a regulated warmth that felt too artificial, almost clinical.
Eleanor finally broke her silence. "This isn't random," she said, her voice cutting through the chatter. "We were brought here. Prepared for. Someone designed this place for us—down to the last detail." Her words hung in the air, a chilling counterpoint to the group's imaginative theories.
One of the boys, a wiry teenager named Lukas, dismissed her concerns with a wave. "So what? Maybe it's a social experiment. Or a survival thing. Let's just figure out how to get out of here."
Eleanor shook her head, her gaze steely. "It's not that simple. There's a purpose behind this. We just don't know it yet." Her conviction silenced Lukas and cast a sombre mood over the group.
As the sun climbed higher, its rays filtered through the translucent dome, creating patterns that danced across the room. Eleanor's mind raced, piecing together fragments of her arrival, the meticulously curated

environment, and the inexplicable circumstances that led them here. Scepticism hardened into resolve: she would uncover the truth behind the dome, no matter the cost.

Eleanor started to methodically examine the perimeter of the dome, her sharp gaze narrowing on the curved glass panels encased in metal frames painted a dull gray. She leaned close to one segment, her breath fogging the surface as she inspected the edges where the glass met the metal. Her fingers traced the seams, searching for markings or imperfections that might reveal how—or why—this place had been constructed.

Her attention was drawn to tiny etchings in the metal frames, symbols that appeared deliberate yet unfamiliar. The geometric shapes seemed to interlock, forming a repeating pattern that sparked faint recognition but eluded full comprehension.

"These markings," she muttered, beckoning one of the others to join her. "Do they mean anything to you?"

Lukas, still sceptical but intrigued, crouched beside her and examined the symbols. "Looks like... engineering labels? Or maybe some kind of code?"

Eleanor didn't respond immediately. Her focus shifted to the glass itself; its surface unusually clear despite the harsh sunlight streaming in. As she pressed her face closer, the distorted reflection of the desolate terrain outside loomed large. The landscape, barren and alien, stretched beyond the dome with no discernible landmarks. Not a single structure, road, or sign of civilization was visible.

"This place isn't anywhere near a city," Eleanor muttered, her voice tinged with unease. "It's isolated. Completely."

The heating vents in the floor released a gentle hum, a sound that had blended into the background until now. Eleanor suddenly stood up, her gaze darting between the vents and the panels above. "The heat. The power. It's all controlled externally. The source isn't here."

Lukas frowned. "So, what are you saying? That we're in some kind of... lab?"

"Possibly," Eleanor replied. "But look at the precision of this dome—the materials, the provisions, the climate control. It's like we're being observed, studied... or tested."

The implications unsettled the group. As the others gathered around to inspect the symbols and glass panels, Eleanor turned her focus to the floor. She knelt beside a heating vent, her fingers brushing the smooth wood surrounding it. A faint vibration pulsed beneath her palm, rhythmic and deliberate.

"This floor," she said, more to herself than the others. "It's not natural wood. It's synthetic. Designed for... insulation?"

Lukas squatted beside her again, listening to her muttering. "So what? It's high-tech. What does that mean for us?"

Eleanor locked eyes with him, her voice low and resolute. "It means whoever put us here has planned for every contingency. And we need to figure out what they want before it's too late."

A chilling silence fell over the group as her words lingered. The sun's rays shifted, casting new shadows across the dome. Somewhere in the distance, a faint mechanical hum began to grow louder, as if the structure itself was coming to life.

The scene unfolded with an almost surreal efficiency. A small robot, designed with humanoid features, rolled into view. Its face was a smooth screen displaying a simplistic but emotive digital expression, while one of its mechanical hands extended forward, holding a monitor. The machine's voice was crisp and oddly soothing, calling out names from the group one by one.

"Eleanor Rhodes," it intoned, its artificial gaze locking on her with unsettling precision. "Lukas Grant. Sophie Marlowe." The names continued, each evoking a mix of apprehension and curiosity among the group.

"What the hell is this?" Lukas whispered; his tension palpable. "It's like we're being... processed."

Eleanor stepped forward; her scepticism now laced with open defiance. "What's the purpose of this? Why are you calling our names?"

The robot turned its head toward her, its screen flickering slightly. "The program for today includes discussions on sustenance and reproduction. Your participation is mandatory."

The words hung heavy in the air, causing murmurs to ripple through the group. "Sustenance and reproduction?" Eleanor repeated, her tone sharp. "What does that even mean?"

The robot ignored her question, extending the monitor to display a menu-like interface. Symbols and diagrams flashed across the screen, depicting a variety of food items and ambiguous, clinical-looking graphics related to human anatomy. The robotic voice elaborated; its tone devoid of any emotion:

"Session objectives:

Nutritional preferences and caloric needs.
Behavioural and social dynamics regarding reproductive strategies."
"Reproductive strategies?" Sophie muttered, her face pale. "Are they seriously going to make us talk about... that?"
Eleanor clenched her fists, stepping closer to the robot. "Who programmed you? Who's controlling this? We deserve answers before we engage in any 'sessions.'"
The robot paused, its screen blinking twice before responding. "Your cooperation is essential to the success of the initiative. Non-compliance may result in environmental adjustments."
"Environmental adjustments?" Lukas said, his voice rising. "What is that supposed to mean?"
As if in response, the dome's interior lights dimmed momentarily, and the faint hum of the heating vents grew louder. Eleanor realized this was more than just a benign exercise—they were being conditioned, manipulated into compliance through subtle control of their surroundings.
"Everyone stays calm," she said, turning to the group. "We need to play along for now and figure out their endgame."
Lukas looked sceptical but nodded reluctantly. Sophie hesitated; her arms crossed defensively. Slowly, the group began to gather near the robot, their unease thick in the air.
The robot extended its arm again, revealing a compartment filled with tablets. "You will document your preferences and responses on these devices," it instructed. "Discussion will follow."
Eleanor accepted the tablet, her mind already racing. She knew these sessions weren't about genuine understanding—they were about data collection, control, and, possibly, something far more insidious. She glanced at Lukas, who gave her a slight nod, as if silently affirming that they would uncover the truth together.

The humanized cobot, once everyone had completed their questionnaires, moved with a calculated grace toward a table positioned in the dome's centre. Without warning, its humanoid features folded inward, panels retracting and collapsing with a soft hiss of mechanical precision. Within seconds, it had transformed into a sleek cubic object firmly locked into the base of the table. The metallic cube emitted a faint pulse of light, as though it were still observing the group silently.
The sight left the group stunned, a collective unease settling over them. "What just happened?" Sophie asked, her voice tinged with disbelief.

"It's still active," Eleanor observed, her tone measured. She tapped the table lightly, feeling the faint vibrations emanating from the cube. "Whatever it is, it's not 'off.' It's just... dormant."

Lukas shook his head, rubbing his temples. "This place keeps getting weirder. We're not in control here—not even close."

The group's collective unease gave way to a need for distraction. Slowly, they gravitated toward the section of the dome that housed the kitchen area. It was a curious sight—gleaming countertops, spotless utensils, and an array of food supplies neatly organized in compartments. The absence of alcohol, already noted by Eleanor, reinforced the idea that their captors were monitoring every aspect of their behaviour.

As they prepared simple meals—sandwiches, fruit, and water—conversation returned, but it was tinged with tension. "Maybe they want to see how we cooperate," Bertrand suggested, slicing bread with a precision that hinted at his museum background.

"Or how we survive," Eleanor replied, her tone sharp. "This is all a test—one we didn't agree to."

After their meal, the group continued their exploration. A section of the dome's circumference they hadn't yet examined revealed itself as something altogether different—a "gameplay area," as they began to call it.

This part of the dome had been divided into zones, each marked with glowing lines on the floor. Some areas appeared like obstacle courses, with walls that shifted positions. Others resembled puzzle stations, with panels lit up in complex patterns that responded to touch. A few zones were still inactive, their purpose unclear.

Lukas stepped forward, tentatively touching one of the glowing panels. It reacted immediately, lighting up in a sequence of colours. "Looks like some kind of game," he said, glancing back at the group.

"Games?" Sophie asked sceptically. "This feels more like training."

Eleanor watched closely, her mind racing. "If they're testing us, they're not just interested in our skills. They're looking for something deeper—how we think, how we adapt."

As the group began experimenting with the gameplay zones, the dome's faint hum seemed to grow louder, almost as if responding to their activity. Eleanor remained on edge, her eyes drifting back to the metallic cube at the table's base.

It pulsed faintly, like a heartbeat. And she couldn't shake the feeling that it was watching.

Eleanor, eager to shake off the unsettling tension that had been building all day, decided to engage with Lukas in one of the dome's more familiar activities: a game of ping-pong. The two set up at a sleek table that emerged from one of the gameplay zones, its surface glowing faintly under the dome's ambient light.

Lukas smirked as he picked up the paddle. "You sure about this? I've got reflexes like a cat."

Eleanor arched a brow, smirking. "We'll see about that."

The match started light-heartedly, the small white ball bouncing back and forth in an almost hypnotic rhythm. But it didn't take long for Eleanor's competitive streak to kick in. She tightened her focus, delivering a sharp serve that had Lukas scrambling. He managed to return the shot, but she slammed it back with precision, earning the first point.

"Alright," Lukas said, shaking his head. "No more Mr. Nice Guy."

The match drew attention from the rest of the group, who gathered around, cheering and laughing. For a brief moment, the eerie circumstances of their situation faded into the background. Eleanor ultimately won; her victory punctuated by Lukas's mock groan of defeat.

After the game, Eleanor wandered to another zone, where Bertrand was setting up a game of snooker. The table, like everything else in the dome, was sleek and flawless, its surface lit by soft, overhead lights. Bertrand adjusted his stance, his movements careful and deliberate.

"You play?" Bertrand asked, chalking his cue.

Eleanor picked up a cue, inspecting its weight. "A little. Let's see how rusty I am."

The two began the game, their conversation weaving between strategy and personal anecdotes. Bertrand spoke of his life as a museum employee, his love for history, and the intricate details of artifacts he'd studied. Eleanor, in turn, shared fragments of her life before the dome, her guarded nature softening slightly as the game progressed.

"You're good," Bertrand said as Eleanor sunk a tricky shot. "Where'd you learn to play?"

"My dad," she replied, a faint smile tugging at her lips. "We used to play every Friday night. He called it 'stress relief.'"

Bertrand nodded; his demeanour warm. "Smart man."

Their game ended in a draw, and as the group reconvened in the dining area, the atmosphere felt lighter. They brewed tea from a selection in the kitchen, the rich aroma filling the air as they sat around a communal table. The conversation turned to the day's events, the strange games, and the inexplicable workings of the dome.

Eleanor sipped her tea, her mind still racing with questions. But for the moment, the camaraderie of the group offered a fleeting sense of normalcy in an otherwise surreal world.

When she felt the group pulse them toward sport or discussion, she felt like force of her commilitons could retake her to life.

In the meanwhile, dome has everything she could desire from her dark small apartment and her acquainted office life.

As Eleanor settled deeper into the sofa, the smart screen extended seamlessly from the floor, illuminating the room with the opening scene of a Tom Cruise classic. The familiar voice and action sequences brought an unexpected warmth to the dome, as if anchoring them to a semblance of normal life. The group huddled together; their earlier camaraderie now enhanced by the shared distraction of cinema.

Eleanor let herself relax for a moment, the tension in her shoulders easing as she sipped the last of her tea. The ambient light of the dome dimmed slightly, mimicking the cozy glow of an evening at home. It struck her how perfectly tailored the environment seemed to anticipate their needs—almost too perfectly.

Her thoughts drifted as the movie played. The dome, with its sleek design and endless amenities, felt like a gilded cage. It provided everything her former life lacked: comfort, companionship, even excitement. Yet it was artificial, a curated illusion that made her long for the gritty imperfection of her tiny apartment and the routine monotony of her office.

When the movie ended, the screen retracted into the floor with the same quiet elegance it had emerged. The group exchanged sleepy smiles, their earlier tension softened by the shared experience. Lukas yawned loudly, stretching his arms. "Well, that was... not how I thought today would end," he said with a chuckle.

Bertrand nodded. "Feels strange, doesn't it? Like someone's watching us, testing how we unwind."

Eleanor's gaze sharpened. "That's because they are," she said flatly. "Every action, every choice we make here is being recorded and analysed. This isn't just a shelter—it's an experiment."

Her words cast a shadow over the group's relaxed mood. Sophie hugged her knees to her chest, her voice small. "But why us? What do they want?"

Eleanor stood, pacing slowly across the room. "That's the question we need to answer. Why us? What connects us? Until we figure that out, we're just playing along with their game."

The faint hum of the dome's systems seemed louder in the silence that followed. Eleanor glanced at the cubic cobot still dormant at the base of the table, its faint pulse a reminder of the invisible hand controlling their world.

"Tomorrow," she said, turning to the group. "We start asking real questions. No more games, no more distractions. We need to figure out who's behind this and how we get out."

As the others nodded hesitantly, Eleanor felt a flicker of determination reignite within her. The dome might offer the illusion of comfort, but it couldn't suppress her will to uncover the truth—and to escape, no matter the cost.

Eleanor found herself caught in the warmth of the day, the ease of the group's shared moments, and the comforting routine that had emerged within the dome. Despite her earlier scepticism, she felt her guard lower. For the first time in what seemed like forever, the pressure to analyse and resist softened, replaced by the allure of simply being.

Rowland, with his calm demeanour and quiet humour, had drawn her attention throughout the day. His steady presence felt grounding, a rare constant in their surreal environment. As the others began retreating to their designated spaces for the night, Eleanor lingered, catching Rowland's eye with a knowing glance.

The two moved toward the quieter corner of the dome, their conversation slipping into softer tones, punctuated by laughter and the occasional silence that spoke volumes. As they settled into the plush sofa, Eleanor felt herself drawn closer, her defences melting away as she traced his features with her fingertips.

It had been too long since she had allowed herself this kind of vulnerability. Here, under the artificial stars projected on the dome's ceiling, she let the moment take over. The embrace was gentle at first, but soon their connection deepened, breaking through the isolation each of them had felt since arriving in this strange place.

Rowland responded with equal tenderness, his touch reassuring in a way that reminded her of the humanity they still shared, even within the

confines of their fabricated reality. For one night, the questions, the fears, and the hidden agendas of their captors could wait. Eleanor allowed herself to feel, to love, and to hope, if only fleetingly, that this connection might help her endure the challenges ahead.
As the dome's lights dimmed further, they drifted into a peaceful sleep, wrapped in each other's arms, unaware of the silent cube at the table's base glowing faintly, recording every moment.

The two made love with taste and passion, only the silence of others could lead them to surpass that threshold, that desire to explore other people's bodies.
The intensity between Eleanor and Rowland grew in the privacy of the dimly lit dome, a fleeting escape from the mounting uncertainties surrounding their confinement. Their connection, unburdened by the weight of survival and surveillance, was an act of rebellion against the sterile environment they were thrust into.
The night offered them solace, a rare moment to rediscover their own humanity amid the artificial constructs around them. Passion bloomed as they let down their emotional walls, allowing themselves to be vulnerable in ways that seemed impossible during the day. The warmth between them pushed aside the eerie silence of the dome, the mechanical hum of the structure fading into the background.
But as they crossed the threshold of intimacy, the unshakable reality of their situation lingered at the edges of their minds. The dome's lights dimmed almost completely, but the faint glow of the cube at the base of the table pulsed intermittently—a quiet, omnipresent observer of their actions. For now, they ignored it, consumed by the moment.
In the hours that followed, their bond felt solidified, yet Eleanor couldn't entirely suppress the creeping suspicion of being watched. Even in Rowland's arms, the unspoken questions returned: who was orchestrating all of this, and to what end? For now, those answers remained as out of reach as the world beyond the dome. But as Eleanor drifted into an uneasy sleep, one thought crystalized in her mind: tomorrow, they would have to face the truth—together.

## Chapter 7: The Human Experiment

The night in the dome offered rare solace, a fleeting reprieve from the constructed artifice enclosing their lives. Beneath the filtered glow of distant stars projected on the dome's ceiling, Eleanor and Rowland had let their guards down, finding comfort in each other's presence. For a few precious hours, they rediscovered their humanity—the raw, unguarded emotions buried beneath layers of survival instinct.

The mechanical hum of the structure faded as their connection deepened, the cold sterility of the dome momentarily displaced by shared warmth. Vulnerability replaced the calculated caution that had marked their days, and in their embrace, Eleanor allowed herself to hope.

But even as their bond solidified, a shadow of unease crept in. The dome's lights dimmed to near darkness, the faint glow of the cube on the table pulsing with a steady rhythm—a silent, omnipresent observer. Eleanor tried to ignore it, to lose herself in Rowland's arms, but the feeling of being watched lingered like a whispered warning.

The week had passed in a slow, surreal blur, but Friday brought a new level of strangeness. They were ushered into a rectangular machine, its walls smooth and seamless, glowing faintly as the chamber sealed shut around them. A disembodied voice explained the procedure, clinical and detached, though its words only deepened Eleanor's unease.

The process began with a gelified solution that coated their bodies, its touch cool and oddly comforting as it cleansed them thoroughly, scrubbing away every trace of dirt and dead skin. Pulses of electrical stimulation followed, causing their muscles to tense and relax rhythmically, as if they were performing invisible exercises. The sensation was strange but oddly invigorating, leaving their bodies tingling with newfound strength.

Next came their teeth. Eleanor winced as precise jets of liquid cleaned and repaired them with startling efficiency, erasing imperfections she hadn't realized were there. A gentle mist enveloped them afterward, delivering a spirulina-based solution directly into their bloodstream. The voice assured them this would restore their natural acidity and replenish lost nutrients.

Finally, a fragrant gel was massaged into their hair and scalp, soothing and strengthening each strand. The machine's hands—soft yet firm—worked with mechanical precision, easing away tension Eleanor didn't know she carried. By the end, her hair felt stronger, her scalp refreshed, as if every follicle had been rejuvenated.

When the machine finally released them, Eleanor stepped out, feeling both revitalized and strangely violated. Her body buzzed with newfound energy, her senses sharper, her muscles taut. But beneath it all, a question gnawed at her: why? Why this invasive, meticulous care? What purpose did it serve, beyond sustaining them as pieces on an elaborate chessboard?

As the day wore on, Eleanor couldn't shake the sense that the dome was preparing them for something—something far more profound and far more dangerous than they'd yet imagined.

The group appreciated the "regenerative" therapy created by the pharmaceutical giant, and the room immediately began to echo with shouts and amused jokes.

"Well, that was... thorough," Rowland muttered, running a hand through his now-silky hair. His usual sarcasm couldn't mask the flicker of relief in his voice.

"Thorough? I feel like a shiny new car fresh from the assembly line!" Alex quipped, flexing his arms exaggeratedly. "What's next? A wax and polish?"

Laughter rippled through the room, cutting through the tension that had settled in the past few days. Eleanor managed a smile, but her thoughts lingered on the purpose behind the procedure. It wasn't just about keeping them healthy—there was something calculated about the precision and care, as if they were being prepared for something specific.

"They could at least offer us dinner and a show after that spa day from hell," Clara joked, leaning against the wall. Her humour, though light-hearted, couldn't completely hide the unease in her eyes.

"Who needs dinner?" Alex countered, patting his stomach. "That spirulina injection has me feeling full of... whatever the hell spirulina is."

"Algae," Eleanor murmured, distracted. "It's algae. High in protein and nutrients."

Alex raised an eyebrow. "Great. So, we're algae-filled, hair-reinforced superhumans now. Fantastic."

The group chuckled again, but their voices carried an edge of nervous energy, as if everyone was pretending that this was normal.

Eleanor's eyes drifted to the faint glow of the cube on the table in the corner of the room. It pulsed rhythmically, the quiet, watchful presence they had all learned to ignore—or at least pretend to. She wondered if it recorded their laughter, their banter, their fears. She wondered if it cared.

Rowland caught her staring. "Still thinking about it, huh?" he said softly, his voice cutting through the background noise of conversation.

She glanced at him, startled. "I can't help it. Everything here—it's too calculated. Too perfect. Every step feels planned."

Rowland shrugged, though his nonchalance was forced. "Whatever the plan is, we'll figure it out. Together."

The words were meant to reassure, but they only deepened her unease. It wasn't just the machine, or the dome, or the cube. It was the gnawing feeling that all of this—the regenerative therapy, the controlled environment, even their growing camaraderie—was part of something far bigger than they could comprehend.

The laughter died down as the group settled into an uneasy quiet, the day's events weighing on their minds. As the dome's artificial lights dimmed, signalling nightfall, Eleanor lay awake, staring at the faint patterns on the ceiling. Her body felt stronger, her mind sharper, but her heart was heavy with unanswered questions.

Tomorrow, she thought, would bring more tests. Not just the ones they were subjected to, but the ones they would have to face within themselves—and with each other.

The room immediately began to echo with shouts and amused jokes.

"Well, that was... thorough," Rowland muttered, running a hand through his now-silky hair. His usual sarcasm couldn't mask the flicker of relief in his voice.

"Thorough? I feel like a shiny new car fresh from the assembly line!" Alex quipped, flexing his arms exaggeratedly. "What's next? A wax and polish?"

Laughter rippled through the room, cutting through the tension that had settled in the past few days. But behind the amusement, a quiet unease lingered. Eleanor could feel it—she wasn't the only one questioning the intent behind such an invasive yet precise procedure.

What none of them voiced was the nagging awareness of the machine's purpose. While the gel and electrical stimulation revitalized their bodies, Eleanor couldn't ignore the subtle hisses and faint vibrations as sensors scanned them. It wasn't just a treatment—it was an analysis. Every touch of the machine's unseen mechanisms seemed designed to probe deeper, to extract something hidden.

Heart rate. Blood pressure. Body temperature. Respiratory parameters. Eleanor felt sure it had recorded it all. The accuracy with which the machine operated left little doubt: it was measuring their entire physiological makeup, every heartbeat, every shiver, every shift in their breath.

That night, as she drifted into a restless sleep, Eleanor couldn't shake the feeling of the machine's presence, its glowing hum etched into the corners of her mind.

When morning came, the group gathered reluctantly in the same room. The machine waited for them, its rectangular frame gleaming with an almost predatory stillness.

"Round two already?" Clara muttered; arms crossed over her chest. "I don't know about you guys, but I was hoping for at least a day off after yesterday's 'spa treatment.'"

"Think of it as a subscription plan," Alex joked, though his voice lacked its usual bravado. "First, they deep-clean us, and now they're upgrading us. Soon we'll get wings."

The disembodied voice returned as they approached. *"Step inside. Today's treatment will enhance vitality, physical resilience, and core strength."*

"Sounds promising," Rowland said, though his unease was clear.

The group exchanged hesitant glances before stepping inside the machine one by one. Eleanor entered last, her stomach tightening with apprehension as the door sealed behind her.

This time, the process felt different. More intense. The gel, thicker and warmer, clung to her skin as pulses of energy coursed through her muscles, deeper and more targeted than before. The sensation wasn't painful, but it was far from comfortable—like a workout compressed into seconds.

Jets of mist delivered concentrated vitamins and minerals, seeping into her pores and leaving her skin tingling. An unfamiliar pressure gripped her chest briefly, as if her lungs were being tested for capacity. Her heart raced, and she was sure the machine noted every beat.

By the time it ended, Eleanor's body hummed with energy, her limbs brimming with vitality she hadn't felt in years. Her muscles felt denser, her breath deeper, her mind sharper.

When she stepped out, she glanced at the others. Alex flexed his fingers, his brow furrowed. Clara pressed a hand to her chest as if measuring her heartbeat. Rowland simply stood still; his expression unreadable.

But it was Eleanor who noticed the most unsettling thing. The machine didn't power down after they left. Instead, its lights dimmed slightly, and its faint hum continued—a patient, watchful presence waiting for them to return.

Whatever this treatment was building toward, it wasn't over. Tomorrow, the machine would demand more.

And somewhere in the back of her mind, Eleanor wondered if they'd have a choice.

By the end of the second treatment, the changes were undeniable. Their physiques had begun to transform—not subtly, but in ways that were impossible to ignore. Alex, who had always been lean and wiry, now carried broader shoulders and arms thick with newfound muscle. Clara, who had complained of knee pain since the start of their ordeal, moved with a grace and ease that seemed almost unnatural.

Eleanor caught her reflection in a mirrored surface and blinked in surprise. Her figure had shifted noticeably—her posture straighter, her limbs leaner but undeniably stronger. Even her face seemed sharper, more vibrant, the shadows beneath her eyes erased.

And it wasn't just her. Everyone was taller, their frames more robust, their muscles defined in ways that suggested not just fitness, but purpose. Whatever the machine had done to them, it wasn't just maintenance. It was enhancement.

The group began to murmur among themselves, their voices buzzing with a mixture of excitement and speculation.

"This has to mean something," Alex said, rolling his shoulders as if testing his new strength. "Maybe they're getting us ready to send us back home. Like… they're fixing us up, making us better before we go."

Clara nodded, her expression hopeful. "It makes sense, doesn't it? Why else go to all this trouble? They want us to leave here... better than we came."

Rowland remained quiet; his brow furrowed as he stared at the ever-present cube in the corner. He didn't look convinced, but Eleanor couldn't ignore the stirrings of hope rising within her.

It had been a week since they'd arrived in the dome. A strange, disorienting, invasive week—but one marked by gradual improvements. The treatments, the controlled environment, even the strange nutritional cocktails they were given—it all seemed designed to perfect them, as though they were being prepared for something beyond the dome.

And for the first time, Eleanor allowed herself to believe that Alex and Clara might be right.

"Maybe this is it," she said aloud, her voice soft but steady. The others turned to her, surprised by the rare optimism in her tone. "Maybe they're sending us back soon. In a couple of weeks, even."

The idea took hold, spreading among the group like wildfire. Conversations became lighter, filled with talk of life beyond the dome, of families, friends, and futures waiting for them. Eleanor found herself swept up in their energy, though a small, cautious voice inside her whispered a warning: don't get carried away.

But it was hard not to. The physical transformations were undeniable, and the prospect of returning home as something stronger, better, even extraordinary, was intoxicating.

As the lights dimmed that evening and the group settled into their quarters, Eleanor let herself linger on the thought of home. The dome, with its calculated precision and cold mechanical hums, felt farther away for the first time.

Yet, as sleep began to take her, the faint glow of the cube caught her eye. Its rhythm was unchanged, its presence quiet yet heavy with intent. Eleanor shivered despite the warmth in the room.

Even with their growing hope, a question still lingered in her mind: what if this wasn't a preparation to leave? What if it was just the beginning of something they couldn't yet understand?

Step by step, their physiques continued to grow, their bodies transforming in ways that felt both exhilarating and unsettling. Heightened musculature made every movement feel powerful, almost effortless. Their postures straightened, their endurance sharpened, and even their senses seemed enhanced. But the changes didn't stop with their bodies.

Their minds shifted too. Eleanor noticed it first in the others, though she was reluctant to admit it was happening to her as well. Their personalities, once cooperative and grounded in shared survival, became more volatile. Small disagreements that had once ended in laughter now sparked into heated arguments. Voices grew louder, gestures more aggressive, as if their growing strength demanded to be expressed.

It started with little things. Alex and Clara bickered over who had taken more of the nutrient packs. Rowland snapped at Eleanor when she pointed out his pacing during one of their forced "rest" periods. By the end of the day, the air between them felt charged, like static electricity waiting for a spark.

And it didn't take long for the first spark to ignite.

"Get out of my way, Alex," Clara snapped, shoving him back with a force that startled everyone in the room.

"Your way?" Alex shot back, stepping forward and planting himself in front of her. "Since when do you own the whole dome?"

"Since I've had to listen to your endless whining," Clara retorted, her eyes narrowing.

"Enough!" Rowland barked, his voice booming louder than Eleanor had ever heard it. For a moment, the room fell silent. But even as the others reluctantly stepped back, their anger lingered, crackling in the air.

Eleanor stayed quiet, but the knot in her chest tightened. It wasn't just them. She could feel it too—a heat building inside her, a restlessness that was harder to contain with each passing day. It was as though the enhancements to their bodies were also feeding something darker within them.

The machine seemed to sense this shift, and its treatments adapted accordingly. Every day, its voice described the next steps as *necessary calibrations* to increase *vitality and stability*. But the group wasn't stabilizing.

If anything, they were unravelling.

By the week's end, Eleanor found herself snapping at Clara over something she couldn't even remember a few hours later. The sound of her own raised voice had startled her, but what frightened her more was the way it felt—good. Powerful.

And she wasn't the only one. The fights became more frequent, more intense, with hands clenched into fists and eyes blazing with challenge. Eleanor tried to calm herself, to remind the others of who they had been just days ago, but her words felt hollow. Each person seemed locked in their own struggle, a mix of defiance and an almost primal need to assert dominance.

The dome, for all its sterile serenity, was starting to feel like a cage. And the group—once bound by a shared desire to escape—was turning on itself.

One night, as Eleanor sat alone near the faintly glowing cube, she allowed herself to admit the truth she had been avoiding: the treatments weren't just enhancing them. They were changing them, reshaping them into something they couldn't yet understand.

And if the process continued, Eleanor feared there might not be anything of their former selves left to go home.

The tensions in the group reached a boiling point, but before another fight could break out, the machine's voice interrupted with cold, mechanical precision.
*"Treatments temporarily suspended. Proceed to next phase."*
The group froze, their anger momentarily overshadowed by confusion. The machine's hum grew louder, its glow intensifying as panels opened along its sides, revealing rows of gleaming instruments.
"What's the next phase?" Alex muttered; his voice tinged with unease.
No one had an answer, but the machine didn't wait for their consent. Robotic arms extended, each one holding a thin, metallic device resembling a needle. The group backed away instinctively, but the voice returned, calm and authoritative:
*"Remain still. The procedure is necessary for stabilization."*
Eleanor felt her heart race as one of the arms approached her. She wanted to run, to fight, but her body refused to move, frozen by a mix of fear and some unseen compulsion. The device pressed against her neck, cool and sharp, and she winced as it punctured her skin.
Around her, the others were being similarly subdued. Clara cried out as a needle sank into her leg, while Alex swore under his breath as one was inserted just beneath his collarbone. Rowland stayed eerily silent; his jaw clenched as a device attached to the side of his torso.
The moment the needle withdrew, Eleanor felt a strange warmth spreading from the puncture site, accompanied by a deep, aching pressure. She pressed a hand to her neck and gasped as something began to swell beneath her skin. A bubo, large and discoloured, pushed outward, its presence both grotesque and terrifying.
"What… what is this?" Clara stammered, clutching her leg as the same swelling appeared.
"No idea," Alex grunted, his voice strained as he doubled over, the bubo on his chest throbbing visibly. "But it doesn't feel like 'stabilization.'"
The pain grew sharper, radiating outward in waves that made Eleanor's vision blur. The group staggered, their movements sluggish, as though their bodies were shutting down. The air in the dome felt heavier, the faint hum of the cube now a deafening pulse in her ears.
One by one, they began to collapse. Alex fell first, his body hitting the ground with a dull thud. Clara followed moments later, her breaths shallow and ragged. Rowland tried to stay upright, gripping the edge of

a nearby table, but his knees buckled as his bubo darkened and swelled
further.

Eleanor fought to stay conscious, her hand still pressed against her neck
as the throbbing intensified. Her limbs felt like lead, her thoughts
sluggish and disjointed. The last thing she saw before darkness claimed
her was the cube's glow, brighter and more insistent than ever, as if it
was watching, recording, waiting.

The cube's eerie luminescence seemed to pulse in rhythm with their
fading heartbeats, its cold light casting long shadows across the room.
As consciousness slipped away, Eleanor had a fleeting thought that the
cube was not just an object, but a sentient entity, hungry for their
suffering. In their final moments of awareness, the trio felt an
inexplicable connection to one another, as if their shared agony had
forged an unbreakable bond that transcended even death. The awakening
was a harrowing experience, marked by excruciating physical
sensations. A terrible headache pounded relentlessly, while painful aches
radiated through their bones. As awareness slowly returned, they found
themselves in an unfamiliar and disorienting environment.

The surroundings were vastly different from what they remembered.
They were enclosed within a circular dome, creating a sense of
confinement and isolation. Each person was immobilized, secured to a
lounge chair by leather restraints that bound their arms and legs. The
restrictive nature of their situation added to the overall feeling of
helplessness and confusion.

This stark contrast between their last memories and current
circumstances likely intensified their discomfort and disorientation,
leaving them struggling to comprehend their new reality. The
individuals began to languish, moaning as they attempted to tear the
restraints that confined them to their chairs. Suddenly, a peculiar figure
wearing a shirt appeared across the room and started speaking, their
demeanour stern and imperious.

The scene depicts a distressing awakening, characterized by intense
physical discomfort and confusion. The subjects experienced severe
headaches and widespread bodily pain. As they regained consciousness,
they found themselves in an unfamiliar and bewildering setting, vastly
different from their previous recollections.

They were enclosed within a circular dome, which created a sense of confinement and isolation. Each person was immobilized, secured to a lounge chair by leather restraints binding their arms and legs. This restrictive situation amplified their feelings of helplessness and disorientation.

The stark contrast between their last memories and current circumstances likely intensified their distress, leaving them struggling to comprehend their situation and surroundings.
Suddenly a strange figure in a shirt across the room and began to speak, frowning and arrogant.
"Their presence was fundamental to the society to understand and explore; the science has made enormous steps since 800' and once and again it was important develop new models based on human intelligence"

Ten minutes later, the heavy silence was broken by the soft hiss of a sliding door. A figure in a white uniform entered—a nurse, their face obscured by a sleek, featureless mask. They moved with precise efficiency, carrying a strange device that emitted a faint hum. It resembled a laser tool, its tip glowing with an eerie blue light.
Without a word, the nurse approached Eleanor first. She recoiled instinctively, but the nurse raised a hand in a calming gesture. The blue light scanned over the swollen bubo on her neck, and Eleanor felt an immediate, soothing warmth. The sharp ache subsided, replaced by a tingling sensation as the device worked. Within moments, the swelling began to recede, the discoloration fading.
"It's... healing," Eleanor murmured, her voice a mix of awe and apprehension.
The nurse moved systematically from one to the next, treating Clara's leg, Alex's chest, and Rowland's torso. Each of them experienced the same rapid relief, their pain dulled and their strength slowly returning. Yet despite the physical improvements, an oppressive unease lingered.
Alex flexed his arms, testing his restored mobility. "Alright, that's better," he said, though his tone was cautious. "But why do I feel like we've just been patched up for something worse?"
The nurse finished their work and stepped back, the laser tool powering down with a faint whine. Without a word, they pointed toward a secondary door that had gone unnoticed until now. The message was clear: it was time to move.

"Wait," Clara said, her voice trembling. "Where are you taking us?"
The nurse didn't respond. Instead, they gestured again, more insistently.
The group exchanged wary glances but knew they had little choice.
They stood, their legs still shaky but functional, and began to follow.
As they passed through the door, the sterile, clinical environment of the
dome gave way to something far more disquieting. They found
themselves in a dimly lit corridor, the walls bare and metallic, stretching
endlessly in both directions. There were no signs, no windows, and no
visible exits. The air was colder, heavier, and carried an unsettling
silence broken only by the distant hum of unseen machinery.
"This place feels... wrong," Clara whispered, clutching her arms as they
walked.
"Wrong doesn't even cover it," Alex muttered, glancing over his
shoulder. The nurse followed a few steps behind, their presence both
reassuring and menacing.
Eventually, they reached another door, which slid open to reveal a small,
spartan room. Inside were four simple cots, a single table, and a faint
overhead light that flickered intermittently. No windows, no amenities—
just isolation.
"This is it?" Rowland asked, his voice filled with disbelief. "We're
supposed to stay here?"
The nurse finally spoke, their voice filtered and mechanical through the
mask. "This will be your station. You will remain here until further
notice. No outside communication is permitted. Meals and essentials
will be delivered."
"And what if we need help?" Eleanor demanded.
The nurse turned to leave, pausing only briefly at the door. "You won't."
With that, the door closed, the sound of its lock echoing through the
room. The group stood in stunned silence, the weight of their new reality
sinking in.
"No facilities, no answers," Clara said, her voice barely above a
whisper. "We're prisoners."
Eleanor sat heavily on one of the cots, her mind racing. "Not just
prisoners," she said, her jaw tightening. "We're experiments. And
whatever they've done to us, it's not over."
The others nodded, their fear mingling with a growing sense of resolve.
In this silent, isolated place, they knew they could trust only each other.
Their survival depended on understanding their captors' intentions—and
finding a way to escape before it was too late.

The figure's voice was cold, clinical, as they continued to speak. "You were chosen because you are... exceptional," they said, their tone carrying a faint trace of contempt. "Your resilience, your capacity for adaptation—it all serves a greater purpose. You should consider yourselves fortunate."

Eleanor's head throbbed with each word, her vision still swimming from the residual pain. She squinted, trying to focus on the logo stitched onto the figure's jacket. It was an abstract design, a swirling pattern that seemed to shift under the stark white light of the dome. Recognition flickered at the edge of her consciousness, but it remained just out of reach.

"What... do you want from us?" Eleanor rasped; her voice weak but defiant.

The figure's eyes narrowed. "Your compliance. Your cooperation is not merely requested—it is expected. You are now part of something far beyond your comprehension, a system that will redefine humanity's place in the cosmos."

Alex groaned, struggling against his restraints. "And if we refuse?"

The figure's lips curled into a thin smile. "You misunderstand. Refusal is not an option. The procedure you experienced was just the beginning. Your bodies are now hosts to a unique symbiosis—one that grants you access to knowledge, to power, but also binds you to us. Any attempt to resist or escape will result in... catastrophic consequences."

Clara gasped; her eyes wide with fear. "You've turned us into experiments," she whispered.

"Experiments?" the figure echoed; their voice almost amused. "No, my dear. You are pioneers. The bubo you see is not a disease; it is an interface. A gateway. Through it, you will perceive realities and dimensions far beyond your own. Painful, yes, but pain is the price of evolution."

Rowland, who had remained silent until now, lifted his head with visible effort. "What's the endgame?" he asked, his voice steady despite the tremor in his hands.

The figure stepped closer, their shadow falling over Rowland. "The endgame is survival. The universe is a harsh and unyielding place. Adaptation is the only path forward. With your help, we will achieve a new paradigm of existence."

The room fell silent, save for the faint hum of the cube. Its glow seemed to pulse in response to the figure's words, as if in agreement. Eleanor felt a surge of dread. Whatever had been done to them, it was irreversible. They were trapped in a game they didn't understand, their bodies and minds no longer their own.

"We'll never stop fighting," Eleanor said, her voice low but resolute.

The figure chuckled; a sound devoid of warmth. "Fight if you must. It will make no difference. In time, you will see the truth."

With that, they turned and walked away, leaving the group alone in the dome. The cube's light intensified, bathing the room in an eerie brilliance. One by one, the restraints released, but their newfound freedom felt hollow. The warmth spreading from their buboes pulsed stronger now, like a second heartbeat, a constant reminder of the transformation they could not escape.

As the group gathered their strength, a new resolve began to form. They were altered, yes, but not defeated. If they were to survive, they would need to unlock the mysteries of the cube, to turn their forced evolution into a weapon against their captors.

Eleanor clenched her fists, her eyes burning with determination. "We'll find a way out," she whispered. "Together."

As the sterile light of their confinement dimmed, the door hissed open once more. Without a word, the nurse from before returned, gesturing for them to follow. Weary but compliant, the group exchanged tense glances and fell into step behind the masked figure.

Their path led them back through the same dim corridors, but this time, the air seemed charged with anticipation. Eleanor's stomach churned— not just from hunger, but from a growing sense of dread.

When they re-entered the dome, it was unrecognizable. The clinical sterility they had first encountered was gone, replaced by a space teeming with activity and life. Banks of holographic displays lined the walls, each depicting intricate, shifting models of human anatomy. The centre of the dome was dominated by a massive, transparent column filled with a swirling, bioluminescent substance. Inside, shapes moved and shifted, indistinct but undeniably organic.

"What... is this?" Clara whispered; her eyes wide.

"Welcome," a voice rang out, smooth and authoritative. From the shadows stepped a figure in a lab coat, their presence commanding. Unlike the nurse, their face was visible—sharp features, eyes gleaming with an unsettling mix of pride and detachment. The same swirling logo adorned their coat, now glowing faintly in the dim light.

"You stand at the forefront of scientific revolution," the figure said, spreading their arms as if to present the room itself. "What you see here is the culmination of centuries of research, innovation, and sacrifice."

Alex's fists clenched. "Sacrifice?" he repeated. "What kind of sacrifice?"

The figure smiled faintly, as though amused by the question. "Every breakthrough requires a cost," they said. "You have been selected to bear witness to the future of medicine—no, the future of life itself."

They gestured toward the central column. The substance within shifted, and suddenly, the shapes inside became clear. They were human organs—hearts, lungs, and brains—suspended in the glowing fluid, pulsing as though alive.

"These," the figure continued, "are fully synthetic, yet biologically indistinguishable from their natural counterparts. They grow, adapt, and even self-repair. With these advancements, we can eliminate disease, extend life indefinitely, and even rebuild the human body from the ground up."

Rowland stepped forward, his voice low and steady. "And what about us? What did you put in us?"

The figure's smile didn't falter. "You are hosts to the next phase of our research. The interfaces within your bodies allow you to seamlessly integrate with these new systems. Your pain, your fear—they were temporary side effects of adaptation. Now, you are part of something far greater."

Clara shook her head, taking a step back. "You're playing god," she said, her voice trembling. "This isn't medicine—it's manipulation."

"Medicine has always been manipulation," the figure replied calmly. "A battle against nature's flaws. We have simply perfected it."

Eleanor's eyes were drawn to a nearby hologram. It displayed a human figure, overlaid with data streams and diagnostic readouts. As she watched, the figure's damaged organs were systematically replaced by the glowing synthetic versions from the column. The process was seamless, efficient—and deeply unsettling.

"What happens if we refuse to participate?" she asked, her voice cold.

The figure's expression darkened slightly. "Refusal," they said, "is an inefficient use of resources. But understand this: your cooperation ensures the survival of humanity. Your resistance would only hinder progress."

The weight of their words hung in the air, heavy and oppressive. The group stood in silence, the enormity of their situation sinking in. They were no longer just individuals; they were cogs in a vast, incomprehensible machine, one that sought to reshape life itself.

As their stomachs growled with hunger, the irony struck Eleanor. Even in the face of such monumental scientific advancements, their most basic human need remained. Yet what they had witnessed had fundamentally altered their perception of science and its role in shaping the future.

"We'll eat," she said finally, her voice steady but filled with quiet defiance. "But this isn't over."

The figure inclined their head slightly, as if acknowledging a challenge. "Of course," they said. "For now, you must nourish yourselves. The journey ahead will demand much of you."

With that, they gestured toward a nearby table that had silently emerged from the floor. It bore plates of food—simple but sufficient. The group hesitated only briefly before approaching, driven by hunger but wary of what lay ahead.

As they ate in uneasy silence, the glowing column continued its relentless, hypnotic dance. The future of life, they realized, was not just being observed—it was being manufactured.

# Chapter 8: A dangerous pursuit

The Siberian winds howled through the trees as Braham and his entourage made their way through the snowy terrain. Despite the biting cold, their spirits were buoyed by the warm reception they had received from the locals of Brekvenny. The villagers had offered food, shelter, and invaluable knowledge of the land, a generosity that left the group feeling both humbled and fortified.

But the mission could not wait. Time was their greatest adversary, and the stakes were too high to linger. Brekvenny was more than a simple village—it sat at the crossroads of a mystery that had drawn Braham and his team across continents. Somewhere in the dense forests and treacherous mountains surrounding the area lay answers they desperately needed.

"Remember," Braham said, his voice low but firm as they gathered just beyond the village's edge, "our objective is clear. We need data—any signs of the anomalies reported in this region. Stay alert, stay together, and document everything."

The group nodded, their expressions a mix of determination and apprehension. Each carried specialized equipment: thermal scanners, portable drones, and radiation detectors, all designed to capture and analyse environmental irregularities.

As they moved deeper into the wilderness, the landscape grew more forbidding. Towering pines loomed overhead; their branches heavy with snow. The ground beneath their boots was uneven, a mix of frozen earth and hidden roots. The air was thick with the scent of pine and the faint, metallic tang of impending snow.

An hour into their journey, the first signs of the unusual began to surface. A faint hum, barely perceptible, seemed to emanate from the ground. Braham knelt, pressing a hand to the icy surface. "It's warmer here," he noted, frowning. "Too warm for this time of year."

Mira, the team's geologist, activated her thermal scanner. The device emitted a soft beep as it registered a heat signature below the surface. "He's right," she confirmed, her eyes narrowing at the display. "There's something down there—possibly geothermal activity, but the readings are... odd."

"Odd how?" asked Eamon, their tech specialist, as he set up a drone for an aerial sweep.

"The heat is concentrated in irregular patches," Mira explained. "Natural geothermal vents usually show a more consistent spread."

Eamon sent the drone skyward, its small rotors buzzing as it ascended. The live feed displayed on his tablet revealed a stark contrast between the frozen landscape and the warmer zones Mira had identified. But something else caught his attention—a series of faint, circular depressions in the snow, forming a pattern that radiated outward from the central zone.

"Take a look at this," Eamon said, tilting the tablet for the others to see. "These formations—too uniform to be natural."

Braham's brow furrowed as he studied the screen. "Set a waypoint," he ordered. "We'll investigate on foot."

The group moved cautiously, the eerie hum growing louder with each step. When they reached the nearest depression, they found not just a simple indentation but what appeared to be the remnants of a structure. Broken stone, weathered metal, and fragments of machinery lay half-buried in the snow, their purpose and origin unclear.

"This isn't local," Mira said, running her hand over one of the stones. "The material composition is completely foreign—could be centuries old, or... something else entirely."

Braham's eyes scanned the horizon. The forest was still, almost unnervingly so, as if holding its breath. "Document everything," he said. "Whatever this is, it's significant."

As they worked, a sudden gust of wind swept through the clearing, carrying with it a faint, almost human-like whisper. The group froze, their eyes wide.

"Did you hear that?" Clara, the team's linguist, asked, her voice barely above a whisper.

Braham nodded, his hand instinctively moving to the radio on his belt. "We keep moving," he said, his tone more resolute than ever. "We're getting closer to the truth, but we need to be ready for whatever lies ahead."

The team pressed on; their resolve unwavering. The anomalies they sought were no longer just rumours—they were real, and they were waiting to be uncovered.


The Siberian winter was as unforgiving as ever. By night, temperatures plummeted to as low as -20°C, and even during the day, the mercury barely climbed above -10°C. The snow fell in relentless waves, covering the landscape in thick, blinding white. At least three to four days a week, the snowstorm raged without pause, burying paths and turning every journey into a treacherous ordeal.

Braham stood at the edge of the village, watching the snow swirl under the dim light of a nearby lantern. His breath came out in frosty puffs, and despite his heavy fur-lined coat, the cold bit through to his bones. His team gathered around him; each member visibly wearies from the harsh conditions.

"This isn't going to work tonight," Braham said, his voice heavy with pragmatism. "Visibility's down to nothing, and the roads are ice traps. We push forward tomorrow."

The group murmured their agreement. The idea of navigating the snowbound wilderness in such conditions was not only reckless but potentially fatal.

"I've arranged for a vehicle from the village," Braham continued. "They've outfitted it with studded tires. It should handle the ice and snow better than we could on foot. If the storm clears overnight, we'll have a much better chance of making progress."

Clara shivered, pulling her scarf tighter around her face. "That's a relief. The thought of getting stranded out there in this weather..."

"We'd never make it back," Alex finished grimly.

Braham nodded. "Exactly. We need to conserve our strength and work smart. Get some rest tonight. We'll regroup at first light."

The team dispersed, retreating to the warmth of the village's communal hall. The Siberians had been more than generous, providing not only shelter but also hearty meals to sustain them. Bowls of steaming borscht and plates of dark rye bread were set out, and the scent of smoked fish and fresh herbs filled the air.

As they ate, the tension in the room eased slightly. The fire crackled in the stone hearth, and for a moment, they could almost forget the harshness waiting outside.

"Think we'll find anything out there tomorrow?" Eamon asked, breaking the silence.

"We'll find something," Braham replied, his tone resolute. "We've already seen signs of the anomalies. Tomorrow, we get closer. But we need to be prepared for anything."

The team nodded in silent agreement. They knew that the real challenge lay not in surviving the elements, but in uncovering the secrets hidden beneath the snow—and whatever dangers might come with them.

The first light of dawn cast a pale, silvery glow over Brekvenny, illuminating the snow-covered village as it stirred to life. Braham and his team gathered near the mechanic's workshop, their breath fogging in the frigid air. Two Niva Ladas, rugged and reliable, stood ready for the journey. The mechanic had worked through the night, fitting them with studded tires and reinforcing their undercarriages to handle the treacherous terrain.

Mira climbed into the driver's seat of the first vehicle, her hands steady despite the cold. Braham took the wheel of the second, his sharp eyes scanning the horizon as the team loaded their gear into the back. They brought everything they might need: thermal blankets, first-aid kits, and an array of scientific instruments to capture data on the anomalies. This wasn't just an expedition—it was a step into the unknown.

"Everyone ready?" Braham called out, his voice cutting through the crisp morning air.

A chorus of affirmations followed as the team bundled into the vehicles. The engines roared to life, a low, guttural sound that seemed almost defiant against the harsh Siberian winter. With a nod from Braham, the convoy began its slow crawl toward the scientific centre.

The path ahead was the only route available, a narrow and winding trail that had not seen proper maintenance in years. Snow and ice had claimed large sections of the road, and the rest was a mixture of frozen mud and jagged rocks. Fallen trees and the remnants of old landslides loomed on either side, making the journey feel like threading a needle through the wilderness.

Mira kept her eyes on the trail, her hands gripping the steering wheel tightly. The Niva bucked and jolted over the uneven terrain, but she maintained control. Behind her, Braham followed at a cautious distance, his focus unwavering.

"Any signs of trouble ahead?" Braham asked over the radio.

"Not yet," Mira replied, her voice calm. "But the road's getting worse."

The further they travelled, the more the landscape changed. The trees thinned, giving way to an expanse of frozen marshland. The air grew heavier, and the faint hum they had detected the day before returned, more distinct now, resonating through the vehicles.

"We're getting close," Eamon said from the passenger seat of Braham's Niva, monitoring the readings on his tablet. "The anomalies are stronger here."

Clara, seated in the back, leaned forward. "Let's hope the centre isn't completely buried under all this snow. "The street was interrupted by a ruined bridge that
they managed to dredge a hundred meters downstream thanks to the low river level
After another gruelling hour of driving, they crested a small hill and finally caught sight of their destination. The scientific centre, a group of low, dome structures, sat partially obscured by the forest. Its once-sleek facade was now weathered and covered in frost, but it remained intact—a relic of a forgotten past.
"We've made it," Braham said, relief evident in his tone. "Everyone stays sharp. We don't know what we'll find inside."
They parked the vehicles a short distance from the building, wary of getting too close in case of structural instability. As they stepped out, the cold hit them with renewed force, but adrenaline and determination kept them moving.
"Let's gear up," Braham said, pulling his hood tighter against the wind. "This is where the real work begins."

Concealed beneath the dense canopy of the forest, Braham and his team carefully observed the scientific centre from a safe distance. The complex consisted of several domes, their surfaces a dull gray that blended almost seamlessly with the snowy landscape. From their position, they could make out patrols moving methodically between the structures, their figures occasionally silhouetted against the pale light. Armed defences were apparent—guards stationed at key entry points and elevated platforms equipped with what looked like automated turrets.
Eamon adjusted his binoculars, focusing on the perimeter. "There's a pattern to their patrols," he muttered. "Two-man teams, rotating every ten minutes. And those turrets—they're motion-activated. We'll need to be careful."
Clara crouched beside him, her camera clicking softly as she captured the layout. "See that?" she whispered, pointing toward a partially obscured section of the dome nearest to them. "Looks like some kind of ventilation system. If we're going to get inside, that might be our best bet."
Braham nodded, taking mental notes. "Good spot. We'll scout closer tonight."

Suddenly, a distant, mournful howl cut through the quiet, sending a shiver down their spines. The sound was followed by another, this one closer. The group tensed, their eyes scanning the treeline. The howls were joined by a low growl, and then a sudden, guttural roar.

From the shadows emerged a massive white bear, its powerful frame cutting through the snow with alarming speed. Its coat was thick and matted with ice, and its black eyes locked onto the group. For a moment, it seemed to hesitate, then charged toward them, its massive paws thundering against the frozen ground.

"Scatter!" Braham barked; his voice urgent.

Clara, quick on her feet, raised her rifle and fired a shot into the air. The loud crack echoed through the forest, startling the beast. It skidded to a halt, its head jerking upward in confusion. Clara lowered her rifle, grinning despite the adrenaline coursing through her veins.

"False alarm, guys," she said, laughing nervously. "Just a bear trying to stake its claim."

The bear let out a final huff before turning and lumbering away, its massive form growing smaller with each passing second. The team regrouped; their breaths visible in the cold air as they watched the creature disappear into the distance.

"Lucky it backed off," Mira said, her voice shaky. "That could've gone a lot worse."

"We can't afford any more distractions," Braham said, his tone serious. "Gunfire could draw attention. We stick to the plan—quiet and precise."

They moved deeper into the forest, putting at least a kilometre between themselves and the dome. From this new vantage point, they continued their surveillance, piecing together the layout of the complex and identifying potential weaknesses.

"We strike by surprise," Braham reiterated, his voice low but resolute. "No second chances. Let's make it count."


The snow-covered forest provided a natural fortress of concealment, its towering pines and thick underbrush masking the group's presence.

After the excitement with the bear, Braham decided they should remain hidden for a while longer, both to continue their reconnaissance and to ensure they weren't being followed.

They settled in a small clearing at the edge of the woods, where the trees formed a dense canopy, offering shelter from the falling snow. Mira and Alex worked quickly to assemble a small bonfire, using dry kindling they had packed along with fallen branches. Within minutes, a modest flame flickered to life, casting a warm orange glow that pushed back the cold and shadows.

The team gathered around the fire, grateful for the warmth. Clara, ever resourceful, set up a snare earlier in their trek, and now she returned triumphantly with a wild rabbit. It was a small catch, but in the freezing conditions, any fresh food was a blessing.

"I'll clean it," she said, already reaching for her knife.

The rabbit was prepared with efficiency, skinned and spitted over the fire. The scent of roasting meat soon mingled with the crisp forest air, a welcome distraction from the cold and tension.

As they ate, they spoke in hushed tones, sharing observations and refining their plan for the next infiltration attempt.

"Did you see how the guards avoided the northeastern dome?" Mira asked, her voice barely above a whisper. "Something's going on there."

"Could be a secure lab or storage area," Eamon speculated, wiping his hands on a cloth. "We'll need to investigate that first."

Clara nodded. "The ventilation system there might give us a way in without tripping any alarms."

Braham listened, his eyes on the distant domes barely visible through the gaps in the trees. "We'll confirm everything tonight. Once we're certain of the weak points, we'll make our move."

As the fire dwindled, the group extinguished the embers carefully, ensuring no trace of their presence remained. The forest returned to its natural quiet, the only sounds now the whisper of wind through the trees and the crunch of snow underfoot as they packed up.

Feeling reinvigorated, they began their trek back to the village under the darkening sky. The warmth of the fire and the hearty meal had given them the strength they needed for the challenges ahead. The village of Brekvenny awaited, its people unaware of the dangerous secrets lurking just beyond the forest's edge. The return was quickest than ever, they didn't put attention to frozen edges, frozen trails of water in the road and they arrived in a flash.


As twilight descended over Brekvenny, the village came alive in its unique, heartwarming way. Warm light spilled from the small windows of the wooden cabins, and the scent of hearty stews and freshly baked bread filled the crisp air. Despite the unforgiving Siberian winter, the villagers carried a warmth that could chase away even the deepest cold.

Braham and his team returned to the communal hall, their faces flushed from the cold and exertion. Inside, the atmosphere was vibrant, with laughter and conversation filling the room.

Long wooden tables were lined with steaming dishes of food—roasted game, thick soups, and stacks of dense rye bread. Jugs of homemade vodka and berry-infused spirits made the rounds, adding a festive spark to the gathering.

The villagers welcomed the group with open arms, eager to hear tales of their exploits in the forest. Mira found herself seated beside an elderly man who regaled her with stories of Brekvenny's history, tales of resilience and survival passed down through generations. Clara joined a group of younger villagers who were already tuning their instruments— an accordion, a balalaika, and a set of drums. Before long, the hall was filled with the lively sounds of Siberian folk music.

The melodies were infectious, and soon the entire room was clapping along. A few villagers began to dance, their movements fluid and rhythmic despite the confined space. Alex, initially reluctant, was pulled into the circle by a boisterous villager, and before he knew it, he was laughing and stomping in time with the beat.

Eamon, meanwhile, engaged in a friendly drinking contest with a wiry man who claimed to have never been bested. The table erupted in cheers as they downed shot after shot, their faces glowing with equal parts pride and vodka-induced warmth.

Braham, ever the observer, stood near the fire, watching his team blend seamlessly with the villagers. Despite the weight of their mission, he found himself smiling. This moment of joy and camaraderie was a rare reprieve, a reminder of the human spirit's resilience even in the harshest conditions.

As the evening wore on, the celebration took on a more reflective tone. Villagers shared songs of old, their voices harmonizing in hauntingly beautiful melodies. Stories were exchanged—some humourous, others filled with the quiet wisdom of those who had lived through countless Siberian winters.

By the time the night grew late, the group felt more connected to the village and its people than ever before. The sense of community, the shared laughter, and the warmth of the fire left an indelible mark on them, a powerful contrast to the cold and danger they faced in the wilderness beyond.

The hall buzzed with life as the celebration carried on well into the night. The villagers' voices rose in song, blending harmoniously with the lively tunes of the balalaika and accordion. Feet stomped and hands clapped in rhythm, the wooden floor vibrating with the energy of the dance. The warmth of the fire, combined with the joy in the air, created a refuge from the cold reality waiting beyond the village.

Braham and his team immersed themselves in the festivities. Plates of steaming Maral stew and hearty onion soup were passed around, their rich, savory aromas filling the room. The soup, with its tender chunks of venison and caramelized onions, was a particular favourite, its warmth spreading through them like a comforting embrace. It was sustenance not just for the body, but for the soul—a taste of home in a foreign land.

Between songs, villagers raised their glasses, toasting to life, resilience, and their honoured guests. The dried vodka, sharp and invigorating, flowed freely, fuelling laughter and loosening even the most reserved among them. The drink's warmth settled in their chests, dulling the bite of the Siberian chill and heightening the festive mood.

But as the night deepened, fatigue began to creep in. The combination of a full day's work, the rich food, and the potent vodka slowly took its toll. One by one, the group began to feel the weight of exhaustion.

By the time the clock struck two, the songs had slowed, and the dancers had retired to their seats, their movements now a gentle sway. The fire crackled softly, its light casting long shadows across the room.

Braham stood, stretching with a tired but contented smile. "Time to call it a night," he said, his voice low but resolute. The others nodded in agreement; their eyes heavy with sleep.

The villagers bid them goodnight with warm smiles and firm handshakes, their gratitude for the shared evening evident. The group made their way through the snowy paths back to their rooms, the village now quiet under the serene blanket of night.

As they settled into their beds, the memories of the evening lingered—a rare moment of warmth and joy amidst the harshness of their mission. The sounds of laughter and song seemed to echo softly in their minds as sleep claimed them, preparing them for whatever challenges the next day would bring.

The next day, Braham met with the cook he had chatted with on his first evening, who was known as "a sherpa" for the community, and the town's priest. Both were deeply concerned about the strange "alien" centre and eager to gather as much information as possible. They shared alarming news: at least a dozen people had disappeared in that area, and they had seen military vehicles, all with Russian license plates, entering the block of buildings.

Braham listened intently as the cook and the priest recounted their observations. The cook, a man with a wealth of local knowledge, detailed how he had noticed unusual activities around the centre, including nighttime deliveries and heavily guarded entrances. The priest added that several parishioners had mentioned seeing strange lights and hearing disturbing noises coming from the facility.

"We need to uncover what's really happening in there," Braham said, his voice resolute. "If people are disappearing and there's military involvement, we can't ignore it."

The cook nodded. "We've already started keeping a closer watch. Anything suspicious, we'll note down and report to you."

The priest agreed, his expression grim. "We must protect our community. I'll speak to others and see if anyone else has information." As they parted ways, Braham felt a renewed sense of purpose. He knew that the information they gathered could be crucial in exposing the truth behind the "alien" centre and ensuring the safety of the townspeople. With the support of the cook and the priest, he felt more determined than ever to uncover the sinister motives lurking behind the facility's walls.

To conquer the fortress, Braham knew they needed to procure weapons and bulletproof vests. He turned to the cook and the priest, his tone serious. "Do you know anyone who can help us get the supplies we need?" he asked.

The cook nodded thoughtfully. "There are a few people in the town who might be able to help. I'll reach out to them discreetly."

The priest added, "I'll speak to some of the parishioners. There's a small network of people who are sympathetic to our cause. We should be able to gather what you need."

As they discussed the plan, the rest of the group joined them. Clara, ever the caretaker, was handing out steaming cups of tea and dry biscuits to everyone. The warmth of the tea was a small comfort in the midst of their tense discussions.

"We need to move quickly but carefully," Braham said, addressing the group. "Once we have the supplies, we'll need to plan our next steps. We can't afford to rush this."

Clara nodded; her expression determined. "We'll make sure everyone is ready. We can't let fear stop us now."

With the cook and the priest working to secure the necessary supplies, and the group united in their resolve, Braham felt a flicker of hope. They had a plan, and they had each other. It was time to take action and confront the dangers that lay ahead.

## Chapter 9: A moment of truth

The days passed with increasing energy and camaraderie. The group's bond grew stronger, and the cobot's cheerful presence kept everyone entertained with a constant stream of quizzes, pastimes, and thought-provoking questions reminiscent of Hamlet.
Eleanor, although still harbouring a quiet affection for Rowland, found herself spending more time with Lukas, the ever-dreamy brunette. Lukas' imaginative nature and philosophical musings provided Eleanor with a comforting distraction from the complexities of their situation. The group, now united and more resilient than ever, faced each challenge with a renewed sense of purpose. With each passing day, their resolve to uncover the truth behind the mysterious centre grew stronger, driven by the support and strength they found in each other.
Their enormous circular room always revealed new scenarios, transformed objects into wardrobes, enriched their days with fun and interest. Eleanor was already certain that, step by step, she had to abandon the idea of belonging to an experiment, whether it was scientific, cultural, or pharmaceutical. She had to escape from that centre.
But escape was no simple matter. The room itself seemed alive, shifting and rearranging itself as if responding to her every move. The walls would pulse softly, emitting a hum that reverberated in her chest. Sometimes, she would wake up to find the entire space reconfigured—a once-cozy corner now a stark laboratory, the soft cushions replaced by sterile metal surfaces.
Eleanor had tried to communicate with the others. There were voices, faint and distant, echoing through hidden corridors, but they were never clear, never consistent. It was as though the centre wanted to keep them apart, to isolate them in their own evolving environments.
One day, the room presented her with a peculiar object: a key. It was unlike anything she had seen before, a shimmering blend of organic and metallic material. It pulsed lightly in her hand, almost as if it were alive. She knew instinctively that this was a turning point, a gift—or perhaps a challenge—from the room itself.
With the key in hand, Eleanor began to explore the room more boldly. She touched the glasses, searching for hidden seams or doors. The room

responded, its surface rippling like water under her fingertips. Finally, a section of the wall slid away, revealing a dark passage.

Her heart pounded as she stepped through. The air was cooler here, the hum of the room replaced by a distant, rhythmic thudding—like the heartbeat of some colossal creature. The passage was lined with symbols that glowed faintly as she passed, their meanings just beyond her grasp. As she moved deeper, Eleanor felt a growing sense of purpose.

Whatever lay at the end of this journey, she was determined to uncover the truth. The centre had controlled her for too long, but now, with each step, she was reclaiming her freedom.

The passage opened into a vast chamber, its ceiling stretching so high it disappeared into darkness. At its centre stood a towering structure, a monolithic console adorned with the same glowing symbols. Eleanor approached cautiously, the key in her hand vibrating with increasing intensity.

She placed the key into a slot at the console's base. The chamber trembled as the symbols on the console flared to life. A voice, calm and resonant, filled the space.

"Welcome, Eleanor. You have reached the core. Your journey has only just begun."

Vromm ! a large metal door opened itself to a subterranean passage probably used to grow plants and fishes in a heated environment with artificial illumination;

the canal contained freshwater fish such as sturgeon and trout, their sleek bodies gliding effortlessly through the crystal-clear water. Algae clung to the submerged stones, their emerald strands swaying gently with the current, visible through a half-height glass wall that ran along one side of the path. The water shimmered under soft, ambient lighting, creating a tranquil yet vibrant ecosystem.

On the opposite side of the path, an entirely different environment thrived. Rows of leafy greens, tomatoes, and herbs flourished under a canopy of ultraviolet lights, their purples and blues blending into a surreal glow. The vegetables were arranged in a precise, almost geometric pattern, each plant connected by a network of irrigation pipes that dripped water and nutrients at regular intervals. The air smelled fresh, a mix of earthiness from the soil and the faint tang of chlorophyll. The stone floor beneath Eleanor's feet was cool and textured, grounding her in the strange yet harmonious blend of nature and technology. The internal temperature hovered comfortably between 18 and 20 degrees

Celsius, carefully controlled to maintain the delicate balance of both aquatic and terrestrial life.

Eleanor paused to observe the interplay of ecosystems, her mind racing. This wasn't just a contained environment; it was a symbiotic system, self-sustaining and meticulously engineered. The canal and the vegetable beds weren't mere decorations—they were part of a larger design, one that hinted at something far more complex than she had initially imagined.

She ran her hand along the smooth glass, watching as a sturgeon swam past, its ancient eyes seeming to meet hers for a fleeting moment. On the vegetable side, the rhythmic drip of water from the pipes was almost hypnotic. It was as though the entire place was alive, not just with the pulse of life but with intent.

What was this place really? Eleanor couldn't shake the feeling that it was more than an experiment. It was a model, a prototype for a new way of living, perhaps even survival. And she was an integral part of it, whether she liked it or not.

travelled at least 150 meters of the canal; all the plants were cared for daily as was evident from precise cuts and fruits and vegetables with precise ripeness. She was about to taste a strawberry when a voice made her jump; "it is not allowed to remain in the underground cultivation area" the group quickly headed towards her, fully armed with camouflage uniforms and dark helmets.

Eleanor was blocked, her frantic attempts to resist met with swift precision. Strong hands bound her wrists and ankles with coarse cords, their grip unyielding. She thrashed, but it was no use; the restraints dug into her skin, forcing her into submission. Two figures, their faces obscured by featureless masks, hauled her to her feet and began escorting her down a dimly lit corridor.

The passage twisted and turned, disorienting her further. The air grew colder, the soft hum of the canal and the vibrant glow of the vegetable garden now distant memories. They passed rooms filled with strange machinery; their purposes unfathomable. Shadows flickered on the walls, cast by the faint, pulsing light of symbols that seemed to watch her as she was dragged past.

After what felt like an eternity, they reached a massive door. It slid open silently, revealing the directional centre.

The room was vast and sterile, its walls lined with screens displaying data streams, maps, and incomprehensible symbols. At its centre stood a raised platform, bathed in a cold, white light. Surrounding it were several figures, their faces illuminated by the glow of the monitors. Unlike her captors, these people wore no masks. Their expressions were a mix of curiosity, calculation, and something Eleanor could only describe as detachment.

She was brought to the platform and forced to her knees. One of the figures, an older man with piercing gray eyes, stepped forward. He held a device in his hand, a sleek, metallic instrument that hummed softly as he approached.

"Eleanor," he said, his voice calm but firm. "You've seen more than we intended. You've begun to piece together the nature of this place."

She glared at him, her breath ragged. "What is this? Why am I here?"

The man tilted his head slightly, as if considering how much to reveal. "You were chosen for your resilience, your ability to adapt. This facility is more than an experiment—it's a proving ground. Humanity is on the brink, and we are preparing for what comes next."

His words hung in the air, heavy with implication. Eleanor's mind raced, trying to make sense of it all. "Preparing? For what?"

The man's gaze didn't waver. "For survival. This centre is a microcosm, a controlled environment designed to test the viability of coexisting ecosystems and human adaptability. You are part of that test."

Eleanor's pulse quickened. "And if I don't cooperate?"

The man sighed, as though he had hoped she wouldn't ask. "Then we will reset your memory, as we've done before. But I suspect this time, you will resist even that. You are…unique."

Eleanor's eyes widened. *Reset my memory? How many times had they done this?* Panic surged through her, but beneath it, a spark of determination ignited. If they had underestimated her before, they wouldn't make that mistake again. She would find a way to escape, to expose whatever this place truly was.

But for now, she remained still, silently plotting her next move.

"We recreated an ecosystem designed to sustain the livelihoods of those within the centre," the man explained, his voice steady but tinged with unease. "However, presence was not intended during the journey."

He paused, watching Eleanor nervously, his hand tightening around a sleek device. Without warning, he lifted it—a compact, gleaming taser—and aimed it at her neck. The electric pulse struck, and her body went rigid before collapsing in a heap. Her consciousness faded for what felt like only a minute, just long enough to disarm her will without causing lasting harm.

When Eleanor awoke, she was slumped in a new chamber within the directional centre. The air here was cooler, almost briny. She blinked rapidly, her vision sharpening to reveal the walls—thick glass panes enclosing an enormous aquarium.

On one side, shadows loomed large as sharks glided by, their dark, streamlined forms exuding a quiet menace. Their movements were graceful, their sharp eyes scanning their environment with primal intensity. Near the bottom, a pair of crabs scuttled between clusters of shells, their claws clicking softly against the glass as they worked to establish dominance over their shared territory.

On the opposite side of the room, the mood shifted entirely. A riot of colour exploded before her: tropical fish in every hue imaginable, darting through vibrant coral formations. Their scales shimmered in the artificial light, creating a mesmerizing display. Some travelled in synchronized schools, while others navigated the tank solo, weaving in and out of sea anemones and sponges.

Eleanor pushed herself upright, her head still spinning from the shock. The tranquil beauty of the fish was at odds with the cold, clinical atmosphere of the centre. She couldn't shake the feeling that even this stunning display was part of the larger experiment—a controlled spectacle meant to distract her or, perhaps, to intimidate her.

"You see," the man's voice echoed from behind her. "We've ensured that life in all its forms can thrive here. The aquatic section, like the others you've encountered, is part of our grand design. But the question remains—how will humanity adapt when confined to such constructs?"

Eleanor turned her head slowly, her eyes narrowing. "You keep talking about survival, adaptation, but at what cost? You treat us like variables in your equation."

The man stepped closer; his expression unreadable. "The cost is irrelevant if the alternative is extinction." He gestured toward the aquarium, where a shark circled lazily. "Even the fiercest creatures know when to submit to the system."

Eleanor's jaw tightened. She didn't plan on submitting—not now, not ever. This place may have been designed to test limits, but they hadn't seen the full extent of hers yet.

"Our core system," the man continued, his tone shifting to one of pride, "is the production of drugs designed to enhance well-being and mitigate the discomfort caused by stress, external agents, bacteria, and infections of any kind."

Eleanor followed him into a sterile laboratory, its white walls reflecting the soft hum of activity. A dozen small, automated machines lined the room, each one tirelessly churning out boxes of tablets. The tablets varied in shape—some circular, others rectangular—but all bore the same sleek brand: a minimalist logo that seemed almost too polished, too perfect.

She observed as the conveyor belts carried the neatly packaged products to a sorting area. The efficiency of the operation was mesmerizing. Labels were applied with precision, detailing the contents, dosages, and benefits of each drug.

The man gestured toward the machinery. "Our tablets are formulated with cutting-edge active ingredients. They target stress hormones, bolster the immune system, and neutralize harmful agents before they can take hold. But that's just the beginning."

Eleanor listened as he delved into the specifics, explaining the composition of their latest formulas. He spoke of bioengineered compounds designed to outperform natural remedies, of synthetic peptides tailored to improve cellular regeneration, and of adaptive antibiotics that evolved in real time to combat resistant strains.

He walked to a nearby console and brought up a detailed diagram on a large screen. "Here," he said, pointing to a molecular structure, "is where we plan to improve. Our competition relies heavily on outdated methods, which limits the bioavailability of their products. By tweaking the binding agents and optimizing the release mechanisms, we'll achieve a faster, more potent response. A single dose of our new line will outperform a week's worth of their treatments."

Eleanor nodded, masking her growing unease. There was no denying the brilliance of their technology, but the implications were troubling. These weren't just ordinary medications; they were tools of control. In the hands of the centre, they could be used to manipulate both body and mind.

"And what about side effects?" she asked, her voice calm but probing. The man hesitated, a flicker of something unreadable crossing his face. "Minimal, of course," he said smoothly. "Any adverse reactions are carefully monitored and mitigated in real time."

Eleanor's gaze shifted back to the machines, watching as they continued their relentless production. Each box that emerged felt like a small piece of the larger puzzle—a puzzle she was determined to solve.

His reaction was precise, his questions meticulously crafted, each one peeling back layers of detail. The officer, standing rigidly beside the man, occasionally interjected, emphasizing his expertise in the field. He was sharp, his gaze unyielding, and every statement carried the weight of authority.

Yet, despite his confidence, Eleanor could sense the underlying tension. His presence here was more than a formality—it was a necessity. The research hinged on his involvement, but the stakes were clear: neither the centre's resources nor the complex, labyrinthine structure of the underground facility were details he could be allowed to divulge.

The officer's tone hardened as he continued, drawing invisible lines in the air with his words. "Your contributions are invaluable, but remember this: the information you're privy to does not extend beyond these walls. The conformation of the underground, the systems we've built, and the resources we command are classified at the highest level."

Eleanor, silent but attentive, absorbed every word. It was clear that the centre operated under strict, almost paranoid control. Knowledge was power here, and power was carefully rationed. The officer's warnings were not mere formalities—they were promises of consequences should anyone stray too close to the truth.

The man nodded; his expression unreadable. He understood the gravity of the situation, yet Eleanor could see a flicker of something beneath his composed exterior—curiosity, perhaps, or defiance. She wondered how far he would push, and how much he truly knew.

For now, the room fell silent, the hum of the laboratory machinery the only sound.

Eleanor forced herself to maintain a calm demeanour as the officer's warnings echoed in her mind. The stakes were higher than she had anticipated, and the centre's oppressive control was palpable. But beneath her composed exterior, her mind raced. She wasn't just here to observe; she had her own agenda.

Taking a steadying breath, she stepped forward, her voice steady but laced with an edge of determination. "I appreciate the gravity of this operation, and I understand the necessity of discretion," she began, meeting the officer's gaze. "However, I believe my expertise could be of value in advancing your medicinal development."

The officer raised an eyebrow, clearly intrigued but wary. "And what exactly do you propose, Dr. Quinn?"

Eleanor gestured to the molecular diagram still displayed on the console. "Your compounds are cutting-edge, but there's room to refine the bioengineering process further. Specifically, in the area of adaptive peptide synthesis. My team has been working on a proprietary algorithm that enhances peptide evolution by simulating thousands of potential mutations in real time. This could significantly reduce the development cycle for your adaptive antibiotics."

The man she'd been speaking with earlier leaned in, his interest piqued. "Simulated peptide evolution? How does it handle variability in host environments?"

"It's designed to factor in multiple variables," Eleanor replied smoothly. "From genetic predispositions to environmental stressors. The algorithm predicts how the peptides will interact within different biological systems, allowing us to pre-emptively mitigate potential side effects."

The officer exchanged a glance with the man before nodding slowly. "Impressive," he said. "But offering your algorithm would require integration into our systems—a significant risk for both parties."

"I'm aware," Eleanor said, her tone unwavering. "But I'm prepared to work within your secure environment. I'll collaborate directly with your team, ensuring the data remains on-site and under your control."

The officer studied her for a long moment, weighing the risks. Finally, he gave a curt nod. "Very well. You'll have limited access to our systems, under strict supervision. Any data shared will be subject to the centre's protocols."

Eleanor inclined her head in acknowledgment, masking her relief. "Understood. I look forward to contributing to your efforts."

As the officer stepped away to relay the decision, the man beside her leaned in slightly. "You've just volunteered for one of the most scrutinized positions here," he said quietly, his tone a mix of caution and admiration. "I hope you're ready."

Eleanor allowed herself a small, confident smile. "I've been ready for a long time."

But as she turned back to the console, her thoughts darkened. She wasn't just here to help. She was here to uncover the truth—and to ensure that this technology, however brilliant, wouldn't become a weapon of control.

Eleanor's eyes flicked back to the glowing display on the console. In bold letters, the words *Code 129 – Phase 3* loomed at the top of the screen. This was no ordinary project. The centre had invested vast resources into reaching this critical juncture: designing a production process that could transform their experimental formulas into a stable, safe, effective, and patient-friendly pharmaceutical product. It was the final step before mass production, and they were close—closer than she had anticipated.

The man beside her, now more at ease with her involvement, brought up another screen displaying a series of reports. "As you can see, we've already produced several small pre-series batches. These samples have undergone initial testing for stability and bioavailability."

Eleanor scanned the data, her analytical mind quickly picking out the key metrics. The results were promising. The compounds retained their potency under a range of conditions, and the delivery mechanisms showed consistent performance. Yet, there were anomalies—small, but significant enough to warrant further investigation.

"These stability results are impressive," she remarked, her tone neutral, "but I notice a slight variance in bioavailability under extreme pH conditions. Have you accounted for this in your formulation process?"

The man nodded. "We've identified it as a potential issue. The next step is to adjust the buffering agents to maintain efficacy without compromising patient safety or comfort."

"And the pre-series testing?" she pressed. "What's the patient response so far?"

"Encouraging," he replied. "The test subjects reported a noticeable improvement in their symptoms within hours of administration, with minimal side effects. However, these are controlled conditions. Scaling up production introduces new variables, and that's where we'll need to focus."

Eleanor folded her arms, her gaze thoughtful. "Scaling up means refining not just the formula, but the entire production process. Equipment calibration, environmental controls, and even the packaging could affect the final product. Have you tested these variables yet?"

"Not extensively," he admitted. "That's why we're here. Phase 3 is about fine-tuning every aspect before we move to full-scale production."

She nodded, already considering how her expertise could streamline this process. "I'll need access to the pre-series production data, including the testing protocols and environmental parameters. If we want to ensure stability and safety, we'll need to simulate real-world conditions as closely as possible."

The officer, who had been listening quietly, stepped forward. "You'll have access to the data you need, under supervision. Remember, Dr.

Quinn, this project's success hinges not only on its effectiveness but also on our ability to maintain control over every aspect of its development." Eleanor met his gaze, her expression resolute. "Understood. My goal is to make *Code 129* a success—on all fronts."
As the officer left the room, Eleanor turned her attention back to the console. This was her chance to make a real difference, but she knew the stakes went beyond science. The success of *Code 129* could redefine the balance of power, and she was determined to ensure it served the right purpose.

## Chapter 10: The assault

The valleys north of Brekvenny lay shrouded in the serene stillness of the Siberian winter. A thick blanket of snow draped over every surface, muffling sound and motion. The towering pines, their branches heavy with frost, stood like silent sentinels over the frozen expanse. Amidst this quiet, the only sign of life was a set of enormous lynx tracks, their deep impressions cutting through the unbroken whiteness.

The lynx itself had paused, its sharp eyes and tufted ears alert. Its sleek, muscular form blended seamlessly with the snowy landscape, save for the dark tips of its ears and tail. It stood in the open tundra, its breath visible in the frigid air.

A low, distant hum began to rise, growing louder by the second. The lynx's ears twitched, and its gaze shifted sharply to the south. Over the horizon, a snowmobile came into view, its engine shattering the winter's calm as it raced toward the animal. The machine plowed through the snow, sending up a spray of ice and powder as it closed the distance with alarming speed.

The lynx hesitated for only a moment before it bolted, powerful legs propelling it into the trees. It moved effortlessly, each leap leaving fresh prints in the snow. The snowmobile roared on, its rider hunched low over the handlebars, intent on the pursuit.

Braham and Jimmy barrelled into the snowy tundra, their snowmobile kicking up a swirling cloud of frost behind them. The hum of the engine echoed across the desolate expanse, a stark contrast to the otherwise tranquil Siberian landscape. Ahead, the lynx bounded with effortless grace, its sleek form vanishing in a blur of motion as it darted toward a cluster of jagged rocks.

With a final, powerful leap, the feline disappeared into a dark crevice—a cave carved into the rocky hillside, likely its den. Braham eased off the throttle, letting the snowmobile coast to a stop. Jimmy hopped off, scanning the cave's entrance.

"Looks like we scared it off," Jimmy muttered, pulling his scarf tighter against the biting wind.

Braham nodded, but his focus was elsewhere. They hadn't come all this way for a lynx. The cave was a curious find, but it wasn't their quarry. They were after bigger game—roe deer, red deer, or, with luck, an elk like the one they'd been treated to upon their arrival in the remote outpost. The memory of that feast, the rich, savory taste of the elk meat, spurred them on.

Braham reached into his pack, pulling out a pair of binoculars. He scanned the horizon, eyes narrowing as he searched for signs of movement amid the endless white. "Let's keep moving," he said after a moment. "The lynx isn't what we're here for. There's got to be better prey further in."

Jimmy nodded, climbing back onto the snowmobile. The engine roared to life again, and they set off, their tracks cutting fresh lines through the pristine snow. The hunt was far from over.

Braham and Jimmy circled wide around the quarry, navigating through the snow-covered terrain with practiced ease. The snowmobile hummed steadily as they weaved between clusters of pine trees, their sharp eyes scanning the landscape for any sign of movement. The cold air bit at their faces, but the thrill of the hunt kept them sharp and focused.

As they rounded a dense thicket, Braham suddenly raised a hand, signalling Jimmy to stop. The snowmobile slowed to a crawl, then went silent. The two men dismounted quietly, their boots crunching softly in the snow. Braham pointed toward a stand of trees ahead, where the faint sound of rustling reached their ears.

There, amidst the shadows of the pines, a magnificent deer emerged. Its powerful frame was cloaked in a thick, russet winter coat, and its antlers spread wide, their sharp points glinting in the pale light. The deer moved with cautious grace, its head low as it scraped its antlers against the rough bark of a tree, marking its territory or perhaps shedding the velvet that still clung to its crown.

Jimmy's breath hitched, and he slowly raised his rifle, but Braham placed a firm hand on his shoulder, shaking his head. The deer, sensing something, paused mid-scratch. Its ears swivelled, and its large, dark eyes scanned the forest around it.

Then, in an instant, it bolted. Powerful legs kicked up clouds of snow as it darted through the trees, its antlers slicing through low-hanging branches. Braham and Jimmy watched it go, the adrenaline of the moment making their hearts pound.

"Beautiful," Braham murmured, lowering his binoculars. "Let's track it. If we're quick, we might catch up before it reaches the deeper woods." Jimmy nodded, and the two men climbed back onto the snowmobile. With a roar, the machine sprang to life, and they set off in pursuit, the hunt now truly underway.

Braham and Jimmy closed in swiftly, the snowmobile cutting through the drifts like a knife. The red deer, a towering specimen with sprawling antlers, had slowed slightly, its powerful strides hindered by the dense snow. The men seized the opportunity.

At just fifteen meters away, Jimmy steadied himself, his rifle braced against his shoulder. He exhaled slowly, his gloved finger tightening on the trigger. The crack of the gunshot shattered the quiet.

The bullet struck true, hitting the deer square in the chest. The beast reared up, its massive antlers slicing through the air as it let out a single, thunderous bellow—a sound that seemed to reverberate through the valley. Then, as if in slow motion, the deer collapsed, its great body sinking into the snow with a muffled thud.

Braham and Jimmy skidded to a stop a few meters away. The snowmobile's engine purred softly as they dismounted, their breaths visible in the icy air. They approached the fallen animal cautiously, its lifeless form now motionless against the pristine white backdrop.

"The king of the forest," Jimmy murmured, awe mingling with the weight of their success.

Braham nodded solemnly. The deer's eyes were closed, its antlers sprawling majestically in the snow—a fitting end for such a magnificent creature. "It's a clean kill," he said, his voice low. "No suffering."

They stood in silence for a moment, paying quiet respect to the fallen animal before setting to work. The hunt had been long and arduous, but now, their efforts had borne fruit.

The red deer was a heavy prize, but Braham and Jimmy worked efficiently, tying its massive body securely to the back of the snowmobile. Thick ropes looped around its legs and antlers, ensuring it wouldn't shift during the ride. The snow beneath it was stained dark where the animal had fallen, but soon the pristine white expanse swallowed the trail as fresh snow began to fall.

With the deer securely fastened, Braham mounted the snowmobile, while Jimmy gave the ropes a final tug for good measure. "That should hold," Jimmy said, stepping back and nodding.

Braham nodded in agreement, then revved the engine. The snowmobile roared to life, its treads digging into the snow as it began to move forward, dragging the enormous red deer behind it. The fresh tracks they left snaked back through the tundra, carving a path toward the distant village.

The journey was slow but steady. The weight of their prey was a constant reminder of their success, and the sight of the massive antlers bouncing gently with each bump in the terrain filled them with a sense of pride. This was a respectable catch—one that would be talked about in the village for weeks, perhaps longer.

As they neared the edge of the forest, the outline of the settlement began to emerge from the white haze. Smoke curled lazily from chimneys, and the faint glow of lanterns flickered in the encroaching twilight. Braham eased the snowmobile to a halt just at the village's edge, where a few onlookers had already gathered, drawn by the distant hum of the engine.

"Impressive," one of the villagers called out, his voice tinged with admiration as he eyed the massive deer. Others murmured in agreement, their eyes widening at the sight of the antlers.

Braham dismounted, a satisfied smile tugging at the corners of his lips. "Tonight, we feast," he said, clapping Jimmy on the back.

Together, they began the task of unloading their prized catch, the village abuzz with anticipation of the stories and celebration to come.

As Braham and Jimmy continued their journey back to the village, the snowmobile carving a steady path through the tundra, Jimmy's sharp eyes caught a flurry of movement in the distance. A small flock of pheasants had emerged from a patch of undergrowth, their vibrant plumage stark against the snow.

"Look there!" Jimmy shouted over the hum of the engine, pointing toward the birds as they scattered across the open field.

Braham slowed the snowmobile to a crawl, and Jimmy quickly dismounted, rifle in hand. The pheasants, startled but not yet fully airborne, darted and fluttered just above the ground, their wings beating furiously as they attempted to flee. Jimmy raised his rifle, steadied his aim, and fired twice in quick succession.

The first shot missed, kicking up a puff of snow. The second found its mark, and one of the pheasants dropped instantly. Another shot rang out as Braham, now standing beside Jimmy, took his turn, felling a second bird with a precise hit.

The rest of the flock disappeared into the trees, their calls echoing briefly before fading into the quiet. Jimmy jogged over to retrieve their catch, holding up the two plump pheasants with a grin. "Not a bad bonus," he said, tossing them gently onto the snowmobile's cargo area, where they landed beside the massive red deer.

Braham smirked, nodding in approval. "We're bringing back a feast and then some."

With their haul now even more impressive, they remounted the snowmobile and resumed their journey. The village was close, and they could already imagine the warm reception waiting for them—a night of shared stories, good food, and well-earned rest.

As the snowmobile rumbled into the village, a small crowd of curious onlookers began to gather. Among them stood Aleksandr, known as "the Sherpa," the leader of their small base. A tall, broad-shouldered man with a thick beard and eyes that seemed to see through the very landscape, Aleksandr had earned his nickname through years of guiding hunters and explorers across the unforgiving Siberian wilderness.

He approached as Braham and Jimmy brought the snowmobile to a halt, his boots crunching over the snow. His sharp gaze immediately locked onto the massive red deer tied behind the vehicle. A wide grin spread across his weathered face, and he let out a low whistle.

"Impressive," Aleksandr said, his voice carrying the rough edge of a man accustomed to the wild. "That's a prize fit for legends. The village will eat well tonight."

Jimmy, still grinning from their successful hunt, reached into his leather bag and pulled out the two pheasants they had shot earlier. Their plumage was vibrant even in the dimming light—deep bronze and gold feathers that shimmered with iridescent greens and purples. He held them up for Aleksandr to see.

"And here's the appetizer," Jimmy quipped, shaking the birds slightly for effect.

Aleksandr chuckled, his laughter a deep rumble that echoed in the cold air. "You two didn't just hunt; you conquered the tundra," he said, clapping Jimmy on the back. "These are beauties. Their feathers alone are a treasure."

He held one of the pheasants by its legs, admiring its vivid colouring. "The elders will be pleased. This is more than a hunt—it's a gift to the community."

Braham nodded, his face calm but his eyes betraying a quiet pride. "We thought it'd be a good haul. The deer will feed many, and the pheasants… well, they're a fine touch."

Aleksandr motioned for the other villagers to help with the deer as he turned back to Braham and Jimmy. "Come, warm yourselves. Tonight, we'll celebrate the land's generosity. But first, we'll prepare this feast together."

With that, the trio headed toward the base, the air filled with a sense of triumph and the promise of a night to remember.

Despite the excitement surrounding the successful hunt, the true purpose of the evening loomed heavily over the village. The feast was only a prelude to a far more serious gathering. As the villagers busied themselves with preparing the deer and pheasants, Braham, Jimmy, and Aleksandr retreated to the base's central hall, where a meeting with the local militias had been planned.

Inside, the atmosphere was tense. A fire crackled in the stone hearth, casting flickering shadows across the rough-hewn walls. Around a large wooden table sat a mix of hardened men and women, their faces marked by years of survival in the harsh Siberian wilderness. These were the leaders of the militias—tough, resourceful individuals who knew the terrain and its secrets better than anyone.

Aleksandr took his place at the head of the table, his usual easy demeanour replaced by a solemn focus. Braham and Jimmy sat on either side of him, their earlier triumph now a distant memory as the gravity of the situation settled over them.

Aleksandr began, his voice low and deliberate. "We've waited long enough. Tonight, we start planning the next phase. We all know what's at stake."

He gestured to a rough map spread across the table, its surface marked with hand-drawn notes and symbols. At its centre was a large, ominous structure—an underground facility that had been the focus of their operations for months. It was heavily guarded, its labyrinthine layout a mystery to all but the few who controlled it.

"This facility," Aleksandr continued, tapping the map, "is our target. We've confirmed that it's the nerve centre for their operations— research, storage, and whatever else they're hiding. If we're going to stop them, we need to get inside."

One of the militia leaders, a wiry man named Viktor, leaned forward. "The problem isn't just getting in," he said, his voice sharp. "It's getting out. They've got patrols, surveillance, and who knows what waiting for us inside."

Aleksandr nodded grimly. "That's why we need a plan that accounts for every variable. We'll need diversions, precise timing, and—most importantly—an escape route."

Jimmy, who had been quietly studying the map, spoke up. "What about their patrols? We've been tracking their movements for weeks. If we can hit their weakest points, we might be able to slip in unnoticed."

Another leader, a woman named Anya, chimed in. "We've identified a supply route they use. It's lightly guarded and leads directly to one of the side entrances. It's risky, but it might be our best shot."

The room fell silent as Aleksandr considered the information. Finally, he spoke. "We'll use the supply route. Viktor, Anya—coordinate with your teams to gather intel on their next shipment. Braham, Jimmy, you'll lead the infiltration. Once inside, we'll rely on you to locate the control room and extract the data we need."

Braham exchanged a glance with Jimmy, both of them aware of the dangers but resolute. Aleksandr's eyes swept across the room. "We move in three days. Make no mistake—this will be our most dangerous mission yet. But if we succeed, it could change everything."

The weight of his words hung in the air. The gathering murmured in agreement, their resolve hardening. The time for preparation was over. Now, the real fight was about to begin.

Aleksandr dismissed the group with a firm nod. "Get to work. We'll reconvene tomorrow to finalize the details."

The team dispersed quickly, each member retreating to their respective posts. The underground bunker buzzed with quiet determination. Maps were pinned to walls, radios crackled with incoming reports, and the faint clatter of weapons being prepped echoed in the background.

Jimmy and Braham stayed behind; their eyes fixed on the map of the fortress.

"Think we'll make it?" Jimmy asked, his voice low.

Braham smirked, though his eyes betrayed a flicker of unease. "We've faced worse odds. Besides, we don't have a choice."

Jimmy nodded, tracing a finger along the highlighted patrol routes. "If we time it right, we'll hit the supply entrance just as the guards change shifts. It's a small window, but it might be enough."

Braham clapped him on the shoulder. "Then we make it enough."

Meanwhile, Anya found Aleksandr in the large dining room. She handed him a dossier containing the latest intel on the supply route.

"Looks like the next shipment is scheduled for Friday night. It's a convoy of three trucks. Light security, as expected, but there's a twist," she said, flipping the pages. "They've added a checkpoint near the outer perimeter—probably in response to our last raid."

Aleksandr's brow furrowed. "How heavily manned?"

"Not much. Four Wagner guards, maybe five. But it'll slow us down."

He tapped his finger against the dossier. "We'll need to neutralize them quickly and quietly. Assign a team to handle it. They'll clear the path for Braham and Jimmy."

Anya nodded. "Consider it done."

For the next two days, the team worked tirelessly, rehearsing every aspect of the mission. They drilled through scenarios, anticipating contingencies and perfecting their approach. By Friday night, everything was in place.

As the clock neared midnight, the team gathered in the staging area. Aleksandr stood before them; his expression steely but calm.

"This is it," he said. "Remember your training, trust your team, and stay sharp. The success of this mission depends on each of you."

A collective nod passed through the group. They donned their gear, checked their weapons, and prepared to move out.

The mission had begun.

The team advanced under the cover of darkness, their movements silent and precise. The forest around the ford was dense, offering plenty of concealment but also limiting visibility. Every rustle of leaves or snap of a twig was scrutinized, the tension palpable.

Jimmy led the way, his sharp eyes scanning for any signs of enemy patrols. He raised a clenched fist, signalling the group to halt. Slowly, he crouched behind a fallen log and peered through his night-vision goggles.

"There," he whispered, pointing toward a faint glimmer of light in the distance. "Two sentries by the ford. Looks like they've set up motion sensors along the path."

Braham crept up beside him, squinting through his own goggles. "Laser tripwires, too. They've fortified this place more than we expected."

Behind them, Aleksandr and Anya joined the observation. Anya pulled out a small device from her pack, activating a signal jammer.

"This will buy us some time once we're in range," she said quietly. "But it won't take them long to notice the interference. We'll need to move fast."

Aleksandr nodded. "We'll neutralize the sentries first. Anya, can you disable the sensors?"

She gave a confident smirk. "Give me five minutes."

Aleksandr turned to Braham. "You and Jimmy cover her. Once she's done, we proceed toward the ford. Stay low and keep comms to a minimum."

The trio moved into position. Anya began her work, carefully dismantling the sensors one by one. Jimmy kept his rifle trained on the sentries, his finger hovering near the trigger. Braham scanned their surroundings, ensuring no patrols approached from the rear.

Minutes felt like hours, but Anya finally gave a thumbs-up. "Sensors are down. We're clear for now."

Aleksandr motioned for the team to advance. They closed the remaining distance to the ford, stopping just shy of the water's edge. From here, they could see the faint outline of the fortress looming beyond the trees. Its perimeter was surrounded by a high fence, and guard towers stood at regular intervals, each manned by a sharpshooter.

"Next step," Aleksandr whispered. "We'll split into two teams. Braham, Jimmy, you'll infiltrate via the supply route. Anya and I will create a diversion near the main gate. Once inside, we'll rendezvous at the control room."

Jimmy nodded, tightening his grip on his weapon. "Let's make it count."

Aleksandr's gaze swept over his team one last time. "Good luck. We move on my signal."

The real test was about to begin.

Anya froze, her heart pounding despite the cold that seemed to constrict her every breath. The sudden

sneeze echoed louder in her mind than it likely had in reality, but the reaction was immediate and unforgiving.

The infrared headlight swept over the area like a predator's gaze, locking onto her position. She pressed herself into the ground, desperately hoping the surrounding undergrowth would provide enough cover. Her mind raced, but before she could act, she caught sight of the approaching figures—three men moving with military precision, weapons at the ready.

They spoke in hushed, clipped tones as they advanced, their boots crunching against the frozen earth. Anya's training kicked in. *Stay calm. Think.* She slowly reached for the small device in her pocket—a portable EMP designed to temporarily disable nearby electronics, including the headlight.

Her fingers trembled as she activated it. The device emitted a soft hum before a pulse of energy rippled outward. The headlight flickered, its infrared beam cutting out, and the guards hesitated, momentarily disoriented.

But the pulse had been briefing, and the guards were already communicating through their radios. "Sector clear, but possible disturbance," one of them reported. "Proceeding with caution."

Anya knew she had seconds at most. She crawled backward, inch by painstaking inch, toward a cluster of boulders a few meters away. Once there, she pulled out a small mirror and angled it to observe the guards' movements without exposing herself.

The men were now fanning out, methodically sweeping the area. Anya's breathing slowed as she forced herself to think. If she stayed put, they'd eventually find her. She needed a distraction.

Carefully, she pulled a small flare from her belt, set the timer to ten seconds, and lobbed it in the opposite direction. It landed with a soft thud before igniting in a brilliant burst of red light.

"Over there!" one of the guards shouted, and they immediately moved toward the flare.

Taking advantage of the diversion, Anya slipped out of her hiding spot and continued toward the eastern fence, her movements swift but silent. The fence was just ahead, and beyond it lay her objective.

Reaching the base of the fence, she retrieved a set of wire cutters from her pack. With practiced efficiency, she made a small opening just large enough to crawl through. Once on the other side, she radioed Aleksandr in a whisper.

"Eastern perimeter breached. Continuing to target."

"Understood," Aleksandr's voice crackled softly in her ear. "Stay sharp. We're counting on you."

Anya steeled herself, the adrenaline surging through her veins now overriding the cold. The mission was far from over, but she had narrowly escaped detection. For now.

Anya advanced cautiously, her boots making barely a sound on the heated floor of the facility. The warmth inside the complex was a sharp contrast to the freezing cold outside, but it did little to ease her tension. The domed ceiling above her cast strange shadows as the dim overhead lights flickered intermittently, creating an eerie atmosphere.

She kept to the edges of the principal track, slipping from one column to another, blending into the maze of walls and machinery. Her breathing was controlled, her movements fluid. Every step brought her closer to the directional area—the nerve centre of the research facility.

As she reached the central track, her instincts screamed at her to stop, but it was too late. From the shadows, three figures emerged, moving with military precision. Before she could react, two of them grabbed her arms, locking them in a vice-like grip. The third stood in front of her, his face partially obscured by a balaclava, but his eyes gleamed with cold calculation.

Anya struggled, but the men's grip was unyielding. One of them twisted her arm just enough to make her wince, while another frisked her, quickly locating her communication device and tossing it aside.

"Well, well," the leader said, his voice low and laced with menace. "What do we have here? A little mouse sneaking into the lion's den?"

Anya clenched her jaw, refusing to speak. Her eyes darted around, assessing her surroundings. The men had positioned themselves strategically, making escape seem impossible. But she knew she couldn't afford to give up. Not now.

The leader tilted his head, studying her. "You don't look like one of the usual intruders. Who sent you? What's your mission?"

Anya remained silent, her mind racing. *Think, Anya. You've been in tight spots before.* She shifted her weight subtly, testing the grip of the men holding her.

The leader sighed, clearly losing patience. He reached for a knife strapped to his belt. "We can do this the easy way or the hard way. Your choice."

Before he could act, a sudden commotion erupted behind them. The faint sound of footsteps echoed from the corridor, followed by a muffled explosion. The guards instinctively turned their heads, their grip on Anya loosening ever so slightly.

Seizing the moment, Anya drove her knee into the stomach of the man on her right, then twisted sharply, freeing her left arm. She spun around and delivered an elbow strike to the second guard, sending him stumbling back. The leader lunged at her, but she ducked under his swing and landed a solid punch to his ribs.

Without wasting another second, she sprinted toward the nearest cover, grabbing a metal pipe from the ground as she ran. The guards recovered quickly and began to pursue her, but Anya was already formulating her next move.

She pressed a button on a small device hidden in her boot, activating a remote signal. Moments later, Aleksandr's voice crackled faintly in her earpiece from the spare comm she had stashed earlier.

"Anya, report."

"Compromised but still operational," she whispered. "Need extraction assistance. Prepare for diversion."

Aleksandr's reply was calm but urgent. "Understood. Hold your position if possible. We're coming to you."

The game was far from over, but Anya wasn't done fighting yet.

The blaring of the alarm shattered the fragile calm, and in an instant, the entire facility was bathed in harsh white light. Floodlights activated along the perimeter, casting long, sharp shadows. The once subtle hum of the research centre was now drowned out by the klaxon, accompanied by the rapid thud of boots on the ground as guards scrambled into position.

Anya, her arms once again pinned by the two soldiers, was dragged toward the directional area. Her captors moved swiftly; their grip unrelenting. She kept her head down, her mind racing. *Stay calm. They need you alive for now.*

As they entered the directional area, Anya was thrust into a sterile room filled with computer terminals and monitoring equipment. Standing in the centre was a man she immediately recognized from their intel: Colonel Sokolov, the facility's chief overseer. His presence confirmed that this was no ordinary operation.

Sokolov turned to face her, his cold eyes scanning her with disinterest. "You've caused quite a commotion, haven't you?" His voice was icy, each word laced with authority. "Who are you working for?"

Anya said nothing, her gaze fixed on the floor. Sokolov nodded to one of the guards. "Search her again. Thoroughly."

Meanwhile, outside the directional area, Aleksandr and Jimmy had taken cover in the shadows near the facility's inner perimeter. The sudden alarm had complicated their mission, but it also provided a small window of opportunity. The guards were focused on securing the facility, leaving certain routes temporarily unguarded.

"We need to get to her now," Aleksandr said, his voice low but urgent. Jimmy nodded; his face grim. "She's likely in the directional area. High security. If they've taken her there, it means they think she knows something."

Aleksandr pulled out a small device from his pack—a holographic map of the facility. He pointed to a maintenance shaft running parallel to the main corridors. "We can use this. It's not monitored as heavily, and it leads directly to the directional area."

Jimmy grinned despite the tension. "You always have a backup plan."

The two moved quickly, keeping to the shadows. They reached the maintenance shaft and pried it open, slipping inside just as a patrol passed by. The shaft was narrow and claustrophobic, but it provided the cover they needed. They crawled through, their movements deliberate and quiet.

As they neared the end of the shaft, Aleksandr pressed his ear to the grate, listening. He could hear voices—muffled but tense.

"She's in there," he whispered. "We'll need to act fast. Jimmy, you take the left side. I'll cover the right."

Jimmy nodded, gripping his rifle tightly. "Ready when you are."

Aleksandr counted down with his fingers: three, two, one. On his signal, they kicked open the grate and dropped into the room, weapons raised.

"Drop your weapons!" Aleksandr barked, his voice cutting through the chaos.

The guards reacted instinctively, raising their rifles, but Jimmy was faster. He fired two precise shots, hitting the soldiers holding Anya in the legs. They collapsed, groaning in pain.

Sokolov, caught off guard, reached for his sidearm, but Anya was quicker. She lashed out with a well-placed kick, sending the weapon skittering across the floor. Aleksandr closed the distance in a flash, slamming the butt of his rifle into Sokolov's chest, knocking the wind out of him.

"Anya, are you hurt?" Aleksandr asked, keeping his weapon trained on Sokolov.

"I'm fine," she replied, retrieving her gear from a nearby table. "But we need to move. They'll be swarming this place any second."

Aleksandr nodded. "Jimmy, cover our escape. We're not leaving without the data."

Anya rushed to one of the terminals, her fingers flying across the keyboard. "Give me two minutes."

Aleksandr and Jimmy positioned themselves near the entrance, ready for the inevitable firefight. The mission wasn't over yet, and every second counted.

Colonel Sokolov's sinister grin deepened as he levelled the rifle, his composure unnervingly calms amidst the chaos.

"You underestimated us," he said coolly, his finger tightening on the trigger.

Before anyone could react, he fired. The shot grazed Jimmy's arm, drawing a sharp hiss of pain as blood seeped through his sleeve. Sokolov quickly shifted his aim and fired again, this time striking Aleksandr's leg. Aleksandr staggered, collapsing against the nearest console but managing to keep his weapon raised despite the pain.

The echoes of the gunfire ricocheted through the facility, triggering an immediate response. Within moments, the sound of boots pounding against the metal floor grew louder. A squadron of heavily armed militiamen stormed into the directional area; their weapons trained on the trio.

"Drop your weapons!" one of the soldiers barked.

Aleksandr, grimacing from his wound, exchanged a glance with Jimmy and Anya. They were outnumbered and outgunned. Reluctantly, Aleksandr released his grip on his rifle, letting it clatter to the floor. Jimmy followed suit, the blood from his arm staining his gear. Anya raised her hands slowly, her eyes locked on Sokolov.

The Colonel lowered his rifle, his expression one of smug satisfaction. "You fought well, but this is where it ends," he said. He gestured to the soldiers. "Secure them. Make sure they can't cause any more trouble."

The militiamen moved in, binding the hands of Aleksandr, Jimmy, and Anya with heavy-duty zip ties. They were unceremoniously shoved to their knees, their weapons and gear confiscated.

"You'll be taken to a more secure location," Sokolov continued, pacing in front of them like a predator toying with its prey. "There, we'll have plenty of time to discuss who sent you and what exactly you were hoping to achieve."

Aleksandr gritted his teeth, his mind racing even as the pain in his leg throbbed. He knew the mission had taken a catastrophic turn, but his resolve didn't waver. He glanced at Anya, who gave him a slight, almost imperceptible nod. Despite their dire situation, he could tell she was already thinking of a way out.

Jimmy, his face pale from blood loss, managed a weak smile. "You think this is over, Sokolov?" he said, his voice defiant. "You're making a mistake."

Sokolov chuckled, his eyes narrowing. "The only mistake was yours. And now, you'll pay the price."

The squadron began escorting the trio out of the directional area, the alarms still wailing in the background. As they were marched through the facility, Aleksandr silently observed every corridor, every guard station, memorizing details that might aid their escape.

The battle was lost, but the war was far from over.

Braham lay motionless in the tundra, his body partially buried beneath a layer of snow. The cold bit through his gear, but he barely noticed it. His focus was entirely on the scene unfolding through the scope of his rifle. From his vantage point, he could see Aleksandr, Jimmy, and Anya being marched out of the facility, their hands bound, and their heads held high despite the overwhelming force surrounding them. Militiamen in tactical gear flanked them, their weapons trained on the prisoners. Braham's jaw clenched, his finger hovering over the trigger. *Too far to get a clean shot, and even if I hit one, it wouldn't change the odds.*

He muttered a curse under his breath. *I should've been closer. I should've been with them.*

His earpiece crackled faintly, picking up residual chatter from the team's comms. Most of it was garbled or drowned out by the facility's alarms, but he caught fragments of Sokolov's smug voice: "…secure location…plenty of time…"

Braham's grip tightened on his rifle. He could feel the weight of their mission teetering on the edge of collapse. If the enemy managed to extract information from Aleksandr or Anya, it could compromise not just this mission, but their entire operation.

*Think, Braham.* He forced himself to stay calm, his mind racing through options. He could attempt a long-distance assault, but the likelihood of success was slim, and it would only expose his position. Alternatively, he could retreat to regroup and plan a rescue.

His eyes darted to the facility's perimeter. Guards were stationed at every possible exit, but he noticed a gap—an area where the patrols were thinner, likely due to the chaos inside. *That's my way in.*

Braham made a decision. He couldn't help them now, but he wouldn't abandon them either. He activated his secure comm line, hoping the backup team was still within range.

"This is Braham," he whispered, his breath visible in the frigid air. "Primary team captured. I'm going dark to initiate Plan Delta. Stand by for further instructions."

He received a brief, static-filled acknowledgment. It wasn't much, but it was enough.

Braham dismantled his sniper's nest quickly and efficiently, stowing his gear. He would move under the cover of night, using the terrain to his advantage. His mission had changed: it was no longer about gathering intel or sabotaging the facility.

Now, it was about saving his team.

Braham led his team with precision, every move calculated and silent. The seven operatives with him were seasoned, their faces grim under the pale light of the tundra. They knew the stakes: Aleksandr, Jimmy, and Anya's lives hung in the balance, and failure wasn't an option.

The group approached the facility's southern perimeter, where reconnaissance had revealed a weak point in the defences. This section was rarely patrolled, a blind spot in the otherwise airtight security.

Braham had studied the layout meticulously, and now, the plan was in motion.

"Cut the fence," Braham ordered in a low voice.

One of the operatives, Kira, pulled out heavy-duty wire cutters and went to work. Within moments, they had a gap wide enough to slip through. The team moved swiftly, disappearing into the shadows of the compound.

Inside the perimeter, the group halted, crouching low behind a stack of supply crates. Braham signalled for a quick status check.

"Thermal readings?" he whispered.

Another operative, Malik, pulled out a handheld thermal scanner. He swept the device across the area, his brow furrowing as he read the data. "Two heat signatures, 30 meters ahead. Likely guards," Malik reported. "Stationary for now."

Braham nodded. "Take them out silently. Kira, Malik, you're up."

The two operatives moved like shadows, creeping toward the unsuspecting guards. In seconds, the guards were subdued, their bodies hidden behind the crates. The team pressed forward, navigating through the maze of the facility's outer structures.

The closer they got to the central compound, the more intense the tension became. Braham could feel the weight of the mission pressing down on him. He glanced at his watch. Time was critical.

The team reached a maintenance access point—one of the entrances that led into the deeper parts of the facility. Braham motioned for his tech specialist, Yelena, to work on the door.

"Can you override it?" he asked.

Yelena nodded, her fingers flying over a portable terminal she had connected to the control panel. "Give me thirty seconds."

As Yelena worked, Braham kept watch, his rifle at the ready. His thoughts drifted briefly to Aleksandr, Jimmy, and Anya. He could only hope they were still holding out.

The door unlocked with a soft click, and Yelena gave a thumbs-up. "We're in."

Braham led the team inside. The interior was dimly lit, the hum of machinery filling the air. They moved quickly but carefully, following the route Braham had memorized. Their destination was a secure corridor leading to the holding area where captured operatives were typically interrogated.

"Stay sharp," Braham whispered. "We'll face heavier resistance the closer we get."

The team advanced, their footsteps silent on the heated floors. Every corner they turned brought them closer to their comrades—and to the inevitable confrontation with the facility's elite forces.

The rescue was underway, and there was no turning back.

The sudden, booming voice from the control tower echoed across the compound:

**"В разделе 4 обнаружены злоумышленники!"**

(*Intruders detected in Section 4!*)

Braham's heart dropped. He knew what was coming. The enemy's response would be swift and brutal.

"Down! Everyone, stay low!" he barked in a harsh whisper, his voice carrying an urgency that brooked no argument.

The team hit the ground immediately, blending into the shadows and piles of scattered debris. Braham motioned for Malik to use the thermal scanner again.

"Where are they?" Braham asked.

Malik's eyes darted over the device. "Ten heat signatures. Heavy weapons. They're moving fast—two minutes, tops."

Braham cursed under his breath. The situation had escalated. These weren't standard patrol guards; they were elite militiamen, equipped with *mitrailleuses*—heavy machine guns capable of cutting down everything in their path.

"We can't take them head-on," Braham muttered, his mind racing. He activated the comm on a secure channel. "Yelena, options?"

Yelena, crouched behind a nearby crate, glanced at her tablet. "There's a junction ahead—an old ventilation shaft. If we can lure them into the narrow corridor, we'll have the advantage. Limited space means they can't effectively use their firepower."

Braham nodded. "Good. Kira, set up a diversion. Smoke grenades. Malik, cover our retreat to the shaft."

Kira swiftly pulled a pair of smoke grenades from her vest, pulling the pins and tossing them into the open. Within moments, thick plumes of gray smoke billowed up, obscuring the team's movements.

The sound of boots pounding against the metal floor grew louder, accompanied by shouted commands in Russian. Braham could hear the unmistakable clatter of the *mitrailleuses* being prepped.

"Go! Now!" Braham ordered.

The team moved quickly but silently, retreating toward the junction. The smoke provided temporary cover, but Braham knew it wouldn't last.

They reached the ventilation shaft, a narrow corridor with limited visibility. Perfect for an ambush.

"Set up here," Braham instructed. "Yelena, get behind that terminal and jam their comms if you can. Malik, on overwatch. Everyone else, prepare for contact."

They positioned themselves strategically, weapons ready. The tension was palpable, every second feeling like an eternity. Then, the sound of approaching footsteps and muffled voices cut through the haze. The militiamen were closing in.

"Wait for my signal," Braham whispered, his eyes fixed on the corridor ahead.

The first shadow emerged through the smoke, followed by another. The militiamen were cautious, their movements methodical as they advanced, rifles sweeping the area.

Braham's finger hovered over the trigger. "Steady…" he whispered.

The lead militant stepped fully into the shaft, raising his weapon—right into Braham's line of fire.

"Now!" Braham shouted.

The corridor erupted in chaos. Braham's team opened fire with precision, targeting the enemy's vulnerable positions. The narrow space limited the militiamen's ability to manoeuvre, and their heavy weapons became a liability.

Within moments, the ambush had turned the tide. Several militiamen went down before they could even react, their shouts of alarm drowned out by the deafening roar of gunfire. Smoke and sparks filled the air as bullets ricocheted off the metal walls.

Despite the initial success, the fight was far from over. More soldiers were advancing, and Braham knew reinforcements wouldn't be far behind.

"We need to move!" Braham shouted. "Fall back to the secondary position!"

The team began their tactical retreat, maintaining suppressive fire as they pulled back. The mission was on a knife's edge, but Braham's resolve was unwavering. They were going to get Aleksandr, Jimmy, and Anya out—or die trying.

Braham's team continued their suppressive fire as they retreated, taking out three militiamen with precise shots. The enemy forces faltered momentarily, but their response was swift.

From the control turret, the mounted guns roared to life, sending a hail of bullets tearing through the smoke-filled air. The ground around

Braham's team erupted in a storm of ricochets and shrapnel. The metallic clang of bullets striking the facility's structures echoed loudly, drowning out all other sounds.

"Turret's active! We've got to move—*now*!" Braham shouted, his voice barely audible over the chaos.

The team instinctively scattered, each member darting for cover as the turret's fire swept across their position. Braham ducked behind a stack of supply crates, his heart pounding as he assessed their rapidly deteriorating situation. The turret's wild, relentless firing made it clear: staying meant certain death.

"Fall back to extraction point Delta!" Braham ordered through the comms. "We regroup and reassess!"

The team didn't hesitate. One by one, they broke from cover, moving quickly and low to avoid the turret's line of fire. The facility's alarms continued to blare, and the militiamen were regrouping, shouting commands in Russian as they prepared to give chase.

Braham was the last to leave his position, covering his team's retreat with short bursts of suppressive fire. As he moved, a stray bullet grazed his shoulder, but he didn't falter. Pain was secondary now—survival was paramount.

The team sprinted through the compound, weaving between machinery and storage units. Behind them, the turret continued to fire sporadically, but the increasing distance gave them a temporary reprieve. They reached the perimeter fence, where Kira quickly pulled out a set of bolt cutters to widen their earlier breach.

"Go, go!" Braham urged, ushering the team through the gap.

Once they were clear, they took off into the tundra, the cold biting at their faces. The cover of darkness and the uneven terrain worked in their favor, slowing down any pursuers.

After several tense minutes, they reached a small ridge that provided some natural cover. The team dropped to the ground, breathing heavily but alive. Braham scanned their surroundings, ensuring they hadn't been followed.

"Status check," he said, his voice steady despite the adrenaline coursing through him.

"Minor injuries," Kira reported, glancing at Braham's shoulder. "We're intact."

Braham nodded, though his mind was already racing ahead. "We didn't get Aleksandr, Jimmy, or Anya, but we're not done. We'll regroup at the

secondary outpost, rearm, and come back stronger. This fight isn't
over."

The team nodded in agreement; their resolve unshaken despite the
setback. Braham knew the odds were against them, but he also knew one
thing for certain: he wasn't leaving his team behind.

The wind howled through the tundra, biting at their exposed skin, but
Braham barely noticed. The adrenaline had taken over, and the icy
landscape felt like the least of his worries. His mind was already plotting
their next move. They had survived the first wave of enemy fire, but that
was only the beginning.

"Let's move," Braham said, his voice cutting through the cold air. "We
have to make it to the outpost before they regroup. We can't afford to
rest long."

The team nodded in agreement, their boots crunching on the frozen
ground as they made their way across the snow-covered expanse. They
moved in a loose formation, constantly scanning the horizon for signs of
pursuit, but the terrain worked in their favor. The snow was deep, the
wind howling, and the visibility was poor. The militiamen would be
slower to track them in these conditions.

As they reached a small cluster of rocks that provided some additional
cover, Braham took a moment to reassess the situation. His mind raced
through their options. There was no time to dwell on the failures of the
mission so far. Their primary objective hadn't changed: rescue
Aleksandr, Jimmy, and Anya. And it was still possible.

"How are we doing on supplies?" Braham asked, his eyes flicking over
to Yelena, who had been working feverishly with her gear since their
retreat.

"We have enough to hold up for a while," she replied, glancing up from
her portable terminal. "But we need to find a way to either re-establish
comms with command or get reinforcements."

Braham's eyes narrowed. *Reinforcements...*

He knew it would take too long to call in heavy support. They couldn't
risk waiting for backup—they needed to act, and fast. Time was a luxury
they didn't have. The enemy would tighten the noose around their
comrades, and every minute they lost meant a higher chance of
Aleksandr, Jimmy, and Anya giving up vital information under torture.

"Alright," Braham said, turning to his team. "We move to the secondary
outpost, regroup, and prepare for an immediate return. The longer we
wait, the harder this will be. And we're not letting them break our
people."

He could feel the weight of their resolve in the air. They were battered and bruised, but their spirits were far from broken.

The team resumed their trek, moving through the darkness, using the natural cover of the terrain to stay hidden. The winds had picked up, and the world around them was little more than swirling snow and shadows. Yet, Braham felt more focused than ever. They were on a tight timeline, but he had faith in his team.

As they neared the outpost, Braham took a final look over his shoulder. He had no illusions about the danger they were in, but he knew one thing: they weren't going to leave anyone behind. Not on his watch.

Once they reached the secondary outpost, Braham quickly moved to the communications console, while Yelena worked to patch into the facility's satellite uplink. There was a brief silence, and then:

"We have a channel," Yelena confirmed. "It's encrypted, but I can send a distress signal. Backup will take time, but at least we'll get their attention."

"Send it," Braham ordered, his voice resolute.

As Yelena sent out the message, Braham turned to the rest of the team. "We rest for an hour. Then we move back in. This time, we go in with everything we've got."

They huddled together, using the outpost's minimal shelter as a moment to catch their breath and check their weapons. The stakes were higher than ever, but their mission was clear. They would stop at nothing to rescue their comrades—and bring the fight to the enemy.

The silence of the tundra was shattered by the violent crack of gunfire. Braham's team, caught off guard, ducked for cover as bullets from the second control tower tore through the air, biting into the snow and surrounding structures. The facility's gunners had spotted them, and the situation was quickly spiralling into chaos.

"Return fire! Covering fire!" Braham shouted, his voice cutting through the chaos as his team scrambled to respond.

Kira and Malik, closest to the line of fire, immediately raised their rifles, firing back in short bursts. The crack of their shots echoed in the still night, and in the distance, they saw three militiamen drop to the ground in quick succession, the result of their well-aimed fire. For a brief moment, the enemy forces faltered, but the return fire was heavy and relentless.

"Braham, we've got incoming!" Kira shouted, ducking behind a stack of crates as the sound of more reinforcements reached their ears.

"Fall back! Fall back now!" Braham barked, his mind racing. The situation was quickly becoming untenable. They couldn't stay and fight, not with the enemy in full force and reinforcements pouring in.

The team broke cover, sprinting toward the breach in the perimeter fence. The gunfire followed them, relentless, but they kept moving, hearts pounding in their chests. As they neared the breach, they heard the telltale rumble of their all-terrain vehicles (ATVs) in the distance— thankfully still intact, waiting for them at the extraction point.

"Go! Go! Go!" Braham shouted.

One by one, the team scrambled through the gap in the fence, barely making it as a barrage of bullets shredded the area around them. Kira was the last through, barely managing to avoid a grazing bullet as she dove toward the ATV.

They jumped onto their vehicles and started the engines, the roar of the engines providing a momentary relief from the chaos they had just left behind. Braham hit the throttle, and the team surged forward, plowing through the snowy terrain at breakneck speed.

"We're heading for the ancient bridge," Braham called out over the comms. "Delta Plan is compromised, we'll regroup there."

The ATVs tore through the snow, kicking up clouds of powder as they made their way toward the ancient stone bridge that spanned the frozen river—a relic of an older time, but strategically important. The bridge was isolated, an ideal place for a temporary regroups, away from the heavy militiaman presence and the main facility.

The distant sounds of enemy vehicles closing in were a constant reminder of the danger still looming. They had narrowly escaped, but Braham knew that their retreat wasn't a victory—it was just a temporary respite.

By the time they reached the bridge, the team's nerves were frayed, their bodies exhausted. Braham slammed his ATV to a stop and signalled for the team to dismount.

"Set up a perimeter," he commanded, his voice sharp but controlled. "We rest for ten minutes, then we reassess. We're not out of this yet."

The team quickly moved into position, setting up makeshift cover near the bridge's ancient stone supports. They all knew what was coming. The Delta Plan had failed. They'd lost their window of surprise, and the enemy knew they were out there, somewhere. But that didn't mean they were finished. Not yet.

"We'll need another approach," Braham said, his mind already running through contingency plans. "We strike hard and fast. Get in, get Aleksandr, Jimmy, and Anya, and get out. This time, no more mistakes." The team nodded, their resolve steeling once more. They had been through hell, and they were still standing. Whatever came next, they would face it head-on.

# Chapter 11: The battle for freedom

Colonel Sokolov stood resolute, his breath visible in the biting cold, as the early morning light stretched across the frozen tundra. The snow around the research centre had become a map of their enemy's movements, streaked with furrows where vehicles had passed and footprints left by those who had infiltrated the facility. He narrowed his eyes, analysing every detail with the precision of a seasoned tactician. His team of soldiers, experts in tracking and field analysis, were combing through the area methodically. They knew the criminal group responsible for the ambush was still nearby. The fact that they had managed to hit three soldiers, one of them critically, with a Russian-made military rifle only fuelled Sokolov's resolve. This wasn't just an intrusion—it was an affront to their power.

"Colonel, we've found something," a soldier called from the far side of the compound. Sokolov strode over, his boots crunching through the snow. The soldier pointed to a series of footprints leading toward the northern tree line, barely visible but clear enough to make out the direction. "These tracks... they're fresh."

Sokolov crouched down to examine them. The boots were military-grade, designed for extreme conditions. He recognized the style—similar to what Braham's team would wear, a tactical choice often seen in high-stakes operations. The prints were deliberate, calculated. It was no coincidence.

"Keep following the trail," he ordered sharply. "We need to know where they went. And find out who's behind this. They won't get away this time."

The team fanned out, moving cautiously but with purpose, as Sokolov remained on high alert. His mind raced through the possibilities. This was no random raid. Someone with knowledge of the area, and the research centre's defences, was behind this. They had managed to slip past perimeter security, neutralize guards, and steal valuable intelligence. And now they were slipping away like shadows in the snow.

The snow was an asset and a curse. It hid signs but also exposed them. Every piece of evidence, every trace of their movements, could be a key to unravelling the mystery. Sokolov understood that time was critical.

Every moment they wasted meant more time for the intruders to cover their tracks and regroup.

"Lieutenant, did we get a clear reading on the rifle?" Sokolov asked, turning to the young officer who had been monitoring their weapons system logs.

"Yes, sir," the lieutenant responded. "The weapon is Russian-made, a standard issue SVD sniper rifle. We've seen similar weapons in use by militant groups in the region. It's likely that whoever is behind this has ties to organized networks. But we need more to go on."

Sokolov's eyes hardened. "They'll make a mistake. Everyone does."

He turned back to the trail in the snow. His hand rested on the grip of his sidearm, and he adjusted his field jacket to ward off the cold. As he followed the team's progress, the realization settled deep in his gut: the operation was only just beginning. He knew that soon, they would be closing in on Braham and his team—and when they did, there would be no second chances.

Back at the central command hub, the atmosphere was tense. Colonel Sokolov entered the strategic briefing room, where the defines chief, Seriakov, was already surrounded by several high-ranking officers and analysts. Seriakov, a man with decades of military experience and ties to the infamous Wagner Group, exuded a quiet, deadly confidence as he studied the maps and reports in front of him.

He had seen countless insurgents, rebels, and terrorist groups come and go, but this group—this unknown enemy—had struck him as different. They had infiltrated the research centre, neutralized soldiers, and used military-grade equipment with impressive precision. Seriakov knew they had to be dealt with decisively, or the situation could escalate into something far worse.

Sokolov entered the room and immediately locked eyes with Seriakov, who nodded, signalling the officers to step back and allow the two men to take charge.

"Colonel, you've found the trail?" Seriakov asked without preamble, his voice steady but authoritative.

"Yes. The enemy is on the move, and we've traced their tracks toward the north," Sokolov replied, his voice clipped. "They have a well-organized retreat plan, and we believe they are regrouping at an undisclosed location."

Seriakov's eyes narrowed as he analysed the new information. The intelligence was vital, but it was clear that they were dealing with a far more sophisticated enemy than the usual band of rebels or opportunistic raiders. These terrorists knew the land, had military-grade weapons, and likely had experienced operatives among their ranks.

"We'll need a multi-pronged strategy," Seriakov said, his gaze flicking over the intelligence gathered. "First, we'll tighten the perimeter around the research centre. All roads leading in and out must be monitored. We cannot afford to let them slip away."

He turned to the map on the wall, highlighting several locations. "This is where we need to hit them hardest—their primary route to escape. They'll need to cross the Old Bridge on the frozen river if they're planning to head west. It's their only viable route if they intend to avoid our air surveillance."

Sokolov nodded in agreement. "We've already set up check points on the east side. With heavy snowstorms coming in, it'll be easier for us to track their movements."

Seriakov turned toward a nearby officer who was reviewing satellite imagery. "We also need drones and satellite surveillance. If they try to disperse into the tundra, we'll track them from the skies. But we must be prepared for the possibility that they will attempt to blend in with civilian populations or hide in the wilderness."

The room grew quiet as the officers and analysts absorbed the weight of the plan. Seriakov's reputation for military strategy was renowned, particularly his expertise in counterinsurgency. He knew how to use the environment to his advantage—and how to turn even the most chaotic situations to his benefit.

"We'll deploy a strike team to cut off the Old Bridge," Seriakov continued, his voice becoming sharper with purpose. "It's imperative we disrupt their escape route before they can make it through. I'll take command of the northern perimeter myself."

He turned to Sokolov. "You will lead a team to the western flank and prevent any of them from crossing into the deeper wilderness. They'll be trapped between us and the frozen river."

Sokolov gripped the edge of the map, his fingers tightening in resolve. "We can't afford any slip-ups. These terrorists are trained, and they're not afraid to kill to protect their mission."

Seriakov gave a short, cold smile. "This is why we will not underestimate them. We will make it clear that any further resistance is futile. Our men are ready, and the technology is in place. Once we hit them, we hit them hard."

A buzz of confirmation filled the room as the officers began coordinating the final details of the operation. The research centre was on high alert, and all of Seriakov's personnel were now fully mobilized. The cold tundra outside would soon be filled with the sounds of military precision.

"Make no mistake," Seriakov added, his voice cutting through the tension. "This will be their last chance to run. We will find them, and we will eliminate this threat before it escalates further. Get your men ready. We strike within the hour."

As the officers dispersed to carry out their orders, Sokolov took one last look at the command centre before heading out. The storm was intensifying, and time was running out.

The enemy had no idea what was coming. And soon, they would know the full weight of the Russian military machine closing in on them.

Colonel Sokolov wasted no time in escalating the search. With Seriakov's plan in motion and the impending strike on the frozen bridge, he understood that finding the terrorists responsible for the attack on the research centre was a priority. He knew the region well—the villages scattered across the vast tundra held little but isolation and hardship, yet they were a crucial piece of the puzzle. If the group was planning to hide among the locals, they would need to be found quickly.

Sokolov called upon five elite squadrons, well-trained in both urban and wilderness combat, to sweep the villages. These men were highly skilled, experienced in the art of reconnaissance, and ruthless when it came to extracting information. The rumours about the Wagner group's vicious reputation had already spread far beyond the province, and local villagers had learned to fear any unusual movements or foreign faces. They knew how to keep their mouths shut—but they also knew the importance of avoiding the wrath of such notorious forces.

The squads were equipped with all-terrain vehicles, drones for aerial surveillance, and cutting-edge communication equipment. They would cover a large area in a short period, making sure to check every settlement, from the smallest cluster of huts to larger, more established communities, looking for any sign of the insurgents.

"Your mission is simple," Sokolov said to the squadron leaders as they gathered around the command post. "Find them. No matter where they hide, we will find them. We've given the villages a warning. If any of these terrorists are hiding amongst the locals, they will be found—and they will be eliminated. Use any means necessary to extract information. Be relentless."

He turned to face each of them individually, his expression cold. "These people are dangerous. You'll be working against time, so don't hesitate.

Take control of the situation. Make sure that if any resistance is met, it is dealt with swiftly."

The squadron leaders nodded in unison, acknowledging the severity of the task. They knew better than anyone that the Wagner militiamen were a brutal and unforgiving force. If the terrorists were hiding in the villages, they would likely have garnered local support or at least sympathy, as the villages had suffered under years of conflict and instability. But Sokolov was resolute: no one was beyond the reach of the Russian military.

"We move in five minutes," he said, signalling the operation's imminent start. "Remember—time is critical. The longer they remain at large, the more difficult it will be to flush them out."

As the squadrons deployed, Sokolov's mind kept returning to the bigger picture. He knew that the operation could escalate quickly. If the terrorists were in the villages, their attempts to lay low would only work for so long. His men would search every corner of the tundra, leaving nothing to chance.

The military trucks rumbled across the snow-covered plains, disappearing into the morning mist, while the squadron leaders communicated with the local authorities, who had been instructed to cooperate fully in the search. Local informants, most of whom had already heard whispers of the group's activities, were being mobilized to help locate any potential hiding places. In many cases, the villagers themselves had already been through multiple confrontations with the Wagner group's militia. They knew what to look for: strange faces, unfamiliar weapons, and any signs of preparation for a quick escape.

Meanwhile, back at the research centre, Seriakov and Sokolov coordinated their movements through satellite feeds and intelligence reports, awaiting word from the squads on their progress. The plan was still in motion—if the enemy was to be trapped, they needed to know exactly where they were hiding.

But as the search teams spread out, a shadow of uncertainty loomed over Sokolov's thoughts. The terrorist group was well-organized, and if they had infiltrated the region so thoroughly, it was possible they had anticipated the military response. They might not have simply been hiding—they might have already prepared for a counterstrike of their own.

Sokolov couldn't afford to make assumptions. He would need to remain vigilant, ready to adapt to any new information or twists that might come his way. The hunt was on, and the clock was ticking. Every minute brought them closer to either victory or disaster.

The military convoy, a mix of armoured vehicles and well-equipped Land Rovers, made its way through the barren landscape, its engines humming against the eerie silence of the tundra. After hours of sweeping the outskirts, they reached the village of Brekvenny—a small, isolated settlement nestled between frozen hills. The village was quiet, but signs of life could still be seen as people moved about, gathered in the central plaza, and chatted in the shadow of a few old buildings.

The village had a rustic charm, with its wooden houses covered in snow and a cold wind that whipped through the streets. A couple of locals milled around the small plaza, bundled up in thick coats, some with livestock in tow, others carrying tools or wares. A group of villagers lingered at the local locant, the rustic tavern known for serving hearty meals of smoked meats and traditional dishes like bear stew, a local delicacy. The smell of smoked meat wafted in the air, and the warmth from inside the tavern seemed inviting compared to the freezing cold outside.

The Land Rover slowed as it entered the village, its tires crunching the snow underfoot. The squadron leader in charge of this unit, Captain Ivanov, signalled for the vehicle to stop. He was a man of few words but had a reputation for getting things done efficiently—and without hesitation.

"Stay alert," he muttered, his voice steady but edged with the gravity of the operation. "This could be our first lead."

The military group disembarked quickly, four heavily armed soldiers stepping out first and scanning the area. The other soldiers followed, their boots crunching in the snow as they formed a secure perimeter around the group. It was clear that they were here on official business, their presence a stark reminder of the ongoing operation, though the villagers didn't seem overly surprised. Life had always been tensing in these remote parts, and with the ongoing military actions in the region, most had grown accustomed to the occasional patrol.

Ivanov looked around, scanning the plaza. A small group of villagers had gathered by the locant's front, enjoying a moment of peace over lunch. Smoke billowed from the chimneys of nearby homes, and the distant sound of wind chimes mixed with the low hum of the engines. There were no immediate signs of unusual activity—no signs of fear or tension in the air.

But Ivanov wasn't fooled. He had seen the tactics these insurgents used. It was possible they were hiding in plain sight, using the normality of village life to remain unnoticed.

"Speak to the locals," Ivanov instructed one of his soldiers, a fluent Russian speaker with a keen eye for detail. "See if anyone's noticed anything unusual. Someone must have seen something. No one is above suspicion."

The soldier nodded, walking over toward a man at one of the tables near the locant, a middle-aged man with a weathered face. He was eating a bowl of smoked bear stew, his back hunched against the cold, but he looked up cautiously when the soldier approached.

Ivanov, meanwhile, kept an eye on the area, his instincts telling him to be cautious. His squad was on high alert, scanning for any signs of trouble, even as the peaceful appearance of the village suggested otherwise. He knew the Wagner Group had a way of blending into environments like this. They could hide in the open and be undetected for days.

Inside the tavern, the smell of the bear dish—slow-cooked, rich, and smoky—seemed to mock the urgency of their mission. It was a stark contrast to the tension that simmered beneath the surface. There was little time to waste. If the terrorists were hiding here, they wouldn't hesitate to strike when the moment was right.

"Has anyone from the outside passed through recently?" Ivanov's soldier asked the villager in a low voice, trying to avoid drawing attention.

The man looked up slowly, his gaze flicking between the soldier and the others, before taking a long pause. It was clear that the village, though quiet, wasn't completely oblivious to the dangers of the outside world. Even in the remote villages, rumours of the Wagner Group's brutality had spread. The man hesitated again before speaking, his voice cautious. "A few strangers passed through in the last couple of days. No one too unusual... just traders, travellers like any others."

Ivanov's soldier pressed further. "Did they say anything odd? Anything unusual about their appearance?"

The man shook his head. "No... but there were some young men, travellers who didn't seem to fit in. They didn't talk much, kept to themselves. People around here don't ask too many questions... but I did hear them mention the Old Bridge."

That mention made Ivanov's stomach tighten. The Old Bridge—an important crossing over the frozen river, now seen as a key route for anyone trying to escape or infiltrate.

"Where exactly did you see them?" the soldier pressed.

"Headed toward the Old Bridge, over by the eastern end of the village," the man replied, wiping his mouth with the back of his hand.

Ivanov exchanged a look with his squad leader. This was their first solid lead. The terrorist group might have passed through here—or worse, they could still be hiding in plain sight, blending with the villagers. With the Old Bridge in mind, they knew where to focus their next move.

"Gather the men," Ivanov ordered, his voice firm. "We head to the Old Bridge. Stay alert, and don't engage unless necessary. If they're using this village as a hideout, they're not getting away."

The military group moved quickly, their boots crunching through the snow as they made their way toward the eastern edge of the village. The Old Bridge loomed in the distance, and with it, the real hunt began.

The militiamen arrived at Braham's lodge just as dawn broke over the frozen landscape. The small building, a secluded retreat in the wilderness, was tucked away in the dense forest—seemingly the perfect hideout for someone trying to avoid the eyes of the military. However, this morning, the tranquillity of the lodge was shattered by the sound of military boots crunching through the snow and the clang of heavy equipment.

As the militiamen approached the lodge, their presence seemed to stir little reaction. The guard post that typically stood at the front of the building was empty, and there was no sign of movement inside. The air was eerily still. Perhaps, Braham and his team had been too careful, or maybe they had expected the military to be more methodical in their search. Either way, the lodge was eerily silent.

One of the militiamen, a tall, broad-shouldered man with a hardened face, stepped forward and approached the massive wooden door of the lodge. The door itself was a work of craftsmanship, made from thick pine, adorned with intricate carvings of modern-style ferns and rich leather straps. The design, while rustic, carried an air of deliberate elegance—an oddity in the middle of the barren wilderness.

The militiaman reached for the brass bell hanging just beside the door and gave it a few sharp jingles. The sound echoed through the still morning air. No response.

He looked back to his comrades, then, with an impassive expression, banged violently on the heavy door. The sound of fists pounding against the wood reverberated through the small clearing, making the air feel heavy with the threat of violence. The force of the knock made the door shake on its hinges, the loud noise cutting through the quiet morning like a warning.

"Open up!" the leader of the squad barked in Russian, his voice cold and commanding. "We know you're in there. No use hiding. Surrender now, and you won't be harmed."

The minutes passed in tense silence, but there was no answer. The militiamen exchanged uneasy glances. Braham's team was experienced, resourceful, and relentless. They had to have known the risk of staying here, so why wasn't there any sign of life?

"Break it down," the squad leader ordered after a moment, his patience thinning. He gestured to the other men, signalling them to prepare for a forced entry. They moved into position, their rifles ready, but still, the door remained silent, the lodge seemingly undisturbed by their arrival.

As the squad leader looked around, scanning the perimeter for signs of movement, his mind raced. If Braham and his team had been here recently, they knew the stakes. They would not have left without taking precautions. The lodge might be empty now, but there was a palpable sense of something wrong. The lack of guards, the stillness—something was off.

With a sharp motion, the squad leader signalled for one of the militiamen to retrieve a crowbar. The door was about to give way to force.

"Get ready for anything," the leader muttered, his eyes narrowing as he watched the men begin to work. "They might be waiting for us inside."

The tension inside the lodge had reached its peak. Kira, Malik, and Yelena stood in the narrow corridor just beyond the dining room, hidden from view. The faint voices of the five soldiers—now in the main area of the lodge—could be heard as they combed through the space, inspecting every corner, searching for any evidence that might tie the group to the foreign terrorist cells they were hunting.

The oppressive silence in the corridor was broken only by the sound of the soldiers' boots shuffling through the dining room, the occasional clink of metal as they rifled through belongings, and the hushed mutterings of commands in Russian. Every sound seemed amplified in the thick silence, making the atmosphere even more suffocating. Kira's breath was shallow, each exhale deliberately controlled, knowing any wrong move could give them away.

Malik and Yelena, equally alert, exchanged tense glances. They were waiting for the signal from Braham. Their mission was clear: gather intel, identify their pursuers' tactics, and avoid a direct confrontation if possible. But the risk was palpable, especially with the soldiers so close. Braham, from his vantage point in the farthest room of the lodge, had heard the voices growing louder, the distinct sounds of boots scraping the floor. His instincts flared, and he knew they were running out of time. His team had been too complacent—too trusting of the lodge's seclusion. They had underestimated the militiamen's ability to track them down.

"Two Siberians, opposite direction. Move fast, and stay quiet," Braham muttered under his breath, speaking into his comms system. The two soldiers, Nikolai and Sergey, both experienced in covert operations, nodded without hesitation, and quickly slipped into the shadows, retreating toward the back of the building.

Meanwhile, Braham's eyes never left the dining room door. He knew it was only a matter of time before the soldiers would start searching the corridors. His heart raced as he considered their options: stay hidden and wait for an opening, or risk fighting their way out. The second option was tempting, but it would lead to chaos, and he had no intention of leaving anyone behind.

A tremor of nerves ran through the team as they felt the weight of the approaching danger. The soldiers' voices were getting closer now, footsteps drawing nearer to the corridor where Kira, Malik, and Yelena were hidden.

Kira's hand instinctively went to the small knife she carried at her belt, her fingers brushing its cold handle. She could feel the adrenaline building in her veins, her muscles tense and ready. Malik's sharp eyes were fixed on the hallway leading into the dining room, where the soldiers were moving toward.

From the other side of the lodge, Nikolai and Sergey had made it to their position. They crouched low, listening intently for any signs of movement. The tremble in the air, a combined tension of their breath and the soldiers' proximity, was thick enough to feel like static, a pulse running through the lodge's very walls.

Braham adjusted his position slightly, eyeing the door as the soldiers grew closer. He knew their chances of escape were slim, but if they could outmanoeuvre the soldiers just long enough, there might be a way out. The key was to stay undetected until the Siberians could flank the soldiers from the opposite side and create a distraction.

The situation was delicate, and the team's nerves were on edge. The soldiers had no idea how close they were to danger.

But then, the sound of footsteps halting in the dining room reached Braham's ears. The soldiers had stopped moving, and Braham's mind raced to understand why. Had they sensed something? Were they just pausing for a break? His heart beat faster in his chest as he waited for the next move, every muscle coiled, ready to act.

Kira, Malik, and Yelena exchanged a brief glance, silently acknowledging the high-stakes nature of the situation. They were about to face a pivotal moment. The tremble in the air was no longer just the cold—it was the storm that was about to break.

The tension in the lodge reached its breaking point as the door to the dining room suddenly flew open with a violent crash. A young soldier, his eyes wide with panic, burst into the room, rifle raised. His sudden entrance was a shock, but before he could fully react, Braham was already in motion.

Braham had been hiding just outside the lodge, keeping a careful watch on the soldiers through the narrow gaps in the wooden walls. As soon as he heard the boy's rushed footsteps, he knew it was time to act. In a fluid, controlled motion, Braham slipped into the building, his gun trained on the young militiaman. His presence in the room was like a shadow, silent but deadly.

"Drop the weapon," Braham commanded, his voice low and steady. The militiaman hesitated for a fraction of a second, caught between fear and instinct, but the barrel of Braham's gun was unwavering. The young soldier's rifle clattered to the ground, and his hands shot up in surrender.

Braham's team, already positioned, quickly sprang into action. Kira, Malik, and Yelena moved swiftly, disarming the remaining soldiers who had been holding the room. The militiamen, taken by surprise, barely had time to react before they were subdued.

The tension in the room didn't dissipate. Braham's eyes scanned the soldiers, now on the ground with their hands tied behind their backs. They were experienced and dangerous, but right now, they were nothing more than obstacles to Braham's team.

"You're not going to kill us?" the young soldier, still shaken, muttered. His voice wavered with confusion and fear.

Braham's eyes met his with cold resolve. "We're not here to kill you. We're here to complete our mission."

With a sharp gesture, Braham ordered his team to strip the soldiers of their uniforms. It was a tactical move—one that would allow them to blend in with the enemy and get closer to the heart of their target: the pharmaceutical fortress.

Once the soldiers were stripped of their gear, Braham and his team quickly donned the uniforms. The heavy clothing provided both warmth and protection, but more importantly, it would allow them to move through the military perimeter undetected. Their appearance now matched the soldiers they had captured, and it would be difficult for anyone to distinguish them from the real militiamen.

Kira adjusted her new uniform, tightening the straps and making sure her weapon was securely in place. She gave Braham a nod, signalling that they were ready to move.

Braham turned to Malik, who was already positioning himself by the door. "Let's move," Braham said. "We don't have much time before the soldiers realize they've been compromised."

With the sounds of the subdued militiamen's muffled groans behind them, the team moved out of the lodge and toward the perimeter, carefully avoiding any more patrols. Their destination was clear: the pharmaceutical fortress, a well-guarded stronghold where critical intel awaited.

The cold air outside bit at their faces, but the danger ahead was much sharper than the tundra's chill. Their mission was far from over, and the stakes had never been higher.

As they advanced, the team's resolve solidified. They were not just fighting for survival—they were fighting to disrupt the operations of an enemy that would stop at nothing to maintain their grip on power. The fortress awaited, and with it, the chance to strike a blow against the forces that sought to control the region.

Braham quickly surveyed the scene before signalling his team to gather the weapons and uniforms from the subdued militiamen. They worked efficiently, stripping the soldiers of their gear and taking their rifles, sidearms, and tactical equipment. The uniforms were bulky and well-worn, but they would serve their purpose—allowing them to blend in with the enemy forces as they made their way to the pharmaceutical fortress.

Kira and Malik quickly stashed the weapons, while Yelena checked the supplies. Braham grabbed one of the rifles, securing it across his back, and checked the sidearm tucked into his belt. The silence was palpable, as the weight of their mission pressed down on them.

"Let's go," Braham said, his voice firm and steady. The team moved quickly but cautiously, slipping out of the lodge and heading toward the old white Land Rover they had used to reach the area. The vehicle was a bit worn, but still functional, and its presence in the snowy wilderness would attract little attention if they drove carefully.

Braham slid into the driver's seat, turning the key and listening as the engine rumbled to life. The others piled into the vehicle, with Kira and Malik taking the passenger seats and Yelena in the back. The familiar hum of the engine gave Braham a small sense of relief, but he knew the mission was far from over.

"We'll take the back roads," Braham muttered, scanning the terrain ahead. "No need to attract attention until we're in position."

With the vehicle now on the move, they travelled through the desolate landscape, the frozen tundra stretching endlessly on either side. The cold was relentless, but the vehicle's heaters did their best to ward off the biting chill. The journey to the CSM FarmCure fortress was treacherous, but Braham had navigated these roads before, and he knew exactly how to avoid detection.

As they neared the fortress, Braham slowed the Land Rover, carefully watching the road for any signs of movement. The fortress loomed in the distance, a massive, fortified compound surrounded by high walls and patrolled by armed guards. It was a heavily secured site, a hub for the pharmaceutical group's operations, and the team knew that infiltrating it would not be easy.

Braham's mind raced, calculating their best approach. The militiamen had likely already reported their presence, so time was of the essence. They needed to move quickly, slip past the guards, and gain access to the central building where crucial intel was stored.

"We're getting close," Braham said, his voice low but focused. "Once we pass the first checkpoint, we'll need to stick to the shadows. We can't afford to make any mistakes."

Kira nodded, adjusting her rifle and scanning the area. "The outer walls are heavily guarded. We'll have to wait for a shift change or find a weak spot in their patrols."

Braham nodded in agreement. The fortress was well-fortified, but there had to be vulnerabilities—gaps in the patrols, blind spots in the surveillance systems. They had trained for moments like this, and now it was time to put their skills to the test.

The Land Rover rolled up to the first checkpoint, a small guard post where two soldiers stood watch. Braham slowed the vehicle and kept his eyes on the guards, who seemed to be engaged in conversation. He glanced at Kira and Malik, signalling for them to be ready.

"Just act natural," Braham whispered. He put the vehicle into gear and drove slowly past the guard post, his face calm and expressionless. The soldiers glanced up briefly but didn't seem to notice anything unusual. They were too focused on their routine.

Once they passed the checkpoint, Braham exhaled, the tension in his shoulders easing slightly. But he knew it was far from over. They were now inside the compound's outer perimeter, and every step from here on out would be critical.

"We're in," Braham said softly, his grip tightening on the wheel. "Now, we move fast and get to the central building. Stay sharp."

As the Land Rover rolled deeper into the fortress compound, the team's focus sharpened. Their mission was clear: infiltrate, gather intel, and escape without leaving a trace. The fortress was the heart of the CSM FarmCure group's operations, and if they could strike at its core, they could cripple the entire organization.

With the fortress ahead and their hearts racing, the team prepared for the most dangerous phase of their mission yet.

## Chapter 12: A desperate escape

The screech of the eagle above the control centre sent a sharp chill through the air, its cry echoing like a harbinger of change. For Braham and his team, that moment felt like the first signal of a shift—something was about to break, and it wasn't going to be subtle. They could feel it in the air, the tension, the anticipation of what was coming.

Braham's hands tightened around the wheel as he steered the old Land Rover toward the underground parking station, marked with clear signs and bright orange lines. This was a crucial part of the fortress's infrastructure—the parking area for military vehicles. It was heavily guarded, but Braham had studied the layout. He knew the place was a logistical hub that could grant them access to key areas within the compound.

The underground parking was shielded from the eyes of the surface patrols, but it was far from a safe zone. It was still under constant surveillance, and the guards stationed there were trained to spot any anomalies. The Land Rover rolled smoothly over the well-maintained road, the sound of the tires on the icy surface almost lost beneath the low hum of the engine.

Braham's pulse quickened as they approached the entrance, a large metal gate that seemed out of place in such a remote location. The massive steel doors were guarded by two soldiers standing at attention, rifles slung over their shoulders. He knew that getting past them was a matter of timing, finesse, and making sure they didn't arouse suspicion.

"We don't have much time," Braham muttered, his voice low but urgent. Kira and Malik were already scanning the surroundings, alert to any movement. Yelena, ever watchful, adjusted her gear and prepared to act at a moment's notice. They were no longer just infiltrating—they were on the verge of something bigger, something that could change everything for their cause.

Braham slowed the Land Rover to a near stop, his eyes darting to the guards. They hadn't noticed anything unusual yet, but he couldn't afford to let his guard down. His fingers brushed the trigger of the rifle at his side, just in case.

As they approached the entrance, one of the guards turned, glancing over his shoulder at the vehicle. Braham's heart skipped a beat. He kept his face neutral, his eyes fixed on the road ahead as if nothing were amiss. Kira, sitting beside him, mirrored his calm demeanour, her expression unreadable.

The guard took a few steps toward the vehicle, his boots crunching on the snow as he walked around it slowly. Braham's breath caught in his chest, but he didn't panic. Instead, he kept the vehicle moving at a steady pace, praying that the guard wouldn't spot anything strange.

A few agonizing moments passed before the guard nodded and waved them through. Braham exhaled a quiet sigh of relief, but he didn't dare relax. The underground parking garage was just a short drive away, but they weren't out of danger yet.

Once past the guard checkpoint, they rolled into the dimly lit underground parking lot, where rows of military vehicles stood, engines idle and parked in neat lines. The soft hum of machinery and the occasional distant chatter of soldiers working in the facility added to the eerie atmosphere. Braham parked the Land Rover in an inconspicuous spot at the far end of the garage, close to a row of armoured transports. The team quickly disembarked, taking only what they needed—small weapons, comms gear, and their stolen uniforms.

"We move fast. Stay in formation," Braham whispered, his voice tight with urgency. "We need to get to the central building before they realize we've breached the perimeter."

Kira nodded and adjusted her gear, while Malik and Yelena did the same. They moved silently, making their way toward the nearest exit leading to the inner compound of the fortress. The hum of the underground machinery was replaced by the quiet thrum of their own breathing as they navigated the sterile corridors.

The next steps were crucial. They needed to access the control room and gather the intel that could expose the FarmCure group's true operations. But with every step, Braham could feel the weight of their decision pressing on him. There was no turning back now. The fortress was a fortress for a reason—it was designed to be impregnable, but they had already proven that wasn't true.

As they moved deeper into the heart of the fortress, Braham kept his focus. One mistake, one wrong move, and everything they had fought for would unravel. The silence of the underground parking area now seemed like a distant memory. The fortress loomed ahead, its corridors a maze of danger, but Braham knew what they were up against.

The stakes were higher than ever, but the team was ready. The past was about to be shattered, and whatever came next, they were prepared to face it together.

The cold, damp walls of the interrogation room were lined with grim fixtures, the harsh fluorescent lights flickering above. Colonel Solokov stood before the three prisoners, his expression cold and calculating. The sounds of distant military drills echoed faintly through the concrete halls, but in this room, the only sound was the occasional drip of water from the ceiling.

The three captives—Jimmy, Aleksander, and Mirna—were suspended by heavy chains, their bodies bruised and battered from the brutal interrogation tactics they had endured. Despite the relentless beatings, the torture, and the psychological pressure, they remained silent. The pain was immense, but they had been trained for situations like this. They had been through hell before, and they would not break so easily.

Jimmy, his face bloodied and swollen, hung from his chains, his body limp but defiant. Aleksander, though barely conscious, glared at Solokov with hatred in his eyes. Mirna, slumped against the cold wall, wiped the blood from her mouth, her black eye already swelling shut. Despite the physical torment, none of them spoke. Their resolve was unshaken.

"You're wasting your time," Aleksander spat, his voice hoarse. "We won't betray our comrades. Not for you. Not for anything."

Colonel Solokov remained silent for a moment, studying the prisoners. His eyes narrowed, his fingers tapping against the handle of his rifle. He had expected this level of resistance—these were not ordinary terrorists. They were well-trained, well-organized, and most importantly, they were loyal to their cause.

The Colonel moved closer to Mirna, his boots echoing on the concrete floor. He bent down, his face inches from hers, and spoke in a low, menacing tone.

"You think you're so clever," Solokov said. "But everyone breaks eventually. Everyone."

Mirna lifted her head slightly, her eyes flashing with defiance despite the pain. "Do your worst. We'll still never give you what you want."

Solokov's smile was cold, his expression devoid of empathy. "You'll talk. Eventually, you all will. And when you do, the others will follow. I'll make sure of it."

His gaze shifted to Jimmy, who was barely conscious. "You're the worst of them," he sneered, pulling a nearby chair and sitting down slowly, as though he had all the time in the world. "You're a symbol of resistance, aren't you? So stubborn, so confident. But in the end, you're just another broken man."

Jimmy gritted his teeth, trying to keep his eyes open, but his body was wracked with exhaustion from the tortures he'd endured. Solokov's words were meant to break him, but they only fuelled his resolve. He had been through worse, and this wouldn't be the thing to break him.

"You're wrong," Jimmy muttered through clenched teeth. "You won't win. We'll be out of here. You'll regret this."

Solokov stood, his expression darkening. He turned to his subordinates, who were waiting at the door. "Keep them here. Continue with the questioning. We'll see how long their courage lasts."

As Solokov walked out of the room, leaving his prisoners to their suffering, the harsh reality set in. The torture would continue. But Braham was out there, and the mission was far from over. The team had trained for situations like this. Their capture was not the end, but the beginning of a new phase.

Despite the pain, despite the blood, they knew their comrades would come for them. They just had to hold out long enough.

The harsh, flickering lights of the interrogation room cast long shadows across the walls, but the silence was broken as the distinct *ding* of an elevator echoed through the cold concrete halls. The heavy steel door slid open with a hiss, and five armed soldiers entered the room, their boots silent on the floor despite their imposing presence.

Colonel Solokov, standing with his back to the door, froze at the sudden intrusion. He turned, eyes narrowing in confusion as he saw the soldiers. They were dressed in tactical gear, their faces covered by masks, their weapons drawn but steady. Solokov's hand instinctively moved to his rifle, but before he could react, a sharp pain struck his chest. He gasped, eyes widening in disbelief as he looked down.

A clean shot. Right in the heart.

Solokov's body jerked as the bullet tore through him, and in the blink of an eye, the Colonel collapsed to the ground, dead before his body even hit the floor. The soldiers moved with surgical precision, stepping over his body without a second glance.

One of the soldiers, tall and lean, gestured toward the prisoners. "Cut them loose," he commanded in a low voice, and the other soldiers moved quickly, unshackling Jimmy, Aleksander, and Mirna from their chains. The cold, numbing metal cuffs fell to the ground with a metallic *clink*, and the three captives, weakened but still conscious, slumped forward, their limbs stiff from hours of hanging.

Braham, appearing from the shadows, stepped into the room behind the soldiers, his expression grim but resolute. His eyes swept over the prisoners. "We've got you. You're safe, for now," he said quietly.

Aleksander, his face bruised and swollen, managed a weak nod. "Braham... You found us," he rasped, his voice hoarse from the pain and exhaustion.

Jimmy, his eyes blinking in disbelief, looked up at the soldiers, then at Braham. "Thought we were done for..."

Braham nodded briefly, signalling for the soldiers to help the prisoners to their feet. The rescue operation had been a success—Solokov and his forces had underestimated how far Braham and his team were willing to go. The timing had been perfect. They'd infiltrated the compound, taken out key personnel, and freed their comrades.

"We don't have long," Braham said, his voice calm but urgent. "We need to move. Now."

Mirna, though clearly in pain, managed to stand with the help of a soldier, her gaze sharp and focused. "Where to?" she asked, her voice low but determined.

"Out," Braham replied simply. "We get you to the extraction point. Then we regroup. We're not done yet."

Braham turned to lead the way, followed closely by the soldiers, the three freed prisoners now on their feet but still weakened from the torture. They moved quickly through the sterile hallways, the muffled sounds of chaos and confusion from the base's sudden lockdown barely reaching them.

As they moved, Braham's mind raced. The success of this rescue was just a small victory, but the war was far from over. They still had to neutralize the rest of the compound's forces, gather the intel they needed, and most importantly, survive.

They reached the elevator and ascended silently, the tension palpable in the confined space. Once the doors opened, they emerged into the heart of the fortress, where the real danger awaited. They were close, but the hardest part was still to come.

Braham's team moved swiftly toward their next goal—getting the intel from the central control room before the enemy realized the breach. But with Solokov and his men out of the picture, it seemed the odds had shifted in their Favor. For now, they had the element of surprise, and that was enough to push forward.

The battle was far from won, but they were one step closer.

As the team entered the next corridor, a deep, resonant alarm suddenly blared through the facility. The piercing wail of the siren echoed off the steel walls, accompanied by flashing red emergency lights that bathed the hall in an ominous glow. The lockdown had been triggered.

"Damn it!" Braham hissed, spinning around to assess their surroundings. Heavy steel doors began to descend from the ceilings, sealing off every exit with an ear-splitting clang. The sound reverberated through the compound, sending a chill down everyone's spine.

"Move!" he barked. "We need to find another way out—now!"

Jimmy, still leaning on one of the soldiers, forced himself to straighten. "What's the plan, Braham? These doors are fortress-grade."

Mirna, her sharp mind still processing despite the pain, pointed to a nearby console inset into the wall. "That's a control terminal. If we can access it, we might override the lockdown."

Braham nodded. "Aleksander, can you—?"

"Give me a second," Aleksander interrupted, already hobbling toward the terminal with the help of another soldier. He slumped against the wall and began to examine the interface. "This is high-level encryption. It'll take time."

"We don't have time," Mirna snapped. Her voice was sharp, but her concern for their survival was evident.

Braham signalled to one of the soldiers. "Watch the corners. The alarm means reinforcements are coming, and we're not exactly in fighting shape."

The soldier nodded and moved to the edge of the corridor; weapon raised. The rest of the group formed a defensive perimeter around Aleksander as he worked, their nerves taut as the relentless siren continued its assault on their ears.

"Come on, come on," Aleksander muttered, his fingers trembling as he navigated the unfamiliar system. "This is taking longer than I'd like."

"It always does," Jimmy said, forcing a weak smile despite the tension.

Suddenly, the sound of approaching footsteps echoed down the hall. Braham raised his fist, signalling silence, and the team immediately dropped into defensive positions. The soldiers adjusted their grips on their rifles, readying for the inevitable confrontation.

"They're coming," whispered one of the masked operatives.

Braham's jaw tightened. "Hold your fire until I give the order. We can't afford to waste ammo."

The footsteps grew louder, closer. Then, without warning, a flashbang grenade clattered to the floor just meters from their position.

"Cover!" Braham shouted, shielding his eyes and ducking behind a nearby column.

The grenade detonated with a blinding flash and deafening bang, disorienting the group. Shouts rang out as the enemy soldiers surged into the corridor; weapons drawn.

Through the chaos, Braham's voice cut through. "Engage! Take them down!"

The corridor erupted into a firefight, bullets ricocheting off the steel walls as the two sides exchanged fire. Aleksander ducked low, shielding himself as sparks flew from the console he was working on.

"Almost there!" he yelled over the chaos, his fingers flying across the controls.

Jimmy, despite his injuries, grabbed a pistol from one of the fallen guards and fired off several shots, forcing the advancing enemies to take cover. "Keep working, Aleksander! We've got this!"

Mirna, crouched behind a crate, exchanged a glance with Braham. "This isn't sustainable. If Aleksander doesn't crack that terminal soon, we're dead."

"I know," Braham growled, firing a burst from his rifle. "Just hold the line."

Finally, with a triumphant beep, the terminal's screen lit up green. Aleksander slammed his fist on the control panel. "Got it! Doors are unlocking!"

As the steel barriers began to rise, Braham shouted, "Fall back! Move, now!"

The team retreated down the now-open corridor, firing sporadically to keep the enemy at bay. They ran as fast as their battered bodies would allow, adrenaline fuelling their every step.

"We're not out of this yet," Braham said grimly as they reached the central control room. "But we've got a fighting chance."

The team regrouped inside, locking the heavy doors behind them. For a moment, there was silence, save for the distant sounds of chaos.

Braham turned to Aleksander; his eyes hard but filled with determination. "Find the intel. We're ending this tonight!"

Aleksander leaned heavily on the terminal, his fingers trembling as he input a serial code he knew was often used for this type of system. He hesitated for a fraction of a second, muttering under his breath, "This better work…" Then he pressed the final key.

The screen blinked red for a moment before flashing green, accompanied by a loud metallic *clang*.

"SBAMM!" The doors slid open violently, the mechanisms groaning as they released.

"We're in!" Aleksander shouted; his voice strained but triumphant. Without hesitation, Braham waved his team forward. "Move! Now!" The group charged down the open corridor and into the garage, their boots pounding against the cold concrete. But as they burst through, they came to a sudden halt. The massive, dimly lit space was eerily silent, and every parking bay was empty. No vehicles. No escape.

Jimmy swore under his breath, his frustration boiling over. "No cars? Are you kidding me?"

"Stay alert," Braham warned, scanning the shadows. "This feels wrong." From behind a stack of crates, slow, deliberate clapping echoed through the garage, the sound cold and mocking. The team turned sharply, weapons raised, as a tall figure emerged from the darkness, his face illuminated by the faint overhead lights.

"Bravo," Seriakov drawled, his voice dripping with condescension. He stopped in the middle of the open space, flanked by five heavily armed soldiers. Their weapons were trained on Braham and his team, their postures confident and unyielding.

"You made it further than I expected," Seriakov continued, a smirk curling his lips. "But then again, you've always been resourceful, haven't you, Braham?"

Braham's eyes narrowed; his rifle trained on Seriakov. "This isn't over, Seriakov. Step aside, or your arrogance will cost you."

Seriakov chuckled, slow and deliberate, as though Braham's words amused him. "You're in no position to make threats. You're outnumbered, outgunned, and…" He gestured around the empty garage. "…out of options."

Aleksander gritted his teeth, his hand tightening around his pistol. "You think this ends here? You're a fool if you do."

"Oh, I'm not the fool," Seriakov replied coolly, his smirk fading into a cold, calculated glare. "You underestimated me. Just like Solokov did. And look where that got him."

Mirna, her body tense despite her injuries, spoke up. "We've dealt with worse than you, Seriakov. Your little power play won't mean anything when we're done."

Seriakov's expression darkened, and he took a step forward, his soldiers moving in unison behind him. "You've already lost. You just don't know it yet. But don't worry—I'll make it quick. Maybe even painless, if you're lucky."

"Funny," Braham said, his voice low and steady. "I was about to say the same to you."

At that moment, a faint, distant hum began to grow louder, reverberating through the garage. Seriakov's smirk faltered as he glanced toward the source of the sound. The team exchanged quick, knowing glances.

"What is that?" one of Seriakov's soldiers muttered, his grip tightening on his weapon.

The hum grew into a roar as a sleek, armored vehicle burst through a concealed side entrance, its engine revving like a beast unleashed. The headlights blazed, momentarily blinding everyone in the garage. Behind the wheel, one of Braham's operatives grinned fiercely, gesturing for the team to get in.

"Get down!" Braham barked, diving for cover as the vehicle's mounted turret opened fire, cutting through Seriakov's soldiers like a scythe through grass.

Chaos erupted as bullets ricocheted off the concrete and the team scrambled toward the vehicle. Seriakov shouted orders, his voice barely audible over the cacophony.

"Go, go, go!" Braham yelled, hauling Jimmy into the backseat as Aleksander and Mirna followed close behind. The remaining soldiers provided covering fire, retreating in tight formation.

As the team piled into the vehicle, Braham turned back, locking eyes with Seriakov one last time. The Colonel's face twisted with rage as he raised his weapon, but before he could fire, the vehicle's turret swung toward him.

Braham's voice was cold and unyielding. "Drive."

The vehicle roared to life, tearing through the garage as the turret unleashed one final barrage, forcing Seriakov to dive for cover.

As they sped out of the compound, the sounds of the chaos fading behind them, Jimmy let out a ragged laugh, leaning back against the seat. "Now *that* was a close call."

Braham, his expression still grim, turned to the driver. "Head for the extraction point. We're not safe yet."

Mirna glanced out the rear window, watching the compound shrink into the distance. "Seriakov won't let this go."

Braham nodded, his jaw set. "Let him come. We'll be ready."

Braham stood in the dimly lit corridor, his team regrouped and battered but far from defeated. The blaring sirens and red emergency lights made every second feel heavier, like the walls were closing in. He stared at the blueprint of the scientific centre displayed on Aleksander's stolen tablet, his mind racing.

"We can't keep running blind," Mirna said, her voice low but urgent. "This place is a fortress, and they know it better than we do. We need a plan—one that doesn't involve walking into a death trap."

Braham exhaled sharply, his hand running through his hair. "You're right. This isn't working. We need to rethink everything."

Aleksander leaned against the wall, still catching his breath, his bruised face lit by the screen's glow. "This centre isn't just well-guarded—it's a labyrinth of traps and defences. Every path out is locked tighter than a vault, and they've got armed patrols covering every corner."

"And don't forget the defence systems," Jimmy added, wincing as he adjusted his injured arm. "Sensors, automated turrets... The whole place is designed to keep people like us from escaping."

Braham stared at the blueprint, his finger tracing the winding hallways and choke points. Every route seemed impossible. His instincts told him that charging through wasn't just reckless—it was suicide. Seriakov's men weren't like the typical guards they'd faced before. These were Weiner's elite, and their orders were clear: no one leaves alive.

"We need to stop thinking like soldiers," Braham said finally, his voice steady but resolute. "This isn't about overpowering them. It's about outsmarting them."

Mirna raised an eyebrow. "Outsmarting them? How? They have control over every system in this facility."

"Exactly," Braham replied, his mind churning. "And that's their weakness. They're too reliant on those systems. If we can disrupt their control, we create chaos—and chaos is our way out."

Aleksander frowned, scrolling through the schematics. "Disrupt how? This place is networked into a central hub. If we could access it, we could disable their automated defences and maybe unlock a few doors... But it's buried deep in the heart of the centre. And it's heavily guarded."

"We don't need to control the entire system," Braham countered. "We just need to create enough of a distraction to draw their attention away from us."

Mirna's eyes narrowed as she considered his words. "You're suggesting we hit them where it hurts. Force them to focus on something bigger than us."

"Exactly," Braham said. "Aleksander, is there anything in the system we can overload? Something that would demand their full attention?"

Aleksander's fingers flew across the tablet, his eyes scanning line after line of data. After a tense moment, he stopped, a slow grin spreading across his face. "The main reactor. It's the core of this whole facility. If we can tamper with the control protocols, it'll trigger a containment breach alarm. They'd have no choice but to prioritize it—no one wants to be anywhere near a reactor meltdown."

Mirna's lips pressed into a thin line. "That's a gamble. If they realize it's a bluff, they'll come for us anyway. And if we screw up..."

"We won't screw up," Braham said firmly. "Aleksander, can you do it?"

"It won't be easy," Aleksander admitted. "I'll need direct access to the control terminal in the reactor room. And it's probably the most secure place in this whole facility."

"Then we make it less secure," Braham said, his voice carrying the weight of his decision. "We create diversions along the way. Force their forces to spread thin."

"And if it works?" Jimmy asked, his voice sceptical.

"If it works," Braham replied, his eyes hard, "we'll have just enough chaos to slip out unnoticed."

The team exchanged uncertain glances, the weight of the plan settling on their shoulders. It was risky, dangerous, and relied on perfect timing— but it was their best shot.

Braham straightened; his determination clear. "Gear up. Aleksander, map the fastest route to the reactor. Mirna, you're with me—we'll secure the path. Jimmy, you and the others prepare the diversions. We move in five."

As the team scattered to prepare, Braham stared at the blueprint one last time, committing it to memory. This wasn't just about survival anymore—it was about proving that even in the face of impossible odds, their minds were their greatest weapons.

"Weiner's men might think they've won," Braham muttered to himself, "but they've underestimated us. And that's going to be their biggest mistake."

Braham leaned against the wall, the faint hum of the emergency alarms still vibrating in the background. His eyes darted between his battered team and the ominous red glow of the hallways ahead. Each route seemed like an open invitation to death. But amidst the chaos, a single thought began to crystallize in his mind.

They couldn't fight their way out. They couldn't run. But they could *disappear*.

"Hiding," Braham said aloud, his voice cutting through the tension.

Jimmy frowned; his face bruised but alert. "Hiding? We're trapped in a fortress. Where the hell do, we hide?"

Mirna, leaning heavily against the wall to steady herself, looked at Braham sceptically. "You're saying we stop running and just... vanish? That's your plan?"

"Yes," Braham said firmly. "Look around. Every corridor is a death trap. Every move we make feeds into their defence systems. Automated turrets, sensors, patrols—they're all designed to track and corner us. If we keep giving them targets, we'll never get out alive."

Aleksander, still tinkering with the stolen tablet, raised an eyebrow. "So, what, we just sit tight and hope they forget about us?"

"Not forget," Braham corrected. "Confuse. They're expecting us to act like desperate soldiers trying to fight or escape. What they won't expect is for us to vanish completely—no reference points, no signals, nothing to guide their systems or their men."

Mirna tilted her head, starting to see where he was going. "You mean turning the fortress against them."

"Exactly," Braham said, his voice gaining momentum. "This place is a machine, and like any machine, it's only as good as the data it's fed. If we give them nothing—no sound, no movement, no heat signatures— their systems will falter. Their men will start doubting the tech, maybe even panicking."

Jimmy crossed his arms. "And how do we pull that off? We can't just turn invisible."

Braham turned to Aleksander. "You're good with systems. Can you find blind spots in their sensors? Places where their coverage is weak?"

Aleksander nodded slowly, his fingers flying over the tablet. "Give me a second… There." He pointed to a section of the map. "Maintenance tunnels. They're not covered by the main security grid, probably because they're considered low-risk. We could use them to stay out of sight."

"Good," Braham said. "Now we need to control our exposure. No open spaces, no noise, and no heat. Strip anything that gives off a signal. If we have to move, we do it slow and silent."

Mirna frowned. "What about patrols? We're still going to run into them."

"That's where the surprise comes in," Braham said. "If we're forced to engage, we strike fast and vanish before they can react. No prolonged fights. No gunfire unless absolutely necessary. We make them think we're ghosts."

Jimmy let out a low whistle. "It's risky. One wrong move, and we're cornered."

"It's better than running headfirst into their traps," Braham countered. "This isn't about winning a fight. It's about surviving long enough to find a real opening."

Aleksander studied the map again. "If we make it to the maintenance tunnels, we might be able to loop around to the power core or even find an exit they're not guarding heavily. But it's a maze down there. If we get lost…"

"Then we don't get lost," Braham said sharply. "Mark every turn, and keep the map updated. This isn't a sprint; it's a game of patience. We're going to make them think we're everywhere and nowhere at once."

Mirna adjusted her gear, her expression resolute. "All right. Let's make them regret ever trying to trap us in here."

"Good," Braham said. "From this point on, no more running. We're ghosts now. We move only when we have to, and when we do, we leave nothing behind."

The team nodded, the weight of the plan sinking in. It was risky, but it played to their strengths: precision, discipline, and the element of surprise.

As they slipped into the shadows, Braham's voice carried softly over the tense silence. "They think they're hunting us. Let's see how they like being hunted instead."

Mirna steadied herself on Braham's shoulders, her bruised hands gripping the edge of the vent grate as she worked it loose. With a final, sharp pull, the metal cover clattered to the ground. The hollow sound echoed faintly, and everyone froze, listening for any sign that the noise had drawn attention.

"Clear," Aleksander whispered, his eyes darting toward the hallway behind them.

Mirna peered into the ventilation shaft, her flashlight illuminating the narrow passage. The vent was at least 1.5 meters wide and half a meter high—just big enough for them to crawl through single file. The downside was immediately obvious.

"It's thin," she muttered. "Feels like the whole thing could give way if we're not careful."

Braham steadied her as she climbed down. "Can it hold anyone?" he asked, his voice low but calm.

Mirna shook her head. "Not for long. The panels will buckle under too much weight. If we're going in, we need to spread out and keep our movements light."

Jimmy knelt next to the opening, inspecting the shaft. "If this thing can't hold us, what's the plan? We can't afford to fall through and end up in the middle of a patrol."

Mirna rubbed her temples, thinking quickly. "We'll need to brace against the sides—use the walls to distribute our weight. Hands and knees won't cut it."

Aleksander nodded, already adjusting his gear to fit the confined space. "It's risky, but it's better than staying here. The vents lead to the maintenance tunnels. If we're careful, this might get us out of the grid entirely."

Braham glanced at the vent and then at his team. The tension in the air was palpable, but there was no other choice. The walls were closing in, and every second spent deliberating was another chance for Seriakov's men to find them.

"All right," Braham said. "Aleksander, you go first. You know the schematics, so you'll guide us through. Jimmy, you're next. Mirna and I will follow. We move slow, stay quiet, and keep the weight distributed. Got it?"

The team nodded; their expressions grim but determined. Aleksander climbed into the shaft, his movements deliberate as he pressed his back against one wall and his feet against the other. The thin metal creaked slightly but held as he inched forward.

Jimmy followed, his larger frame making the process more cumbersome. Each shift of his weight made the vent groan ominously, but he adjusted quickly, finding a rhythm.

Mirna turned to Braham. "You're going to hate this," she said, her lips curving into a faint, humourless smile.

"Not as much as I hate this place," Braham replied, gesturing for her to go.

As Mirna disappeared into the shaft, Braham took one last look down the hallway. The sirens were still blaring, and the red emergency lights cast long shadows. There was no sign of pursuit yet, but he knew that wouldn't last. Seriakov and his men would be hunting them relentlessly.

With a deep breath, Braham hoisted himself into the vent. The narrow space was claustrophobic, the air stale and metallic. Each movement had to be precise to avoid putting too much pressure on the fragile panels below.

They crawled in silence, the only sounds the faint scrape of clothing against metal and the occasional creak of the vent. Aleksander led them through a maze of turns and junctions, his focus unshakable.

After what felt like an eternity, they reached a junction where the vent split into two directions. Aleksander stopped, checking his tablet.

"This way," he whispered, pointing to the left. "It'll take us closer to the maintenance tunnels."

As they moved, Braham's mind raced. They were buying time, but it wasn't enough. They needed a way to stay ahead of their pursuers—a way to turn the tide in their favour.

For now, though, survival came first. The ventilation system was their best chance, and they would have to make every inch count.

Mirna's breath hitched as she pressed her feet firmly against the fence-like structure on the wall. The metallic noise from the external tunnel echoed ominously, freezing the blood in her veins and sending a ripple of dread through the group.

Aleksander clenched his jaw, his eyes darting nervously. "What the hell was that?"

"No idea," Braham muttered, his voice barely above a whisper. "Keep quiet. Mirna, what do you see?"

Mirna strained her neck to peer through the faint gap in the tunnel wall. The faint glow of artificial lighting shimmered below. "There's something down there… looks like a maintenance area. Maybe storage?"

Without waiting for confirmation, Mirna gritted her teeth and pushed off the wall, launching herself into the unknown. The drop was about three meters, and she landed hard, rolling to absorb the impact.

The team held their breath as they watched her stand, brushing off dust. She turned back to them, her face lighting up with something unexpected—hope.

"Yes, yes, yes!" she shouted, her voice echoing in the dim, cavernous space. "It's a tunnel! A way through!"

One by one, the team followed her lead, climbing down cautiously until they stood together in the expansive underground chamber. At first, it was hard to make out their surroundings in the dim, green-tinged light. Then their eyes adjusted, and what they saw left them stunned.

They were in what appeared to be a self-sustaining agricultural system. Rows of plants, vegetables, and fruits stretched across the room in neatly organized hydroponic beds. A shallow channel of water snaked along the floor, teeming with fish and algae. The air was humid and faintly sweet, the sound of trickling water creating an almost serene atmosphere.

Jimmy let out a low whistle, his expression a mixture of awe and disbelief. "This… this is their food source. It's how they've been sustaining themselves."

Aleksander crouched next to a patch of tomatoes, his fingers brushing one of the leaves. "They've recreated external conditions. Light, humidity, even the nutrient cycles. It's... impressive."

"It's genius," Mirna corrected, her eyes scanning the room. "They've built an ecosystem down here. Plants, fish, algae—everything in balance. They could live off this for years without needing outside supplies."

Braham's gaze hardened as he stepped forward, his boots splashing slightly in the water channel. "It's more than just a food source. This is strategic. It's why this fortress can operate independently for so long." The team stood in silence for a moment, each of them processing the implications. The fortress wasn't just a stronghold; it was a living organism, designed to thrive even in isolation.

Jimmy broke the silence. "So, what do we do? Destroy it? Use it?"

Braham shook his head. "Not yet. Right now, this is an opportunity. We can regroup here, maybe even find supplies or tools to help us. But we don't have time to sit around. Seriakov's men will figure out we're not in the vents soon enough."

Mirna's eyes flicked toward a control panel embedded in the wall. "If this system is automated, there might be a way to access the fortress's broader network. It could give us an advantage—a way to override defences or at least track enemy movements."

Aleksander nodded, already moving toward the panel. "I'll see what I can do. Keep an eye out. If they find us down here, we'll be sitting ducks."

Braham gestured for Jimmy and Mirna to fan out and secure the perimeter. As they moved, his eyes lingered on the lush greenery and the shimmering water.

This hidden oasis was a testament to the enemy's ingenuity—but it might also be their undoing.

The team moved cautiously through the corridor; their footsteps muffled against the damp floor. The walls were lined with pipes and faintly glowing conduits, adding an eerie light to the already tense atmosphere. The corridor stretched on for what felt like forever—nearly 500 meters—before they reached its end, where a strange steel door loomed in front of them.

The door was massive, smooth, and featureless save for a faint seam in the centre, suggesting it might be a sliding mechanism. No visible handles, buttons, or panels gave any clue as to how it operated. It stood silent and imposing, an unyielding barrier to whatever lay beyond.

Jimmy placed a hand on the cool metal, tilting his head as if listening for a sound. "It's thick," he muttered. "Feels reinforced. Probably locked tight from the other side."

Mirna frowned, crouching to inspect the floor and edges of the door. "No obvious mechanisms. No hinges. This thing wasn't meant to be opened easily."

Braham stepped forward, scanning the door's surface intently. "There's got to be something. Sliding doors like this don't just open by magic." He ran his fingers along the smooth steel, searching for any sign of a biometric scanner, keypad, or hidden activation point.

Aleksander joined in, tapping the walls near the door. "If it's automated, there's a control system somewhere. Could be hidden or connected remotely. We're looking for a keystone area—something that triggers it."

Jimmy sighed, stepping back to give Braham room. "I don't like this. If it's sealed this tight, there's probably something important on the other side. Whatever it is, they don't want us getting to it."

Mirna glanced over her shoulder nervously, her voice low. "Or it's a trap. Seriakov and his men could be herding us here, waiting to ambush us as soon as we figure it out."

Braham ignored the growing tension, his hands continuing to glide over the surface of the door. He paused for a moment, then pressed against a faint indentation on the left side. Nothing. He moved to the right, trying another spot. Still nothing.

Frustration began to creep into his movements as he tapped and pushed at random points on the door. "There's got to be a way," he muttered.

Aleksander suddenly crouched, noticing something near the base of the door. He pointed to a small groove running along the floor. "This could be the mechanism's track. If we can figure out how to engage it—"

Before he could finish, Braham's hand brushed against a cold, raised section near the top-right corner of the door. It was barely noticeable, but it had a faint metallic texture different from the smooth steel around it.

"Found something," Braham said, pressing against it.

Nothing happened.

He pressed again, harder this time, and then tried to slide his fingers around the edges. Still nothing.

Mirna stepped beside him, her eyes narrowing. "Let me see." She reached into her pocket, pulling out a multitool. Carefully, she wedged a thin blade into the raised section, prying it loose.

The small panel popped off, revealing a recessed compartment with a glowing scanner and a narrow slot. Aleksander leaned in, inspecting it. "Looks like it's for a keycard... or something biometric."

Jimmy groaned. "And we don't have either."

Braham's mind raced as he stared at the scanner. "If this is part of their internal system, there might be a way to bypass it. Aleksander, can you hack it?"

Aleksander frowned, pulling out a portable interface device from his pack. "Maybe. But if I screw this up, it could trigger an alarm—or worse, lock us out completely."

"Do it," Braham ordered. "We don't have time to waste."

Aleksander nodded, plugging his device into the scanner. The small screen on the interface flickered to life, displaying lines of code. He began typing rapidly, his fingers flying across the keyboard.

As the seconds ticked by, the rest of the team stood tense, their eyes flicking between Aleksander and the corridor behind them. Every faint sound or distant echo sent a jolt of paranoia through their nerves.

Finally, after what felt like an eternity, Aleksander let out a small laugh. "Got it."

The scanner beeped, and the steel door hissed as it began to slide open, revealing a dimly lit room beyond.

Braham stepped forward, his hand on his weapon. "Stay sharp. We don't know what's waiting for us in there."

The team moved cautiously into the room, their eyes scanning every corner. Inside, they found stairs   leading to another locked entrance...

As the team stepped into the dimly lit chamber, their boots echoed off the smooth, metallic floor. A staircase spiralled upward, its structure sleek and reinforced, leading to another door four meters above. This door was even more imposing than the one they had just bypassed.

The new barrier loomed like a sentinel, its surface a polished, dark alloy etched with faint, glowing circuitry that pulsed in an eerie rhythm. Unlike the previous sliding door, this one seemed far more advanced—a fortress within a fortress.

Jimmy tilted his head, his face a mix of awe and frustration. "This... this isn't just a door. It's a damn vault."

Aleksander ran a hand along the edge of the staircase rail, his eyes narrowing as he studied the intricate design. "This isn't just security; it's overkill. Whatever's behind that door is critical. High-value intel or tech—something they'd defend with their lives."

Mirna squinted at the glowing circuitry. "Looks like it's powered by some kind of advanced energy system. We're not brute-forcing this one."

Braham stepped forward, his mind racing. "Aleksander, can you interface with it like before?"

Aleksander hesitated; his gaze fixed on the glowing patterns. "This is different. The complexity… it's on another level. If I try to force my way in, I might trip an automated countermeasure. Alarms, lockdowns, or worse."

Jimmy groaned, leaning against the railing. "So what? We're stuck?"

Mirna's brow furrowed as she stepped closer to the door, inspecting the glowing circuits. "Not necessarily. This kind of system is usually paired with something—an override mechanism, a key, or a specific access code. It might even require two-factor input: biometrics plus a physical key."

Braham frowned. "Then we need to find whatever unlocks this. It's got to be nearby."

Aleksander pointed to a small console embedded in the wall beside the door. The interface displayed a pulsating light, its rhythm in sync with the circuitry on the door. "This console might give us a clue. If I can access it without triggering anything..."

Braham nodded. "Do it. But be careful."

Aleksander knelt by the console, connecting his portable interface device once again. As he worked, Mirna paced the room, her sharp eyes scanning for anything out of place. Jimmy, meanwhile, stood guard near the entrance, his weapon at the ready.

Minutes stretched into what felt like hours as Aleksander typed furiously, lines of code scrolling across his screen. The rest of the team held their breath, every faint clicks of his keyboard magnified in the oppressive silence.

Finally, Aleksander exhaled sharply. "I've got partial access. There's a secondary system—something external. The door won't open unless we activate a switch or trigger hidden within the compound."

Braham's jaw tightened. "So, we're on a scavenger hunt."

Aleksander nodded grimly. "And we need to hurry. If Seriakov's men figure out where we are, this whole place will turn into a death trap."

Mirna's voice cut through the tension. "Then we split up. Some of us look for the trigger, while the rest stay here and secure the area."

Braham hesitated, weighing the risks. "It's dangerous, but we don't have a choice. Aleksander, stay here and keep working on the console. Jimmy, you're with me. Mirna, find that switch. Move fast and stay in contact."

Mirna gave a sharp nod, her eyes blazing with determination. Without another word, she slipped back into the corridor, disappearing into the shadows.

Braham turned to Aleksander; his voice low. "If you see or hear anything, lock this place down and alert us immediately."

Aleksander smirked, though the tension in his face betrayed his nerves. "Don't worry, boss. I'll hold the fort."

As the team moved into action, the clock was ticking. Whatever lay behind that door wasn't just the key to their escape—it was the heart of the enemy's operations. And finding a way inside was their only shot at survival.

As they regrouped in the confined, metallic chamber, the tension among the team was palpable. The door above remained as intimidating as ever, its glowing circuitry a constant reminder of the high stakes they faced. Everyone's thoughts seemed to converge on the same theme: *The Enigma of the Sphinx.*

Mirna was the first to break the silence. "No handles. No keys. Nothing standard. This door is designed to keep out even the smartest intruders. It's a puzzle, not just a barrier."

Jimmy sighed, his hands on his hips. "Yeah, but puzzles have solutions, don't they? Or are we stuck with this thing until the enemy finds us?"

Aleksander, still working at the console, grunted. "Whatever it is, it's meant to stall us. The longer we stay here, the greater the chance they'll catch up."

Braham scanned the room, his sharp eyes searching for anything they might have missed. It was then that he spotted something in the far corner—a strange object tucked behind a cluster of exposed pipes.

"Hold on," he said, striding over to the corner. As he crouched down, he saw it clearly: a large, oddly shaped key. It was unlike any key he'd ever seen—intricately designed, with ridges and grooves that didn't resemble any traditional lock mechanism.

"What the hell is this?" Braham muttered, holding up the key for the others to see.

Mirna stepped closer, her brow furrowing as she examined it. "It's massive. And look at the design—it's not just a key. It's part of an activation system. Maybe even a tool for the door."

Jimmy took the key from Braham, testing its weight. "Feels sturdy. If this thing doesn't open the door, we could at least use it as a weapon."

Aleksander glanced up from his console, curiosity flashing across his face. "Let me see that."

Jimmy handed it over, and Aleksander turned it over in his hands, his eyes narrowing. "This isn't just decorative. These grooves—they look like they're meant to slot into something. But not the door directly. It's too big for the console and doesn't match the interface."

Mirna looked back at the door. "What if it's part of the puzzle? Like a riddle. The door might not open until we activate something else, and this key could be the trigger."

Braham nodded. "It's possible. Let's search the walls, the floor—anywhere this key might fit. It wouldn't be here unless it served a purpose."

The team spread out, examining every inch of the small room. It didn't take long before Mirna called out, her voice sharp with excitement. "Over here! I think I've found something."

The others hurried to her side. She was crouched near a panel on the floor, partially obscured by debris. The panel was circular, with a deep groove running through its centre—an opening that matched the key's ridged design perfectly.

"This has to be it," Mirna said, brushing away the debris.

Braham knelt beside her, holding the key. He glanced at the team, then back at the panel. "Let's hope this doesn't trigger something worse."

He inserted the key into the groove, feeling it click into place. The room was silent for a moment, and then a faint hum began to emanate from the walls.

The glowing circuitry on the door above shifted, its pattern altering as if reacting to the activation. Aleksander's console lit up with new data, and his eyes widened. "It's working! The system's unlocking. Keep turning the key!"

Braham twisted the key further, feeling resistance as the mechanisms engaged. The hum grew louder, and the door above began to shift, its seamless surface splitting down the centre.

With a final twist, the key clicked into place, and the massive door slid open, revealing a darkened hallway beyond.

Mirna let out a breath she didn't realize she'd been holding. "We did it."

Jimmy grinned, gripping his weapon tighter. "And without blowing ourselves up. I'd call that a win."

Braham stood, pulling the key from the panel. "Let's move. Whatever's beyond this door, we're not stopping now."

The team ascended the staircase and stepped through the newly opened door, their nerves on edge as they ventured into the unknown. Behind them, the hum of the system quieted, leaving only the sound of their footsteps as they pressed forward into the heart of the compound.

The team stepped cautiously into the space beyond the door, their breath catching at the sight that greeted them.

It was a vast, breathtaking dome, its metallic framework arching high above them, supporting a network of polygonal glass panes. The structure glowed with a soft, golden light, filtering through the glass and illuminating the space with an almost ethereal warmth. The glass appeared to refract light in subtle rainbows, creating a surreal and dreamlike atmosphere.

Inside the dome, a stark contrast to the harsh corridors and high-tech defences they'd passed, was a massive kitchen and living area. Sleek, modern counters and appliances gleamed under ambient lights, blending functionality with comfort. A group of individuals, clearly European judging by their accents and appearances, was gathered around a large island in the kitchen.

Inside the group, Braham suddenly recognized two familiar faces among the scientists—a young girl named Eleanor and a boy named Lukas. They were among the people who had disappeared in the same area.

"Eleanor, Lukas!" Braham called out, relief and surprise evident in his voice. The two turned around, their faces lighting up with recognition.

"Braham!" Eleanor exclaimed, rushing over. "How did you find us?"

Lukas followed, his expression a mix of bewilderment and relief.

"We've been here for weeks, trying to understand what these people are doing."

Braham quickly briefed them on their mission, while Mirna and the rest of the team continued to secure the dome. Dr. Laroque watched the reunion with a concerned look but didn't intervene.

"Dr. Laroque," Braham said, turning back to the scientist, "these two were reported missing. Why are they here?"

Laroque sighed, his demeanour softening. "They stumbled upon our facility by accident. We couldn't let them leave knowing what we're working on. It was for their own protection, and ours."

Eleanor shook her head. "Protection? We were prisoners. We didn't choose to be here."

Laroque nodded, acknowledging her point. "I understand your perspective, but we are on the brink of discoveries that could change the world. We couldn't risk exposure."

Before the conversation could continue, the automated voice echoed through the dome again: "Warning: Multiple unauthorized personnel approaching. Estimated time to breach: Five minutes."

The team exchanged tense glances. Braham knew they had little time to act.

"Dr. Laroque, if you want our help, we need the full truth now," he demanded.

Laroque took a deep breath. "Alright. We have been developing advanced technologies that could solve global crises—energy, food, water. But not everyone wants these solutions. Some see them as threats to their power. Seriakov was one of those people. He used to be part of our team, but he turned against us, wanting to control these technologies for himself."

Jimmy cut in, "So he's the one trying to breach the facility now?"

Laroque nodded. "Yes. If he gets in, he'll take everything we've worked for. We can't let that happen."

Braham looked at his team. "Alright, we defend this place, but only if we get full cooperation from you and your team."

Laroque agreed. "Deal. We'll do everything we can to help."

The team quickly set up defensive positions around the dome, ready to face the impending threat. As they prepared for the confrontation, Braham couldn't help but think about the thin line between innovation and exploitation. The answers they sought were within reach, but so was danger.

And so, with the fate of groundbreaking technologies and countless lives hanging in the balance, they braced themselves for the battle that would determine the future of the dome—and perhaps, the world.

They appeared relaxed, discussing something animatedly and laughing, as though they were at a weekend retreat rather than deep within a high-security facility.

The group froze for a moment, startled by the newcomers. A man in his mid-40s, with sharp features and greying hair, stepped forward, holding a cup of coffee. He raised his hands in a gesture of peace.

"Ah," he began with a faint accent—perhaps French or Belgian—his voice calm and collected. "You must be the ones who managed to bypass the lower-level security. Quite an impressive feat."

Braham's team exchanged wary glances; their weapons instinctively raised. Mirna's eyes scanned the room for any visible threats, while Jimmy kept his finger on the trigger. Aleksander's hand hovered near his console, ready to hack into any nearby systems if needed.

"Who are you?" Braham demanded, his voice firm but cautious.

The man smiled faintly and took a step forward. "My name is Dr. Étienne Laroque. I lead this small research team here. And you are?"

Braham didn't lower his weapon. "That's not important. What *is* important is why you're here, in the middle of what seems to be a high-security compound."

Laroque gestured around the dome with an almost casual air. "We're scientists. Researchers. This is our lab, our home. We're working on solutions to some of humanity's greatest problems—sustainable energy, advanced agriculture, water purification. What you see here—" he motioned to the kitchen and the dome itself, "—is a fraction of what we've achieved."

Mirna's voice cut in, sharp and sceptical. "That doesn't explain the defences outside or the fact that this place looks like a fortress. What are you really hiding?"

One of the other researchers, a younger woman with auburn hair, spoke up, her tone defensive. "Hiding? We're not hiding anything. The security is to protect us and our work. You've seen the world out there—it's ruthless. People would kill for the technology we're developing."

Aleksander scoffed. "And yet you're all here, laughing over coffee like you're on vacation."

Laroque's expression darkened slightly. "We take our work very seriously. But even in a place like this, we must have moments of humanity. Surely you understand that?"

Braham narrowed his eyes. "We understand that this 'humanity' could be a front for something else. Where's Seriakov?"

At the mention of the name, a ripple of unease passed through the group of scientists. Laroque's composure faltered, just for a moment, before he replied. "Seriakov? He's… no longer here."

Jimmy stepped forward; his tone icy. "That's not an answer."

Before Laroque could respond, a soft chime echoed through the dome, followed by an automated voice:

**"Warning: Perimeter breach detected. Unauthorized personnel inbound."**

The scientists exchanged nervous glances, and Laroque's face paled. "Listen to me," he said urgently, turning back to Braham's team. "If you're here for answers, we don't have much time. Seriakov's men won't stop until they find you—and us. You've already compromised the facility's security."

Braham's grip on his weapon tightened. "Then start talking. What's behind all this? Why is this place so important?"

Laroque hesitated, glancing at his team. Finally, he sighed, his shoulders slumping slightly. "I'll explain everything. But first, we need to secure this area. If they get in here, none of us will survive."

Mirna looked to Braham, her expression tense. "What's the play, boss?"

Braham nodded; his decision made. "Secure the dome. Then we get the truth."

The team moved quickly, locking down the room as best they could while keeping a wary eye on the scientists. Whatever secrets this dome held, they were determined to uncover them.

The silence of the place was abruptly interrupted by a metallic clanking. Three humanoid cobots entered the dome from another entrance, their movements fluid yet distinctly robotic. They glided across the floor with mechanical precision, their sensors scanning the room for any signs of threat.

Braham and his team immediately sprang into action, their training kicking in. "Take cover!" Braham shouted, as they ducked behind the kitchen island and nearby furniture. The cobots, undeterred, advanced toward them, their tasers raised and ready to fire.

Mirna peeked over the counter, her eyes widening at the sight of the cobots. "We've got company, and they don't look friendly!"

Jimmy aimed his weapon, his finger steady on the trigger. "These aren't your average security bots. They're advanced, probably programmed to neutralize intruders."

Aleksander's hands flew over his console, attempting to hack into the cobots' systems. "I'm trying to override their protocols, but it might take a moment!"

Eleanor and Lukas, now part of the team, crouched low, their eyes darting around for any makeshift weapons they could use. Dr. Laroque and his team stood frozen, clearly unprepared for a combat situation.

One of the cobots raised its taser and fired, narrowly missing Braham's shoulder. The crackling sound of the taser echoed through the dome, a stark reminder of the danger they were in.

"Hold them off!" Braham ordered, firing a shot that hit one of the cobots squarely in the chest. Sparks flew, but the cobot continued to advance, seemingly unaffected by the impact.

Aleksander's fingers moved even faster. "Got it! I've managed to disable one of their defense protocols. It should slow them down!"

As the cobots hesitated, their movements becoming slightly more sluggish, Braham saw an opening. "Now! Take them down!"

The team moved as one, a well-oiled machine in their own right. Mirna's precise shots, Jimmy's brute force, and Aleksander's technical skills combined to overpower the cobots. Within moments, the metallic figures lay motionless on the ground, their tasers clattering to a stop.

Braham took a deep breath, scanning the room for any further threats. "Everyone alright?" he asked, his voice steady but tense.

Dr. Laroque nodded, visibly shaken. "Yes, but we need to move quickly. This is only the beginning. If they sent cobots, more reinforcements are likely on their way."

Braham glanced at his team, his resolve firm. "Then let's not waste any more time. Secure the area and find out everything we can. We're not leaving until we get to the bottom of this."

With renewed determination, the team set to work, knowing that every second counted. The secrets of the dome were within their grasp, and they were ready to uncover the truth, no matter the cost.

Braham made a swift decision to convince Eleanor and Lukas to escape with them. However, their immediate priority was to flee the dome, given that the cobots seemed invincible for now. With urgency fuelling their actions, they located an opening on the opposite side and began to navigate through the outer paths of the centre.

The team moved swiftly and silently, the cold air biting at their faces as they sprinted through the dimly lit corridors. Each step was calculated, every movement purposeful. The metallic echo of the cobots' footsteps grew fainter, but the team knew they couldn't let their guard down.

As they emerged into the open, the vast expanse of the desert greeted them, bathed in the pale light of the moon. The chill of the night was in stark contrast to the intense heat they had felt within the dome. The group paused for a moment, catching their breath and assessing their surroundings.

"We need to keep moving," Braham urged, his voice low but firm. "We're not safe yet."

Eleanor and Lukas exchanged a glance before nodding in agreement. They had come this far and weren't about to let fear hold them back now.

Navigating the rocky terrain, the team made their way towards the safer grounds, keeping an eye out for any signs of pursuit. The faint glow of the facility faded into the distance, replaced by the serene vastness of the desert. The silence of the night was punctuated only by their heavy breathing and the crunch of sand beneath their boots.

Eventually, they found a small outcrop where they could rest and plan their next move. The night sky stretched endlessly above them, dotted with stars that seemed to whisper tales of both hope and despair.

Braham gathered the group around, his tone serious but hopeful. "We've made it this far, but we need to find a way to stay ahead of Seriakov's men. We have to use the terrain to our advantage and find a place to regroup."

Mirna nodded, her eyes scanning the horizon. "There's a small town not too far from here. We can head there and figure out our next steps. Maybe even gather some more supplies."

Eleanor, still catching her breath, spoke up. "Thank you for coming back for us. We were starting to lose hope in there."

Braham placed a reassuring hand on her shoulder. "We're in this together now. Let's keep moving and find a way to end this once and for all."

With renewed determination, the team set off towards the town, the moonlight guiding their path. They knew the road ahead would be fraught with challenges, but they were ready to face whatever came their way. Together, they were stronger, and together, they would uncover the truth behind the dome and its secrets.

Their escape route led them towards the vast, unforgiving tundra.

Braham and his team quickly located a section of the fence that seemed weaker than the rest. With efficient precision, they cut a square opening large enough for everyone to pass through.

One by one, they slipped through the fence, stepping cautiously over the thin layer of snow that covered the ground. The cold air bit at their faces, but the adrenaline of their escape kept them moving. The sounds of the facility grew faint as they pressed on towards the tundra.

The landscape before them was a stark contrast to the dome's interior. The wide expanse of the tundra stretched endlessly, a frozen, desolate wilderness. Snowflakes drifted down gently, adding to the surreal beauty of the scene.

As they made their way through the snow, the team huddled close together, using the sparse cover of rocky outcrops and sparse vegetation to shield themselves from view. The tundra, with its icy silence, seemed to swallow their footsteps, offering a temporary sanctuary from the dangers behind.

Braham glanced at Eleanor and Lukas, who were trudging along with determined expressions. "We're almost there," he assured them, his voice steady. "Just a bit further, and we'll be out of sight."

Mirna, ever vigilant, scanned the horizon for any signs of pursuit. "We need to find shelter soon," she said. "The cold will only get worse as night falls."

Jimmy nodded in agreement; his breath visible in the frosty air. "Let's keep moving. There's a cluster of trees up ahead. It might provide some cover."

The team pushed forward, driven by the hope of reaching safety. The tundra, though harsh and unforgiving, held a strange, serene beauty. It was a place of solitude, where the silence was broken only by the crunch of their footsteps and the occasional gust of wind.

Finally, they reached the small grove of trees. It wasn't much, but it offered some protection from the biting wind. They huddled together, sharing body warmth and planning their next move.

Braham looked around at his team, his heart swelling with pride at their resilience. "We made it this far. We'll figure out our next steps from here. For now, let's rest and regroup."

As they settled in for a brief respite, the reality of their situation began to sink in. They were far from the dangers of the facility, but the journey ahead was still fraught with challenges. Yet, in the vast, silent tundra, they found a moment of peace, a brief pause in their relentless pursuit of the truth.

And with that, the team prepared for whatever lay ahead, united in their determination to uncover the secrets that had driven them into this frozen wilderness.

The frozen tundra, though a temporary haven, was still far too exposed for their liking. The cluster of trees provided some cover from the relentless wind but offered little protection if they were to be pursued. Mirna was the first to voice the concern.

"This is too open. If they find us, we won't stand a chance here," she said, her sharp eyes scanning the horizon again.

Braham nodded, agreeing silently. "We need to move. There was a faint track leading south, toward the outskirts of the dome. If we're lucky, it might lead to a road or even a village."

"A village?" Lukas asked, his voice filled with equal parts hope and scepticism.

"It's possible," Braham said. "We're close to the old mining routes. Some settlements still exist out here—barely, but enough to give us some shelter."

Eleanor brushed the snow from her sleeves, her cheeks flushed from the cold. "Whatever we do, we need to decide quickly. The temperature's dropping, and this grove won't keep us hidden for long."

"Alright," Braham said, his voice firm. "We'll follow the track. But we stay close together and keep moving. No stops unless absolutely necessary."

The team gathered their sparse belongings and set off. Jimmy, the youngest of the group, led the way with a quiet determination, his sharp eyes scanning the snow-covered ground for the faint track Braham had mentioned. The cold gnawed at their exposed skin, the wind biting harder as the sun dipped lower on the horizon.

At last, the trail emerged—a thin, barely discernible indentation in the snow, marked by scattered remnants of long-abandoned markers. It wound its way through the tundra, promising a chance at survival, albeit a slim one.

They moved cautiously but swiftly, their breaths clouding the frigid air. Each step brought them closer to the edge of exhaustion, but none of them dared to stop. The tundra, vast and silent, was both their ally and their adversary—a shield from pursuers, but an unrelenting test of their endurance.

Hours passed before they saw it: a faint glimmer of light in the distance. Lukas was the first to spot it, his voice breaking the silence. "There! Over that ridge!"

The team froze, squinting into the dimness. Sure enough, the glow of a small settlement flickered like a distant beacon of hope. Braham felt a surge of relief but tempered it with caution. "We need to approach carefully. It could be friendly—or it could be a trap."

Mirna tightened her grip on her makeshift weapon. "I'll scout ahead," she offered, her tone resolute.

"No," Braham said. "We stick together. If it's a trap, we'll deal with it as a team. But if it's not... it might be exactly what we need."

With renewed determination, the group pressed on toward the light, their hopes pinned on the promise of warmth, shelter, and safety. The village loomed closer with each step, its shape taking form against the desolate tundra—a cluster of modest buildings huddled together against the cold, their chimneys puffing thin trails of smoke into the twilight sky.

Whatever lay ahead, Braham knew one thing: they couldn't turn back. The secrets they carried—and the dangers they fled—left no room for retreat.

As they approached the edge of the settlement, the team paused, huddling close to decide their next move. "If this is a friendly place," Eleanor whispered, "we'll need to blend in. Act normal."

Braham nodded. "Let's hope for the best," he said, though his grip on his knife betrayed his unease.

With cautious steps, they crossed the final stretch of tundra, entering the village and stepping into the unknown.

The village, modest and isolated, consisted of no more than ten houses. The structures were simple and weathered, their wooden walls bearing the scars of countless winters. Smoke curled lazily from a few chimneys, and the faint glow of lanterns lit the interiors. It was a quiet place, nestled against the unforgiving tundra, but it also felt watchful, as though the villagers were accustomed to trouble finding its way to their doorstep.

Braham, knowing the urgency of their situation, stepped forward, his breath frosting in the air. His team huddled behind him; their exhaustion evident but their determination unwavering. Spotting an old woman shuffling across the narrow path with a shawl wrapped tightly around her shoulders, he approached cautiously.

In fluent Russian, he called out, his tone low and urgent. "Excuse me, babushka. We need help. We're being pursued by dangerous men. Is there a place we can hide?"

The woman stopped, turning to study him with sharp, wary eyes. Her face, lined with years of hardship, softened slightly as she took in their haggard appearances. She shifted her shawl and nodded. "Follow me. But be quiet. They mustn't see you."

With a surprising swiftness for her age, the old woman led them through the narrow streets of the village, keeping to the shadows. Her movements were deliberate, her eyes darting to the corners where she might spot potential threats.

As they neared the outskirts of the village, she stopped in front of a dark, unassuming block of concrete. It was a squat, windowless structure, its walls thick and unyielding. The air around it was colder, as if the building itself had absorbed the tundra's chill.

"This place was built during the war," she whispered, her voice barely audible. "It was used to hide those in danger—refugees, deserters, anyone who needed a safe place. It hasn't been used in years, but the walls are solid, and no one will look for you here."

Mirna scanned the block sceptically but nodded in approval. "Looks secure enough."

The woman led them inside through a heavy wooden door reinforced with iron. The interior was as cold and uninviting as the tundra itself, but it was dry, and most importantly, it was hidden. A faint smell of damp earth lingered in the air. The space was sparse—bare walls, a couple of old benches, and a small, rusted stove in the corner.

"You'll be safe here, at least for now," the old woman said, turning to face Braham. "But if these men you're hiding from come here, I can't promise the villagers won't tell them something. People are afraid, you understand?"

Braham nodded; gratitude evident in his expression. "Thank you. You've already done more than enough."

The woman gave a curt nod and handed Braham a small lantern from her satchel. "There's some firewood in the corner. Keep warm, but don't let the smoke be seen from outside."

As the door creaked shut behind her, the team collectively exhaled. Eleanor slumped onto one of the benches, cradling her head in her hands. Lukas and Jimmy began stacking the firewood, their movements methodical.

"We're safe—for now," Mirna said, though her tone carried a note of caution. "But how long can we stay here before they catch up to us?"

Braham didn't answer immediately. Instead, he lit the lantern, the faint glow casting long shadows on the walls. "We'll stay long enough to rest and come up with a plan," he said finally. "But she's right—we can't rely on the villagers to protect us. We'll have to move again soon."

The fire crackled softly in the stove, its warmth a welcome reprieve from the freezing cold. For a brief moment, the team allowed themselves to relax, their breaths slowing as they regrouped in the silence of the block.

But even as they rested, the weight of their mission pressed on them. The tundra might have provided temporary refuge, but the secrets they carried—and the people hunting them—were never far behind.

## Chapter 13: A new beginning

The group remained holed up in the silence of the hidden blockhouse, their breaths shallow and hearts pounding as they huddled together in the dim glow of the lantern. Outside, the tundra stretched vast and quiet, but they all knew danger was closing in.

Seriakov, the ruthless leader of the defense group, had deployed his men to comb the entire perimeter surrounding the scientific centre. They worked methodically, sweeping outward in concentric circles. Armed and alert, the soldiers moved with precision, scanning every crevice, ridge, and drift of snow for signs of the fugitives.

Mirna crouched by the door, listening intently for any sound beyond the thick walls. Her hand rested on the hilt of her knife, her fingers twitching with nervous energy. "They're looking for us," she whispered, her voice barely audible.

Braham nodded grimly. "Seriakov won't stop until he's certain we're dead—or captured. We have to be smarter than him."

Eleanor leaned against the wall; her eyes heavy with exhaustion but her mind still sharp. "We can't just sit here forever. If they expand their search to the village..." She trailed off, the unspoken implication clear to everyone.

Jimmy, huddled near the stove, tightened his coat around himself. "Do you think that old woman would give us up?"

"No," Braham said firmly. "She took a risk to help us. But fear is a powerful thing. If they press the villagers hard enough, someone might slip."

Outside, the muffled sound of a distant vehicle engine drifted on the icy wind. Seriakov's men were deploying drones—small, silent machines equipped with thermal imaging. They hovered low over the snow, their sensors scanning for any signs of heat amidst the tundra's frozen expanse.

"Thermal scans," Lukas muttered, his voice low. He had spotted the drones during their escape from the scientific centre. "If they get close enough, they'll detect us through the walls."

Braham's jaw tightened. He rose from his seat, pacing the small space as he calculated their next move. "We can't wait for them to find us," he said. "We need a distraction—something to draw them away from the village and give us time to escape."

Mirna glanced at him sharply. "You're not thinking of going out there, are you?"

"If we stay here, it's only a matter of time before they find us," Braham replied. "We'll use their own technology against them."

Eleanor frowned. "What are you proposing?"

Braham pulled a small device from his coat pocket—an old transmitter they had scavenged during their escape. It was primitive but functional. "We'll rig this to send out a false heat signal. If we set it far enough from here, the drones will pick it up and lead the search party in the wrong direction."

Jimmy perked up. "I can rig it to simulate a group of people—like we're camped out somewhere nearby. It'll buy us time."

"It's risky," Mirna said, her voice tense. "If they figure out it's a decoy, we'll have even less time to get away."

"We don't have a choice," Braham said. "It's this or we wait for Seriakov to kick down the door."

The group exchanged glances; their fear tempered by determination. Finally, they nodded in agreement.

"Alright," Mirna said. "Let's do it. But we need to be fast."

While Jimmy worked on the transmitter, Braham and Lukas scouted a location to plant the decoy—far enough from the village to draw attention away, but close enough that they could return before Seriakov's men zeroed in.

The snow outside was beginning to fall heavier, a blessing that would obscure their tracks but also hinder their visibility. As the team prepared to execute their plan, the cold weight of the tundra pressed in on them. The fight for survival was far from over, but for now, they had a plan—and in the frozen silence of the blockhouse, that was enough to keep hope alive.

The night was falling fast, the dim light of the overcast sky giving way to the encroaching darkness. The cold grew sharper with each passing minute, its icy fingers creeping through their worn clothing. The group huddled together near the small stove, their breath visible in the frigid air, their bodies trembling from the effort of their escape.

They had walked at least 3.5 kilometres through the woods and snow, their progress slow and gruelling. Hunger gnawed at their stomachs, and the adrenaline that had fuelled their initial flight was fading, replaced by an overwhelming exhaustion.

Braham glanced at the team, their faces pale and drawn. He knew they couldn't afford to linger in their current state—not with Seriakov's men scouring the perimeter and the risk of being discovered increasing by the hour.

"Alright," Braham said, breaking the silence. "We need to decide how to move forward. Staying here much longer isn't an option."

Eleanor raised her head, her voice soft but resolute. "We're too exposed here. Even with the decoy, it's only a matter of time before they expand their search to this area."

Mirna nodded in agreement. "We need to get out of the village entirely. But we can't go far without food or proper shelter. The cold will kill us before Seriakov's men do."

Jimmy, who had been fiddling with the transmitter to perfect the decoy signal, looked up. "I've rigged it to ping a heat signature about a kilometre southeast of here. If they pick it up, it'll pull them in the opposite direction."

"That's good," Lukas said, his voice hoarse. "But where do we go? Do we risk trying to find another village? Or do we head deeper into the tundra?"

The question hung in the air, heavy with uncertainty.

"We'll need supplies if we're going to make it anywhere," Braham said. "I don't like it, but we may need to risk asking for help again. There's no chance of surviving the tundra without proper gear—and food."

Eleanor frowned. "The villagers may not want to help us further. If Seriakov's men come back and find out they aided us, they'll pay the price."

"I know," Braham said, running a hand through his hair. "But if we explain its life or death, someone might give us something. We can't force anyone to help, but we need to try."

Mirna's sharp gaze swept across the team. "If we split up, it might improve our chances. One group can stay hidden here while the other scouts for supplies or an escape route."

"Splitting up is risky," Eleanor countered. "If one group gets caught, that's it for them. And we're weaker without everyone together."

The group fell silent, weighing their options. Outside, the wind howled faintly, a chilling reminder of the harsh environment that surrounded them.

Finally, Braham spoke, his tone decisive. "We'll stay together. Jimmy, deploy the decoy signal now. It'll buy us some time. Lukas and I will approach the far side of the village to see if we can find anything—

supplies, a sled, anything to help us. The rest of you stay here and watch
the horizon. If we're not back in an hour, assume the worst and prepare
to move."

The group nodded, the grim determination in their eyes a testament to
their shared resolve. Jimmy activated the transmitter, setting it to emit its
false signal.

As Braham and Lukas prepared to leave, Eleanor grabbed Braham's
arm, her voice steady despite the fear in her eyes. "Be careful out there."
"We will," Braham promised. "Stay ready."

The two men slipped out into the biting cold, their figures quickly
swallowed by the dark and swirling snow. Inside the blockhouse, the
remaining team huddled closer, their breaths a steady rhythm in the
silence, waiting anxiously for their return—and for whatever came next.

The group knew survival depended on quick thinking and
resourcefulness. After their initial deliberation, hunger and necessity
drove them to action. With the last light of dusk fading into night,
Braham and Lukas ventured into the woods, their senses sharpened by
desperation.

Armed with makeshift tools and their instincts, they stalked quietly
through the snow-covered terrain. The night was deathly still, save for
the occasional rustle of the wind through the branches. It wasn't long
before they spotted movement: a wild boar rooting around for food near
a fallen log and, not far away, the unmistakable fluttering of a pheasant
taking flight.

Lukas crouched low, signalling to Braham. They coordinated their
approach with practiced efficiency. Braham took aim at the boar with a
sharpened spear, while Lukas prepared to intercept the pheasant. With a
quick, decisive throw, Braham struck true, felling the boar. Meanwhile,
Lukas managed to catch the pheasant as it panicked and tried to escape,
trapping it under a net they had fashioned earlier.

The duo worked quickly to secure their catch, knowing every moment
spent in the open increased their risk of discovery. They fashioned a
makeshift sled out of fallen branches to drag the boar back to the shelter.
As they returned, trudging through the snow, they kept their eyes
scanning the horizon for any signs of pursuit. Then they saw it—a faint
blue light hovering in the distance, no more than 150 meters away.

"It's a drone," Lukas whispered, his voice barely audible.

Braham's eyes narrowed as he watched the device zip across the
landscape with alarming speed, its sensors likely searching for heat

signatures or movement. "Seriakov's men are close," Braham said, his tone grim. "We need to move, now."

The two men crouched low, abandoning the trail and slipping into the cover of the bushes. They remained perfectly still, their breath forming small clouds in the freezing air. The drone lingered, its light sweeping the area, before zipping off in another direction.

After a tense moment, Braham whispered, "Let's go. Slowly."

The pair crept back to the shelter, taking a circuitous route to ensure they weren't followed. By the time they arrived, the rest of the team was already on edge, waiting anxiously by the stove.

"We saw one of Seriakov's drones," Lukas reported as they entered. "It's searching the area, but we managed to stay out of sight."

Mirna's expression hardened. "It's only a matter of time before they expand their range. We need to stay sharp."

But the immediate concern was sustenance. Working quickly, they dressed the boar and pheasant, cooking portions over the stove while preserving the rest as best they could in the freezing conditions. The aroma of the roasting meat filled the small space, lifting their spirits and temporarily easing their worries.

As they dined on the hard-won meal, the group felt a renewed sense of strength. The warmth of the food and the camaraderie of shared survival gave them a momentary reprieve from the relentless tension of their escape.

Braham, chewing thoughtfully, broke the silence. "We've bought ourselves a little time, but the drones are a problem. Tomorrow, we need to figure out a way to either evade or disable them. Otherwise, it won't matter how far we run—they'll find us eventually."

The others nodded, the weight of the situation settling over them once more. The precious food provided them with much-needed energy, but the knowledge of Seriakov's relentless pursuit loomed large.

For now, the shelter remained their haven. But the frozen wilderness outside was a constant reminder: safety was temporary, and the fight for survival was far from over.

The aroma of the roasting meat filled the small shelter, a rare luxury in the harsh tundra. The pheasant, carefully cleaned and skewered, turned slowly over the makeshift spit, its juices sizzling as they dripped into the fire. Nearby, the boar's legs, thick and marbled with fat, crackled over the grill, sending wafts of rich, smoky scents into the cold night air.

For the first time in days, the group had a meal that promised not only to satiate their hunger but to restore their strength. They ate in silence, savouring each bite, the warmth of the food banishing some of the chill that had settled deep into their bones.

Eleanor leaned back against the wall, her face relaxing for the first time in hours. "This feels like a feast," she murmured, her voice tinged with both gratitude and exhaustion.

"Enjoy it while we can," Braham said, though his tone wasn't unkind. "We'll need every ounce of energy for what's ahead."

The proteins from the hearty meal worked their magic, revitalizing the group. Tired muscles felt less strained, and their minds cleared from the fog of hunger. As the fire burned low and the last scraps were finished, Braham called them together.

"The village is still our best bet," he said, his voice steady but low, mindful of the need for silence. "We can't stay here much longer, not with drones sweeping the area and Seriakov's men combing the tundra. But heading back to the village won't be easy. We'll need to move under cover of darkness."

Mirna nodded. "The earlier we leave, the better. If we can get ahead of the drones' sweep, we might avoid detection."

"We leave at three," Braham announced, glancing at his watch. "That gives us a few hours to rest and plan. When we move, we stick to the woods as much as possible. The village isn't far, but we can't afford mistakes."

Jimmy looked uneasy. "What happens if we're seen? The villagers won't want a confrontation with Seriakov's men. They might turn us in."

"That's a risk we'll have to take," Braham admitted. "But the village is our only chance for supplies—and possibly information. If we can find someone willing to help us, it might give us the edge we need to stay ahead of them."

The group exchanged weary glances; their determination tempered by the reality of the dangers they faced.

"Alright," Eleanor said finally. "We'll follow your lead, Braham. But we need to be ready for anything."

With their plan set, the group settled in for a brief rest. The shelter was silent except for the soft crackling of the fire and the faint whistle of the wind outside. Each of them knew the risks awaiting them at dawn, but for now, they drew strength from their shared purpose.

As the hours ticked by and the temperature outside dropped further, they prepared themselves for the next leg of their perilous journey. The wilderness had tested their resolve, but it was the uncertainty of human nature—and the looming threat of Seriakov's forces—that would define their fate in the days to come.

Three o'clock arrived like a sharp jolt, cutting through the fragile peace of their brief rest. The small shelter, once a haven from the harsh tundra, now felt oppressive—a trap waiting to be sprung. The time to act had come, and the group stirred reluctantly, their muscles stiff and their minds heavy with fatigue.

Outside, the night was an unforgiving void. The cold was more than a chill; it was a biting, relentless force that seemed to seep into their very bones. The wind howled across the tundra, carrying with it the sharp sting of ice crystals, each gust a reminder of the dangers waiting beyond the fragile walls of their refuge.

Braham stood by the door; his breath visible in the dim light of the lantern. He pulled his coat tighter, glancing back at the others as they prepared to leave. "It's now or never," he said, his voice low but resolute.

Eleanor shivered as she pulled on her gloves, her movements slow and deliberate. "The darkness is both our ally and our enemy," she murmured. "It'll hide us, but it'll also make it harder to see what's ahead."

"The cold doesn't care who it kills," Mirna added grimly, wrapping a scarf tightly around her face. "We'll have to move fast or freeze before we even reach the village."

The group gathered their meagre belongings, their movements efficient despite the oppressive cold. The shelter had served its purpose, but lingering any longer would only bring the enemy closer. Seriakov's forces, relentless and merciless, would have no hesitation in exacting their revenge if they were found.

Jimmy extinguished the lantern, plunging the room into complete darkness. "Let's hope the wind masks our tracks," he said, his voice barely audibles over the howling outside.

Braham pushed the door open, and the icy wind immediately surged inside, biting at their exposed skin. The group stepped out into the night, the tundra an endless expanse of black and white under the faint glow of the moon.

The journey was treacherous. The snow was deep in places, dragging at their legs and slowing their progress. The wind made it hard to hear, even harder to communicate, and the cold numbed their fingers despite their best efforts to stay warm.

Braham led the way, his eyes scanning the horizon for any sign of movement. He knew Seriakov's drones could be hovering nearby, their blue lights invisible until it was too late. The group moved in silence, their breaths shallow to conserve energy, their focus split between staying hidden and simply enduring the brutal conditions.

As they trudged forward, the weight of their situation pressed down on them. The enemy was close—too close for comfort. They had seen Seriakov's brutality firsthand, and they knew he wouldn't hesitate to punish anyone who got in his way.

The village was their only hope, but it felt impossibly far, each step a battle against the elements and their own exhaustion. Yet, as bleak as the night seemed, their resolve remained unbroken. They had come too far to give up now.

The tundra stretched on, endless and unforgiving, but the faint outline of the village on the horizon gave them a glimmer of hope. They pressed on, united by their determination to survive, even as the cold and darkness threatened to consume them.

The GPS flickered faintly in Braham's hand, its small screen a guiding light in the oppressive darkness. The group trudged forward, driven by sheer determination despite the bitter cold and exhaustion. The nearest street was still seven kilometres away—a daunting distance through snowdrifts and unrelenting wind.

Each step was an effort, the snow pulling at their feet and the icy air biting at any exposed skin. Their breaths came out in sharp, shallow bursts, forming clouds that quickly disappeared into the night.

"Two hours," Braham muttered, glancing at the GPS. "If we keep this pace, we'll make it."

Eleanor, walking close behind him, nodded silently. There was no energy for words, only the shared understanding that stopping meant death—whether from the cold or Seriakov's forces closing in behind them.

The darkness seemed endless, broken only by the occasional faint glimmer of moonlight reflecting off the icy terrain. The wind howled through the trees, carrying with it a desolate chill that seeped into their very bones.

Finally, after what felt like an eternity, they reached their goal: a frozen, ice-covered street stretching into the void. It was eerily silent, devoid of life or movement. The ice had shattered the asphalt in places, leaving jagged patches of black rock surrounded by glistening sheets of frozen water.

"No traffic," Lukas said, his voice hoarse and strained. "Not even tracks. It's completely abandoned."

"Probably for the best," Mirna replied, her breath visible in the air. "If there were cars, they might belong to Seriakov's men."

Jimmy crouched down, brushing some of the ice with his gloved hand. "This road hasn't been used in weeks, maybe months. It's frozen solid."

"At least it gives us a clear path," Braham said, scanning the horizon. "If we follow it, it should lead us closer to the next village."

Eleanor frowned, glancing down at the cracked and frozen surface. "Walking on this won't be easy. One slip, and someone could break a leg—or worse."

"We'll move slowly," Braham said, his tone firm. "Stick close together and use whatever we can to steady ourselves. We can't afford another delay."

The group nodded; their faces grim but resolute. They tightened their scarves, adjusted their packs, and prepared to move again. The street stretched out before them like a ribbon of ice, its surface gleaming faintly in the moonlight.

With every step, the crunch of snow underfoot was replaced by the unnerving scrape of boots on frozen asphalt. The ice was treacherous, forcing them to walk carefully to avoid slipping. The cold gnawed at them relentlessly, but the thought of stopping was unthinkable.

As they moved, the street seemed to stretch endlessly into the horizon, a stark reminder of the isolation and danger they faced. Yet, despite the challenges, the group pressed on, their collective will stronger than the harsh tundra around them.

The silence was broken only by the sound of the wind and the occasional muffled curse as someone stumbled. But together, they forged ahead, knowing that every step brought them closer to survival— and farther from the deadly grip of their pursuers.

Ten minutes after stepping onto the frozen road, the group's fortunes shifted unexpectedly. In the distance, they heard the faint rumble of an engine—a sound that seemed almost out of place in the desolate landscape. The noise grew louder, cutting through the icy silence like a beacon of hope.

It was an old pickup truck, its headlights piercing the darkness as it approached. The vehicle was laden with a towering pile of firewood in the back, swaying precariously with every bump in the road.

"Do you see that?" Eleanor gasped; her voice tinged with disbelief.

Braham squinted into the night, his breath catching. "It's a truck. Coming this way."

Without hesitation, the group sprang into action. Desperation overrode caution as they stepped onto the middle of the road, waving their arms wildly and shouting as though they were children excited for the first day of school.

"Stop! Stop!" Lukas yelled, his voice echoing in the cold air.

The truck slowed as it neared, the driver clearly startled by the sight of the ragged group blocking the icy street. The vehicle came to a careful halt a few meters away, the engine idling loudly.

The door creaked open, and a stocky, middle-aged man in a heavy fur-lined coat stepped out. His face, weathered from years of exposure to the harsh tundra, was framed by a thick, graying beard. He held a lantern in one hand and peered at the group with suspicion.

"Who in the hell are you all, and what are you doing out here?" the man asked, his voice rough but not unkind.

Before anyone else could answer, Aleksander stepped forward, his face lighting up in recognition. "Malin!" he exclaimed, his voice cracking with relief.

The man's stern expression softened instantly. "Aleksander? Is that really you?"

"It's me," Aleksander replied, stepping closer. "It's been years, old friend."

Malin laughed, shaking his head in disbelief. "You look like hell! What are you doing out here in this cold? And who are these people with you?"

"It's a long story," Aleksander said, his tone sobering. "But we need help, Malin. Seriakov's men are after us. We're in real danger."

Malin's expression hardened at the mention of Seriakov. "That bastard," he muttered. He glanced at the group, his eyes narrowing as he assessed their condition. "You all look half-dead. Get in the truck. We'll talk on the way."

Without hesitation, the group piled into the back of the pickup, squeezing in among the stacks of firewood. The warmth of the engine and the shelter from the wind felt like a small miracle after the hours spent in the freezing cold.

Malin climbed back into the driver's seat, calling out over his shoulder, "There's a village about ten kilometres from here. I'll take you to my place—it's quiet, and no one will bother us there."

The truck lurched forward, its wheels crunching over the icy road. In the back, the group huddled together, their spirits lifted by this unexpected stroke of luck. For the first time in days, hope felt tangible, like the warmth of the engine beneath them and the promise of refuge just ahead. As they rode through the night, Aleksander leaned close to Malin, his voice low. "Thank you for this. I don't know what we would've done without you."

Malin gave a small nod, his gaze fixed on the road ahead. "You can tell me everything when we get there," he said. "But if Seriakov's involved, you'll need more than luck to get through this. You'll need a plan."

The truck rumbled on, carrying them closer to safety—but also toward the next chapter of their perilous journey.

In just ten minutes, the group arrived at Sibovka, a tiny, snow-covered village nestled amidst the frozen wilderness. The houses were simple, their wooden frames leaning slightly from years of enduring the tundra's brutal conditions. Smoke curled lazily from chimneys, promising warmth and respite from the unrelenting cold.

Malin pulled the pickup into the courtyard of a modest home on the village's outskirts. "This is my place," he said, stepping out and motioning for the group to follow. "You'll be safe here—for now."

Inside, the air was thick with the comforting aroma of woodsmoke and something cooking. Malin's wife, a petite woman with sharp eyes and a warm smile, greeted them at the door. She didn't ask questions, only ushered them inside and pointed to the large table in the centre of the room.

"Sit," she said briskly, ladling steaming soup into bowls. "You all look like you've been through hell."

The group didn't need to be told twice. They crowded around the table, clutching the bowls in their hands as the heat seeped into their frozen fingers. The soup—a hearty mix of potatoes, vegetables, and chunks of meat—felt like a balm to their frayed nerves.

As they ate, Malin leaned against the doorframe, his arms crossed. "There's been talk," he said, his voice low and serious. "Word's been spreading about an attack on the CSM FarmCure Centre. You know, that big scientific facility out in the tundra. Most people here don't even know what goes on there, but the rumours..."

He paused, his gaze flickering to Aleksander. "They're saying it was something serious. Military serious. What happened out there?"

Aleksander hesitated, glancing at Braham, who set his spoon down and wiped his mouth with the back of his hand. "The centre's not what it seems," Braham said carefully. "It's not just a research facility—it's a front for something... darker. Dangerous experiments, unethical practices. We had to get out. But now Seriakov's men are hunting us."

Malin swore under his breath. "I knew that place was trouble," he muttered. "People disappear around here sometimes. No one asks questions, but... it's always felt wrong."

"We didn't just leave," Mirna added quietly. "We took something. Evidence. Enough to expose what they're doing."

Malin straightened, his expression sharpening. "Then you've got more than just Seriakov after you. If the centre's as secret as you say, there'll be people—powerful people—who'll want to silence you. Permanently."

"We know," Braham said grimly. "That's why we need to keep moving. The village is a refuge for now, but we can't stay long. If Seriakov finds out we're here..."

Malin nodded, his mind already working. "I can help you. There's a supply route that runs through the forest—an old smuggling trail. It's not on any official maps, and it'll take you out of the tundra. From there, you might stand a chance of getting somewhere safer."

"How soon can we leave?" Lukas asked, his voice urgent.

"Tomorrow night," Malin replied. "The trail's easier to follow under moonlight, and the snowstorm that's coming will help cover your tracks."

The group exchanged weary glances. Another night in hiding was a risk, but Malin's plan offered their best chance of escape.

"Alright," Braham said finally. "We'll rest here tonight and prepare to move tomorrow. Thank you, Malin. We owe you more than we can say."

Malin waved him off. "You don't owe me anything. Just promise me one thing—whatever you've got on that place, make sure the world sees it. People deserve to know."

The group nodded, their determination solidifying. The path ahead was uncertain, but for the first time since their escape, they had a plan—and a glimmer of hope.

Meanwhile, in Brekvenny, Seriakov's grip on the region tightened. The small town had become a tense and anxious place, overshadowed by the presence of his military squad. Thirty of his best men, hardened by years of brutal tactics and loyal to his every command, had been dispatched to control the situation around the CSM FarmCure Centre. These weren't just ordinary soldiers—this was a specialized unit, handpicked and trained by a shadowy group linked to Wagner, known for their ruthless efficiency. They were deployed to ensure that nothing and no one would threaten the secrecy of the centre.

Seriakov stood in the operations room, surrounded by maps and surveillance screens, his eyes scanning the feeds that were constantly updated. His face was a mask of cold calculation as he watched the movements of his forces. There was no mercy in his mind; the escapees had become a nuisance, and they would not be allowed to slip away. Every corner of Brekvenny, every hidden route, was now under scrutiny.

"Continue tightening the perimeter," Seriakov commanded, his voice low but commanding. "Every road, every exit—leave no stone unturned. They won't get away."

His men, well-versed in the art of pursuit, were already out in full force. The quiet streets of Brekvenny were now patrolled by armed soldiers, their boots crunching through the snow as they searched for any sign of the fugitives. Drones hovered above, scanning the area, their small blue lights flickering through the gloom.

The villagers, despite their knowledge of the increasing military presence, did their best to stay out of the way. Fear rippled through the community like an undercurrent, each resident aware of the danger that came with speaking out or getting involved. Whispers filled the cold air—rumours of an attack on the FarmCure Centre, of strange experiments and the disappearance of people who dared ask questions. Some of the more cautious villagers had even begun to speak in hushed tones about leaving for safer parts, but most of them remained paralyzed by fear. The presence of Seriakov's men was a constant reminder of the power and reach of those who controlled the centre.

Still, despite the quiet murmurs of fear, the villagers kept their distance. They avoided crossing paths with the military personnel, turning their faces away or ducking inside their homes when they saw the soldiers approaching. Sibovka, the small village where Malin had taken the group, was close enough to Brekvenny for anyone to notice strange movements, but far enough away to offer some semblance of safety— for now.

In the midst of this tension, Seriakov's focus remained on the task at hand: finding the fugitives. His military squad worked relentlessly, sweeping through the region, tightening their noose around the villages and the surrounding wilderness. If anyone was even remotely connected to the escapees, they would be interrogated, silenced, or worse.

Back in Sibovka, Malin's small home was becoming more of a sanctuary than the group had hoped for. But the danger was real and growing with each passing moment. The more Seriakov and his forces searched, the tighter the walls of safety seemed to become. The group knew that their window of opportunity was shrinking, and that soon, the warmth and safety of Malin's home would be just another memory. The hunt was on, and their escape was far from certain.

The day in Sibovka was a brief respite from the chaos that had consumed their lives over the past weeks. Inside Malin's small, warm house, the group was able to rest and recover, even if only for a short while. The heat from the stove, the nourishment of the soup, and the safety of the village provided a temporary escape from the harshness of the tundra and the terror that had chased them for so long.

Jimmy, Mirna, and Aleksander, in particular, used the day to recover from the physical toll the CSM FarmCure Centre had inflicted on them. The brutal treatment they had endured—beatings, forced labour, the psychological torment of constant surveillance—had left deep marks, both visible and invisible.

Jimmy, sitting on a worn wooden chair by the fire, gingerly examined his bruised ribs, wincing with every movement. The cold air had exacerbated the pain, but now, with a small fire crackling in the hearth, it was bearable. He had been tortured, beaten down physically and mentally, and though the pain of his body might fade, the scars would remain.

Mirna, still pale from the ordeal, quietly pressed a cloth to a swollen eye. The beating she'd received had been brutal. It had been only days since she'd been struck, but the pain was still fresh. She had been one of the most vocal among them, and in the centre, that had made her a target. Now, sitting in the warmth of Malin's home, her body ached, but the silence gave her the space she needed to heal, even if just a little.

Aleksander, despite his usual stoic demeanour, sat with his back against the wall, his face tired and drawn. His hands were trembling slightly as he gingerly massaged his shoulder, where the guards had twisted his arm during the interrogation. His mind was far from the warmth and safety of the room; it was still back at the centre, replaying the days of imprisonment, the threats, the constant fear. He hadn't spoken much all day, lost in the weight of his memories.

But the rest of the group understood. They too had suffered at the hands of the guards, and though their wounds weren't as deep, they carried their own burdens of guilt, fear, and loss. Braham, ever the leader, kept a watchful eye on them, making sure that no one was alone for too long, ensuring they had what they needed. The group had been through hell, but their bond was only growing stronger, forged through shared suffering.

As night fell, the group gathered around the fire, their quiet conversations breaking the silence. Malin's wife, ever practical, had set out more food for them, but the focus was less on eating and more on the planning ahead. They couldn't afford to relax for too long. Seriakov's forces were still closing in, and they knew the window of safety wouldn't last forever.

"We can't stay here long," Braham said, breaking the quiet. His voice was steady, but the exhaustion weighed on him. "Tomorrow, we start moving again, to the smuggling route Malin mentioned. But we need to be careful."

Mirna, her voice rough, spoke up. "We need to keep our wits about us. I know the trail isn't easy, but it's better than staying here and getting caught. We've got the evidence. Now we need to make sure it gets out."

Jimmy nodded, though his face was drawn. "I'm not going to let them catch us. I've already been through too much."

The group exchanged looks of determination, knowing that tomorrow would bring more danger, but also the potential for escape. For now, though, they needed the rest. The sleep would be restless, haunted by memories of the centre, but it would be necessary for the journey ahead.

As the fire flickered and the night deepened, they leaned into the warmth of the room, trying to let go of the horrors of the past while holding tightly to the hope of survival. Tomorrow, they would rise and keep moving forward, knowing that the road ahead was treacherous, but they were no longer alone.

At noon, the group quietly departed from Sibovka, slipping into the snow-covered forest with the careful, deliberate steps of those who knew the stakes of their escape. The small village was already behind them, swallowed by the vast whiteness of the tundra. They moved quickly, avoiding any unnecessary noise, aware that their time was running out.

Aleksander led them through the forest, his pace steady, despite the physical toll the journey had already taken on him. He had built the refuge years ago, a place he once used to hide those who were fleeing from the oppressive forces of the region. It had been his own safe house, a forgotten spot nestled deep in the woods, where the military's reach could not easily touch. It was isolated, hidden well enough to provide a short respite from the relentless pursuit of those who sought to control the area.

"We should be close," Aleksander muttered, his breath clouding in the frigid air. The trees, thick with snow, created a natural barrier, cloaking the land in a silence that felt both serene and unsettling. The group trailed behind him, their eyes darting about nervously, alert to any sudden sounds or movements.

As they approached the refuge, the familiar sight of a weathered cabin tucked between two large pines came into view. It was humble, with its wooden walls covered in layers of frost, but it was sturdy and had served its purpose for years. Aleksander opened the creaky door with a quiet turn of the knob, and the group quickly filed in. Inside, the small space was dark, but the air was warmer than outside, and a sense of relief washed over them.

The refuge, though modest, had everything they needed for the next ten days: a small stockpile of dried food, a wood stove for warmth, and a couple of cots. There was no electricity, no distractions, just the isolation of the forest and the fragile comfort of knowing that, for a brief moment, they were hidden.

Malin had provided them with enough provisions to last, but the group knew they couldn't grow complacent. The ten days would be critical. They would need to rest, regain their strength, and most importantly, keep low profiles, avoiding detection at all costs. The ultimate goal was to make it to Novosibirsk's airport, where they could find a way out of the country and to safety.

But for now, the forest refuge would have to be their sanctuary.

As the group settled in, Braham wasted no time setting up a guard schedule. "We can't let our guard down. The next few days are our chance to heal and strategize. The forest offers cover, but Seriakov's men will be combing the area soon enough. We'll rest, but we need to stay alert."

Mirna, still nursing her wounds, nodded in agreement. "I'll take the first shift. We need to know if anyone's coming."

The rest of the group divided the tasks—some gathered firewood, others took stock of the food supplies, and a few huddled near the stove, their hands warmed by the crackling fire. Despite their exhaustion, the sense of urgency hung in the air. The days ahead were uncertain, and they knew that every moment of rest they could steal in the refuge was one step closer to their goal, but also one step further into the unknown.

Over the next few days, the group did their best to settle into the rhythm of life in hiding. They tried to keep a low profile, speaking in quiet voices and limiting their movements. The cold, stark beauty of the forest provided a sense of peace that felt almost surreal after the chaos of their escape. But it was also a reminder of how fragile their situation was—the isolation of the woods was both their safety and their prison.

They kept their plans simple. Ten days in the forest, recovering as best they could, and then, when the time was right, they would leave for Novosibirsk's airport. But that goal, as much as they wanted to reach it, still felt far away. For now, all they could do was wait, hidden in the stillness of the forest, and prepare for whatever came next.

The peaceful silence of the forest, which had enveloped the group for the past few days, was abruptly shattered by a deep, guttural roar that seemed to reverberate through the trees. The howl of the brown bear echoed in the distance, sending an immediate wave of tension through the group. It was a terrifying sound—low, powerful, and unmistakably close.

Braham's hand instinctively went to the shotgun that had been placed beside him, resting against the wall of the small hut. His heart raced, but his mind was calm. He had faced danger before, and his training kicked in. The bear, drawn by the smell of food or perhaps the warmth of the fire, was circling closer. The group's breath quickened as the sound of heavy paws crunching the snow grew nearer.

"Stay calm," Braham whispered, his voice steady but urgent. "We don't need to shoot. We just need to scare it off."

Mirna, her hand clutching the small knife she'd been keeping close, looked out the window, eyes wide with fear. "Is it coming closer?"

Braham didn't respond immediately, his eyes fixed on the dark outline of the trees outside. The bear's growls grew louder, the sound vibrating through the walls of the cabin. He knew that shooting would attract unwanted attention and could bring more danger than it was worth. The last thing they needed was to draw attention to their location.

"Everyone, get back!" Braham ordered; his voice sharp. He moved swiftly toward the door, his shotgun held firmly in his hands, but not aimed at the bear. Instead, he kept it low, preparing to fire into the air if needed.

The group quickly retreated to the far side of the cabin, staying out of sight, though the tension was palpable. The roar of the bear echoed again, closer now, and Braham opened the door just enough to catch a glimpse of the massive creature moving slowly through the snow. Its fur was dark, its eyes glinting in the dim light as it sniffed the air, clearly aware of their presence but unsure of what to make of the humans within.

Braham took a deep breath and aimed the shotgun skyward, firing a single blast into the air. The loud crack of the gunshot shattered the calm of the forest, and for a moment, everything went still. The bear, startled but not entirely frightened, paused. It sniffed the air again, seemingly weighing its options. Braham raised the barrel slightly, ready to fire another shot, if necessary, but he held back, knowing the danger of provoking the bear further.

The bear growled one last time, a low, throaty sound, before turning and lumbering back into the shadows of the trees, retreating from the cabin. The forest fell silent once more, save for the crackling of the fire and the steady breathing of the group.

Braham closed the door slowly, his heart still pounding from the close encounter. He didn't need to say anything; the looks on the faces of the others said it all. They were all shaken, their nerves frayed by the bear's proximity.

"That was too close," Jimmy muttered, his voice still edged with fear.

Mirna, trying to steady her breath, looked toward Braham. "How did you know not to shoot?"

"I've been in situations like this before," Braham said quietly, his voice calm now that the danger had passed. "Shooting would have only drawn attention. The bear was just curious. It was looking for food. As long as we don't provoke it further, it will leave."

"Lucky for us," Aleksander added with a shaky laugh. "But I think we're done with wildlife for the night, right?"

The group shared a tense, relieved chuckle. Despite the adrenaline still coursing through their veins, the moment of danger had passed. They huddled back together near the fire, the warmth now a comfort in the aftermath of the bear's visit.

"Let's keep the fire small tonight," Braham suggested, his voice still steady. "And no more unnecessary noise. We stay low until morning."

The group nodded in agreement, silently grateful for the calm that had returned. But in the back of their minds, they all knew that the forest was not only a refuge from the militia but also from the unpredictable dangers of the wild. Tonight, they had been lucky. Tomorrow, they would remain vigilant, for both man and beast could strike at any moment.

The days in the forest refuge passed slowly but steadily, marked by moments of relative peace and the ever-present tension of their situation. The small group had settled into a routine of sorts: Braham, ever vigilant, took the first watch; Mirna and Aleksander ventured out to track wildlife for food; Jimmy, in his own way, tried to lift the group's spirits, and Eleanor and Lukas helped with whatever tasks were needed. One day, as the sun dipped low, casting long shadows over the snow-covered ground, Jimmy found himself sitting in a tall pine tree, his legs dangling carelessly, a momentary escape from the confines of the cabin. His breath clouded in the chill air as he hummed, then began singing softly to himself, "We all live in a yellow submarine, a yellow submarine, a yellow submarine…" His voice, a little off-key but full of heart, floated out over the forest.

Mirna glanced up from where she was crouched near some disturbed snow, eyes scanning the ground for any sign of a wild boar. She smirked despite herself, shaking her head at Jimmy's attempt to bring a bit of cheer. "What are you doing up there, Jimmy?"

"Just keeping the spirits high," Jimmy called back, his voice carrying through the trees. "Might as well make the most of it. At least the wildlife won't mind my singing, right?"

Aleksander, who had been focused on the tracks nearby, rolled his eyes but couldn't help a chuckle. "I think we'll be fine as long as it's only boars and not bears. Keep singing, Jimmy. Maybe the bears will be too confused to bother us."

The light mood, though fleeting, was a welcome relief. For a brief moment, the tension that had gripped them since their escape from the CSM FarmCure Centre seemed to loosen. In the forest, there was a fragile sense of normalcy—even if just for a moment.

Braham, always focused on the bigger picture, glanced toward the horizon. The wind had picked up, and there was a chill in the air. But he wasn't just concerned with the cold. He could feel the weight of the group's thoughts, their hopes and fears, pressing in on him. Everyone, at some level, had begun to long for something more than just survival. They hoped for something beyond the frigid expanse of the tundra, beyond the endless chase, the never-ending threats.

As he stood near the small window of the cabin, watching the trees sway in the wind, Braham felt the weight of his own thoughts. He had been through countless battles, but this was different. The dangers were more insidious. It was no longer just about fighting to survive—it was about getting out, getting back to safety, back to a life that had been lost, and perhaps, for some, back to their homes.

"We'll make it," Eleanor said, breaking his thoughts. She had come to stand beside him, her voice quiet but resolute. "It might not be easy, but we'll make it. We've survived this long."

Lukas, sitting on a nearby cot and cleaning his rifle, nodded in agreement. "We'll find a way out. UK or not, as long as we get out of here, that's what matters."

Braham turned toward them, giving a small nod of acknowledgment. They had come this far together, and despite the ever-present fear and exhaustion, there was a glimmer of hope in their hearts. They could still find a way out. The thought of returning to the UK, where the world was familiar and the dangers were far less immediate, kept them going, one day at a time.

And so, the days continued to pass—quiet, tense, filled with the sound of Jimmy's occasional off-key singing and the low murmurs of plans being made in the shadows of the forest.

As the sun dipped lower each night, they kept hope alive, knowing that soon, they would have to leave the shelter and continue their journey—toward the airport, toward safety, and toward the possibility of a life they hadn't dared to believe in for so long.

The pressure was mounting for Seriakov and his elite military command. For days, his squadron had been scouring every potential hiding spot, from the familiar refuge of villages to the remote forests, but Braham and his group had left no trace. The cold landscape had swallowed their movements, and no sign of their whereabouts had been uncovered. Despite their best efforts, every lead seemed to fade into nothingness.

Frustration simmered within Seriakov as he reviewed reports. His men had checked every shelter, every abandoned building, every track in the snow—and yet, Braham's group had vanished. "They're good," Seriakov muttered to himself, his jaw clenched tight. "Too good." He glanced at the reports on his desk, showing the results of their relentless search. Nothing.

The situation was growing critical. The military presence in the region had been steadily ramping up, but the threat of losing control over the key areas was looming. It was not just about Braham and his group anymore; it was about control. The stakes had escalated. If the groups hiding in the villages managed to slip past their grasp, it could unravel everything.

Then, the final hope appeared: Novosibirsk Airport.

Seriakov's command received word that Braham and his team were most likely heading toward the airport, possibly to escape the region entirely. The idea of blocking them there seemed the only viable option left. The airport, while a busy travel hub, had a few vulnerabilities—especially now that the chaos of the past weeks had thrown the entire system into disarray. If they could intercept them before they reached their flight, it would be the end of their journey.

But Seriakov's command couldn't do it alone. As tensions mounted, he sought reinforcements from a new, highly trained Wagner unit—an elite group of soldiers with experience in dealing with high-value targets in hostile environments. These soldiers, known for their ruthlessness and efficiency, were brought in to ensure that the perimeter around Novosibirsk and the surrounding areas would be locked down tight. Their mission was clear: find and eliminate any threats to the regime, and ensure that Braham's group did not escape.

"Make sure the airport is secure," Seriakov ordered, his voice cold and commanding as he gathered his commanders. "No one gets in. No one gets out."

The Wagner unit took to the task with deadly precision. They set up roadblocks, checkpoints, and surveillance systems around the airport, tightening the noose. No one, whether local or foreign, would pass through without being scrutinized.

As the days wore on, the team's nerves were tested. For Braham and his group, the knowledge that they were being hunted by forces this relentless only made their journey more perilous. Every movement had to be calculated, every stop along the way carefully planned. The goal was clear: survive long enough to reach Novosibirsk, but now, more than ever, the danger was real.

For Braham, the reality of what lay ahead was never far from his mind. He knew they had to stay ahead of the military forces, and that meant finding new, unpredictable ways to move. Their goal—getting out of the country, to the safety of the airport—had become even more crucial. The airport now held the key to their survival. But Seriakov and his growing army were closing in, and every step they took toward their destination brought them one step closer to danger.

The clock was ticking.

After ten tense days in the forest refuge, the group realized that their time in hiding was running out. Seriakov's forces were closing in, and the military presence in the surrounding areas had intensified. Every day brought a greater risk of being discovered. The decision was made: the group would split up in order to maximize their chances of escape. Aleksander and Malin, who had known the terrain and local networks well, took responsibility for getting the Anglo-Saxon members— Braham, Eleanor, and Lukas—to Novosibirsk, where they could board a flight to Moscow. The city, though far from safe, was a more reliable route out of the region. Novosibirsk offered the anonymity and the infrastructure they needed to blend in long enough to make their escape. But the journey would be risky. The checkpoints around the city were tightening, and there was little time to waste.

"We'll take the southern road," Aleksander said, his voice low but firm, as he prepared to leave. "It's the least monitored route. But we need to be careful—everything depends on timing."

Malin, ever resourceful, nodded in agreement. "We'll meet you there, and we'll get you through. But you need to move fast, and you need to stay in the shadows."

Braham looked to his group with a mixture of gratitude and determination. "Thanks, Aleksander. Malin. We won't forget this."

With the plan set, Aleksander and Malin led the Anglo-Saxons down a narrow, concealed path that would take them toward Novosibirsk. The first part of the journey would be the most dangerous—crossing into areas where Seriakov's forces were active, but Aleksander's knowledge of the land gave them an advantage. They had to move quickly, though, knowing that every hour spent in the open was an hour closer to being spotted.

Meanwhile, Mirna and the others—Jimmy, Mirna, and the rest of Braham's close-knit team—took a different route. They relocated to a large village situated on the outskirts of the area now under Seriakov's control. The village, though still vulnerable, was remote enough to avoid immediate attention. It was the perfect place for the team to lie low for a while and regroup.

The settlement was quiet, a mix of old wooden homes and overgrown fields, far removed from the prying eyes of the military. The villagers were wary of outsiders but had a sense of solidarity born from years of living in the shadows of the ever-present conflict. Mirna, who had spent years navigating such territories, negotiated with the locals, convincing them of their need for shelter.

"This place should be safe enough for now," Mirna told Braham as they settled in one of the larger homes, a former farmstead that had been abandoned for years. "We'll rest here and make sure we stay off the radar."

Jimmy, ever the optimist, cracked a joke as he began unpacking supplies. "You know, it's not so bad here. No bears, no military, and definitely no cold sandwiches."

"Let's no

The night had fallen quietly, cloaking the land in darkness, offering the only cover the group could rely on. Aleksander, Malin, and the Anglo-Saxon group—Braham, Eleanor, Jimmy  and Lukas—moved swiftly under the cover of the black sky. The entire transfer was carefully planned to avoid detection by the numerous block points and the sophisticated radar systems employed by the US and Russian forces. Aleksander led the way, with Malin close behind, guiding the others along hidden paths and through thick forests. Their steps were deliberate, measured, as they avoided roads and known checkpoints. They knew that the only way to make it to Novosibirsk undetected was by staying off the beaten path and taking risks few others would dare. Every now and then, Aleksander would raise his hand, signalling the group to stop. He would listen carefully for the faint hum of a distant drone or the crunch of boots in the snow, but the night remained silent. They were in enemy territory, and every movement carried the threat of discovery.

"How much further?" Braham whispered, his breath forming clouds in the freezing air. He was keeping close to Eleanor and Lukas, all of them carrying only the essentials. They had no room for anything that could slow them down.

Aleksander glanced over his shoulder; his face shadowed. "Not far now. We'll cross a ridge soon, then we'll be in range of Novosibirsk. But we can't afford to be spotted."

Malin nodded. "There are blocked roads, and radar systems are watching for any movement. We have to stay off the main routes."

As they pressed forward, they encountered an abandoned barn, just beyond a snow-covered hill. It was a fleeting moment of rest before continuing on their way. They gathered quickly inside, using the barn's decaying walls as shelter, though the cold seeped through the cracks. While they rested, they communicated in hushed tones. It was an unspoken rule that they had to keep moving swiftly, as every second spent in one place increased the risk of detection.

After the brief stop, they set out again, now moving through an old forest path that Aleksander and Malin knew well. The snow crunched beneath their feet, but with the wind howling, they hoped it would mask their movements. Malin took the lead again, his eyes constantly scanning for the slightest sign of danger.

Time seemed to stretch in the freezing cold, but by the early hours of the morning, after several hours of moving without rest, they had crossed the ridge and were in the outskirts of Novosibirsk. The familiar glow of the city's lights gleamed faintly on the horizon, a reminder of the safety that still seemed so distant.

"We're almost there," Aleksander whispered, urging them on.

At this point, the group was not far from the relative safety of the city's outskirts, but they were still vulnerable. The last part of the journey, cutting through the forest and sneaking into the urban area, would be the most dangerous. The forces patrolling the region were becoming more active, and the group had to stay vigilant.

By the time they reached a secluded area just outside the city limits, dawn was beginning to break. The light was weak, barely cutting through the clouded sky, but it gave them just enough to find cover until they could figure out their next move. They had made it through the night. They were in Novosibirsk—just one final push to reach the airport and their escape.

In the quiet moments as they hid among the shadows of the city's industrial outskirts, they allowed themselves a brief breath. They had made it this far, despite the odds. But they knew that the hardest part was yet to come: getting onto a plane out of the country and beyond the reach of Seriakov's ever-growing military presence.

t get too comfortable," Braham replied, his voice steady but filled with a quiet urgency. "We can rest here for a few days, but we need to keep moving toward Novosibirsk. We can't stay in one place too long."

The decision to split up was not without risk, but they knew it was their best chance of survival. With both groups now on separate paths, their hopes rested on reaching Novosibirsk and then on to Moscow, where they would be able to disappear into the relative safety of the city's expat community. The goal remained clear: escape the tightening noose, leave the country, and find safety beyond the reach of Seriakov's regime.

As they settled into their temporary refuge, the reality of their situation weighed heavily on them. The tension of being pursued by a relentless military force was never far from their minds. But for now, in the quiet wood, there was a small sense of peace—a brief, fragile pause before the next leg of their journey. The group used this temporary respite to gather supplies, plan their route, and rest their weary bodies. They knew that the journey ahead would be fraught with danger, requiring every ounce of their strength and cunning to navigate. As they prepared for the next phase of their escape, a mix of determination and fear coursed through their veins, each member silently vowing to see this through to the end.

# Chapter 14: The return flight

The sun dipped low on the horizon, painting the tundra in hues of amber and gold as the group marked their tenth day of respite in the remote wooden house. The harrowing escape from the scientific centre seemed a distant memory, though its shadows lingered in subtle ways. Braham, burdened by the weight of their mission, had turned his attention to Eleonor, seeking to understand the enigmatic woman who had become an unlikely ally. Their conversations were tentative but revealing, each exchange peeling back layers of guarded mystery.

Meanwhile, Jimmy, ever the silent guardian, had retreated into the wilderness. For days, he roamed the snow-dusted expanse, alone but not lonely. The crisp air and unbroken solitude became his sanctuary, a space to mend his frayed spirit and rediscover the inner strength that had carried him through so much. In those moments, he felt a fleeting connection to the unyielding tundra—vast, resilient, and quietly alive.

Inside the wooden house, Malin worked tirelessly, his mind consumed by logistics and strategy. A map of Novosibirsk sprawled across the table, dotted with pencilled notes and potential routes. He knew their journey back to the city would be fraught with danger, yet the thought of staying put was equally untenable. Moscow loomed large in their plans, a beacon of hope and uncertainty. Every move needed precision; every decision carried weight.

But time had run its course. The safety of the tundra was temporary, and the day had come to leave the shelter that had given them refuge. As the group packed their belongings—a few meager supplies, warm clothing, and the unspoken resolve to see their mission through—an unshakable tension settled over them.

Their journey to Novosibirsk would not be easy. The city was a labyrinth of memories and threats, yet it was there that Malin believed they could find the resources to secure a flight to Moscow. The stakes were higher than ever, and each step brought them closer to a confrontation with forces far greater than themselves.

As they prepared to depart, the tundra seemed to watch silently, as if bidding them farewell. The return flight was no longer just a means of travel—it had become a symbol of their resolve to face the unknown, to push forward against all odds, and to reclaim the lives they had been forced to leave behind.

The sun dipped low on the horizon, painting the tundra in hues of amber and gold as the group marked their tenth day of respite in the remote wooden house. The harrowing escape from the scientific centre seemed a distant memory, though its shadows lingered in subtle ways. Braham, burdened by the weight of their mission, had turned his attention to Eleonor, seeking to understand the enigmatic woman who had become an unlikely ally. Their conversations were tentative but revealing, each exchange peeling back layers of guarded mystery.

Meanwhile, Jimmy, ever the silent guardian, had retreated into the wilderness. For days, he roamed the snow-dusted expanse, alone but not lonely. The crisp air and unbroken solitude became his sanctuary, a space to mend his frayed spirit and rediscover the inner strength that had carried him through so much. In those moments, he felt a fleeting connection to the unyielding tundra—vast, resilient, and quietly alive.

Inside the wooden house, Malin worked tirelessly, his mind consumed by logistics and strategy. A map of Novosibirsk sprawled across the table, dotted with pencilled notes and potential routes. He knew their journey back to the city would be fraught with danger, yet the thought of staying put was equally untenable. Moscow loomed large in their plans, a beacon of hope and uncertainty. Every move needed precision; every decision carried weight.

But time had run its course. The safety of the tundra was temporary, and the day had come to leave the shelter that had given them refuge. As the group packed their belongings—a few meager supplies, warm clothing, and the unspoken resolve to see their mission through—an unshakable tension settled over them.

Their journey to Novosibirsk would not be easy. The city was a labyrinth of memories and threats, yet it was there that Malin believed they could find the resources to secure a flight to Moscow. The stakes were higher than ever, and each step brought them closer to a confrontation with forces far greater than themselves.

As they prepared to depart, the tundra seemed to watch silently, as if bidding them farewell. The return flight was no longer just a means of travel—it had become a symbol of their resolve to face the unknown, to push forward against all odds, and to reclaim the lives they had been forced to leave behind. As dawn broke, casting long shadows across their makeshift camp, the group began to stir. They packed their meager belongings with practiced efficiency, erasing all traces of their presence.

The forest around them seemed to hold its breath, as if aware of the gravity of their mission.

Eleonor, the group's unofficial leader, unfurled a crudely drawn map on a flat rock. Her fingers traced the path they would take, lingering on the treacherous mountain pass that lay ahead. "We'll need to cross here before nightfall," she murmured, her voice barely above a whisper. The others gathered around, their faces etched with a mixture of resolve and apprehension.

Lukas, the youngest of the group, nervously fingered the frayed strap of his backpack. "What if they're waiting for us?" he asked, voicing the fear that had been gnawing at all of them.

"Then we'll deal with it," replied Jimmy, the grizzled veteran whose experience had proven invaluable thus far. He checked his weapon one last time, a grim reminder of the stakes they faced.

As they set out, the forest seemed to close in around them, branches reaching out like grasping fingers. Every snapping twig and rustling leaf set their nerves on edge. They moved in silence, communicating through gestures and meaningful glances, each step taking them further from danger and closer to an uncertain future.

Inside the wooden house, Malin poured over maps and notes with relentless focus. Moscow was their ultimate destination, but reaching it required navigating a labyrinth of challenges. Their latest lead had brought them to a precarious conclusion: the only way to secure a safe flight was to enlist the help of an old Yakut man who lived near a river in the valley.

This man, rumoured to speak Turkish, was said to be a former pilot with a knack for navigating the skies under the radar of authorities. Finding him was no small task. His location was vague—descriptions of his hut spoke only of a place "where the river bends and the valley open wide." Yet his knowledge and skills could mean the difference between survival and capture.

The group prepared to leave their sanctuary at dawn. Each member carried a mix of hope and unease, knowing their journey to find the Yakut man was fraught with uncertainties. The valley was a desolate expanse, unforgiving in its isolation, but its hidden dangers were not the only concern. Time was pressing; staying too long in one place increased the risk of being found.

As they trudged through the snow, the landscape stretched before them in an endless canvas of white and grey. The wind whispered secrets of the land, carrying with it the distant scent of the river they sought. Their only guide was Malin's map and the hope that the old man would still be there, living in quiet seclusion.

When they reached the valley, they spotted a small, smoke-curling chimney rising from a cluster of trees near the water's edge. Their hearts quickened. The hut was rudimentary, weathered by time and the harsh elements, but it stood as a testament to resilience.

Braham was the first to knock, his knuckles rapping against the rough wooden door. It creaked open slowly to reveal a man in his late sixties, his face lined with years of survival and a life lived close to the earth.

His sharp eyes darted from one stranger to the next, lingering on Braham before he spoke in accented but clear Turkish:

"You've come a long way. What do you want from me?"

The man's tone was guarded, but his words were a lifeline. The group exchanged glances before Malin stepped forward, explaining their plight and their need for his help. The Yakut man, who introduced himself as Timur, listened intently, his expression unreadable.

"We don't have much time," Malin finished. "Can you fly us to Novosibirsk?"

Timur sighed, stepping back to let them inside. The air inside the hut was warm, filled with the scent of burning wood and a faint hint of tobacco. "It's been years since I've piloted a plane," he admitted, settling into a weathered chair. "But if the stakes are as high as you say, I will do what I can. For a price."

The group nodded in agreement. Negotiations would come later, but for now, the pieces of their plan were beginning to fall into place. The journey to Moscow was far from over, but the first step—the return to Novosibirsk—was finally within reach.

The sun climbed higher in the sky, its heat beating down mercilessly. Sweat trickled down their faces, mingling with the dirt and grime of their journey. Despite the discomfort, they pressed on, driven by a desperate hope for freedom and safety.

The tundra wind howled as Braham and his group stood at the threshold of Timur's modest wooden hut. The old Yakut man, his eyes sharp and calculating, studied them with a guarded curiosity. His weathered face bore the marks of a hard life, each wrinkle a testament to battles fought and years survived in the unforgiving wilderness.

Timur did not seem particularly moved by Malin's plea or the urgency in Braham's voice as they explained their desperate need to reach Moscow. Instead, he leaned back in his creaking chair, a faint smirk playing on his lips.

"I've heard stories like yours before," he said, his voice gravelly but steady. "People running from something. People chasing something. But me? I'm not part of any of that anymore."

Braham frowned, glancing at Malin, who shifted uneasily. "We're not asking you to fight our battles," Braham said. "We just need your skills—your ability to get us where we need to go."

Timur chuckled dryly, shaking his head. "You think I care about where you're going or what trouble you're trying to outrun?" He gestured broadly to the room, his hands rough and scarred. "I've spent most of my life fighting wars that weren't mine. Twenty years as a soldier for Russia. I've seen things that haunt even the coldest of nights out here. But that's behind me now. These days, I worry only about fishing the river and hunting a few mild boars to keep my belly full."

The group fell silent, uncertain of how to sway the grizzled pilot. It was Eleonor who finally spoke, her voice calm but resolute. "You've spent years surviving out here, living by your own rules. But doesn't that mean you know better than anyone how important it is to help when you can? We don't have anyone else, Timur. Just you."

Timur's expression softened slightly, and he let out a long sigh. He rose from his chair and grabbed a coat from a nearby hook. "You're stubborn, I'll give you that," he muttered. "Follow me."

He led them out into the biting cold, trudging across the snow-dusted ground toward a cluster of trees at the edge of his property. The sound of their footsteps crunching in the snow was the only noise as they approached a large, weathered barn-like structure hidden among the trees.

Timur stopped in front of the structure, pulling a key from around his neck. "You're lucky I never got rid of this old thing," he said, unlocking the heavy wooden door. With a groan, the doors swung open to reveal a sight that took the group by surprise: an old, Soviet-era airplane, covered in a thick layer of dust but otherwise intact.

"It's an aNTONOV AN-2" Timur explained, patting the side of the airplane with a mix of pride and nostalgia. "A workhorse from another time. I used to fly this bird on missions no one dared to talk about. And when the wars were done with me, I flew her here, to the valley, and hid her away. Figured someday I might need her again. Didn't think it'd be for this."

The interior of the hangar smelled of engine oil and aged metal. Tools lay scattered across a workbench, and a faint beam of sunlight streamed through a crack in the roof, illuminating the AIRPLANE'S faded green paint.

"Will it still fly?" Jimmy asked sceptically, running a hand over the chipped surface of the airplane

The creaking doors of the hangar swung fully open, revealing a relic from another time. The old Antonov biplane stood before them, its weathered frame and faded paint a testament to decades of survival. The group froze, their breath visible in the frigid air, staring at the aircraft in a mixture of awe and disbelief.

Jimmy was the first to break the silence. "It's from the Second World War!" he exclaimed, his voice echoing in the cavernous hangar. He ran toward the plane, brushing snow off its fuselage. "An Antonov An-2," he added, tracing his fingers along the embossed Cyrillic lettering. "These things are legends! They used them for everything—cargo, passengers, even crop dusting. But this one… this one's ancient."

Timur stepped forward, his face unreadable. "She's older than most pilots still flying," he said with a gruff chuckle, "but she's tougher than anything you'll find in the sky today. They don't make machines like this anymore."

Timur let out a low chuckle as he joined Jimmy, patting the Antonov affectionately. "No, boy," he said. "She's not that old, but her story is long. This here is an Antonov An-2, the most produced aircraft in history. Over 18,000 of them were made, and they've flown in nearly twenty countries. They call it the

*king of the skies*

—and for good reason."

He tapped the wing affectionately, then gestured to the group. "If you've got doubts, speak now. But if we're doing this, you better trust her like I do."

Braham remained silent; his gaze fixed on the Antonov. He admired its sturdy build, its history etched in every scratch and dent. Though the plane's age was undeniable, it radiated a certain strength, a resilience that mirrored their own. After a moment, he nodded, turning to the others.

"We're doing this," he said firmly. "But we're not taking any chances. We need to be sure it's flightworthy."

He pulled a notebook and pencil from his coat pocket and began jotting down a list. His military background had taught him the importance of preparation, and this mission was no exception.

Timur let out a low chuckle. "It'll fly," he said confidently. "She's old, but she's reliable. I've kept her maintained for the past ten years. A man out here needs to be prepared for anything."

The group exchanged hopeful glances as Timur began inspecting the biplane, checking its rotors and fuel levels. "But let me make one thing clear," he added, turning to face them. "I'm not doing this because I care about your adventure. I'm doing this because it's been too long since I've had a reason to take to the skies. You cover the fuel costs and give me a good story to tell, and we'll call it even."

Braham nodded, a faint smile tugging at his lips. "Deal."

As the group prepared for the next leg of their journey, the tension began to lift, replaced by a cautious optimism. The biplane represented more than just transportation—it was a glimmer of hope, a reminder that even in the most desolate corners of the world, unexpected allies could be found.

Timur's gruff demeanour softened as he tinkered with the controls, muttering to himself in a mix of Russian and Yakut. "Looks like we're going to Novosibirsk after all," he said under his breath. "And who knows? Maybe this old soldier still has a few adventures left in him."

*Braham's Checklist for the Flight:*

**Structural Integrity**

Inspect the wings, fuselage, and tail for any visible cracks, rust, or damage.

Check that all bolts and joints are secure.

**Engine and Fuel System**

Ensure the engine starts without sputtering or delays.

Test fuel lines for leaks and ensure the tanks are filled.

Verify fuel reserves are adequate for the trip to Novosibirsk.

**Controls and Navigation**

Test the rudder, ailerons, and elevator for smooth operation.

Check the condition of the cockpit instruments: altimeter, airspeed indicator, compass.

Verify communication equipment is functional, if available.

**Landing Gear and Brakes**

Inspect the tires for wear or punctures.

Test the brakes to ensure safe landings.

**Emergency Supplies**

Pack a first-aid kit, emergency rations, and water.

Secure parachutes, if available, and confirm safety harnesses.

As Braham read aloud the checklist, each item carried the weight of their mission's survival. He assigned tasks to the group. Jimmy eagerly volunteered to inspect the engine, his fascination with the Antonov overriding any hesitation. Malin took the structural check, his sharp eye for detail making him the ideal choice. Eleonor began gathering emergency supplies, while Timur inspected the controls with the practiced ease of a man who had spent decades in the skies.

The hangar buzzed with activity as they worked together, each member contributing to the preparation. The cold air bit at their fingers, but no one complained. Every creak of the aircraft's frame and groan of its old components seemed to echo their collective determination.

As dusk settled over the valley, Braham called them together. "This isn't going to be easy," he said, his voice steady but serious. "But we've done everything we can to make sure this plane is ready. The rest… well, the rest is up to the skies."

Timur smirked, lighting a cigarette as he leaned against the Antonov's side. "You're overthinking it, kid," he said, exhaling a cloud of smoke. "This old girl's seen worse than whatever's waiting for us out there. She'll get us to Novosibirsk. You just sit back and enjoy the ride."

The group exchanged weary but hopeful glances. As they finished the final checks, the Antonov loomed large against the fading light, its silhouette a symbol of their fragile hope. The time to leave the valley was drawing near, and with it, their journey into the unknown.

The frozen air hung heavy with unspoken words as the group gathered near the Antonov, its engine rumbling softly, preparing for takeoff. The long days in the tundra had forged bonds between them, but now the moment of separation had arrived.

The group had decided to divide into two teams to increase their chances of survival. The Siberian group, led by Aleksander, would stay behind to continue their efforts closer to home. Alongside him were Mirna, whose sharp instincts made her invaluable, and Yelena, whose steady resolve masked a quiet sadness. The Anglo-Saxon sequel, as Timur had jokingly referred to them, would take the Antonov and push forward toward Novosibirsk—and ultimately Moscow.

The old Antonov groaned and creaked as Timur ran through his final pre-flight checks. Its powerful engine coughed to life, spewing a puff of smoke into the cold air as it began to warm up. The group exchanged quiet farewells; their voices barely audible over the growing roar of the aircraft.

Mirna's smile was soft, her usual sharpness tempered by the gravity of the moment. "Don't let Moscow eat you alive," she teased, pulling Braham into a brief embrace. "You've got too much left to do."

Aleksander clasped hands with Braham firmly. "We'll hold our ground here," he said with a nod. "But you… you have to see this through. For all of us."

Yelena stood off to the side, her hands clasped in front of her, her face a mask of composure. When she finally spoke, her voice was steady but carried a hint of vulnerability. "The tundra has been kind to us, but it's time. You belong out there, pushing forward. We'll meet again, I'm sure of it."

As the Siberian group stepped back, the Anglo-Saxon team boarded the Antonov. Jimmy's face was a mix of excitement and apprehension as he strapped himself into the passenger seat. Eleonor sat quietly, her eyes scanning the horizon, while Braham took his place next to Timur in the cockpit.

The engine roared louder as the Antonov began to move, its wheels crunching over the frozen ground. Mirna, Aleksander, and Yelena stood together, watching as the aircraft accelerated down the makeshift runway.

The tundra blurred past the windows as the Antonov gained speed, its wings trembling slightly before lifting into the air. Inside, the mood was sombre but resolute. As the ground fell away beneath them, Braham looked back through the small window, catching one final glimpse of the Siberian group standing by the edge of the landing strip. They grew smaller and smaller, until they were just specks against the vast, white expanse.

Mirna waved, a wistful smile on her face. "The destiny wanted it so," she murmured to herself. "And maybe… maybe it's right this way."

Aleksander put a hand on her shoulder, his voice steady. "They'll make it. They have to."

Yelena, standing beside them, looked up at the sky. "It's strange, isn't it?" she said softly. "To feel both sadness and hope at the same time."

The Antonov climbed higher, its steady drone fading into the distance. The Siberian group turned away slowly, their task clear: to hold their ground, to fight their battles in this corner of the world, and to trust that their companions would carry their shared purpose forward.

Inside the Antonov, the mood was heavy but filled with determination. Braham glanced at Timur, who was focused intently on the controls. "Do you think they'll be okay?" he asked.

Timur didn't look away from the cockpit. "They're tougher than you think," he said gruffly. "Just like this plane. Just like you."

Braham leaned back in his seat, watching the endless white of the tundra stretch out below them. Their journey was far from over, but for now, the sky was theirs.

Here's the continuation of the scene:

The view from the skies was nothing short of breathtaking. The sunrise painted the horizon in a cascade of golden hues, blending into soft pinks and fiery oranges that reflected off the endless white snow below. The tundra stretched on like an untouched canvas, its pristine beauty broken only by the winding snake of the Ob River glimmering under the morning light.

As they approached Novosibirsk, the scenery transformed. The vast emptiness gave way to civilization. Skyscrapers rose defiantly against the flat landscape, their reflective windows catching the sunrise and scattering light across the snowy expanse. The Antonov's passengers stared in silence, mesmerized by the sight. Even Timur, who had seen this view countless times, couldn't help but glance out of the cockpit window with a faint smile.

"It's beautiful, isn't it?" Eleonor whispered, leaning toward the small window.

Braham nodded, though his mind was already shifting toward their mission. The sight of Novosibirsk's sprawling city centre brought with it a surge of both relief and urgency. Their journey through the wilderness had been harrowing, but now they were heading into a new kind of challenge—a battle of wits and survival in the heart of Russia.

The Antonov descended steadily, its engine humming as Timur expertly guided it toward a small airstrip on the eastern edge of the city. It wasn't much to look at—just a stretch of cleared snow bordered by a few run-down hangars and a single control tower that looked like it had seen better days.

"Welcome to Novosibirsk's forgotten airport," Timur said with a smirk as the biplane touched down with a slight jolt. He eased the aircraft to a stop, the propeller slowing until it finally came to rest.

The group disembarked quickly, the cold biting at their faces as they stepped onto the snow-packed runway. Braham scanned their surroundings, his sharp eyes noting the lack of activity. The airport appeared deserted, save for a lone figure approaching from one of the hangars.

The man was tall and broad-shouldered, bundled in a heavy coat and fur hat. He moved with purpose, his boots crunching against the snow. As he came closer, his face became visible—a thick beard framed his stern expression, and his piercing blue eyes locked onto Braham and the others.

"That's our contact," Timur muttered, gesturing toward the man. "His name's Sergei. An old friend of mine—trustworthy, but only just."

Sergei stopped a few paces away, his eyes scanning the group before settling on Timur. "You've brought more than I expected," he said in Russian, his voice deep and gravelly.

Timur stepped forward, clapping Sergei on the shoulder. "These are my passengers, and they're in need of your help. They need a way to Moscow—quietly."

Sergei raised an eyebrow, glancing at the Antonov before shifting his gaze back to the group. "Moscow's not exactly a quiet destination these days," he said. "But I might know a way. It won't be cheap, though."

Braham stepped forward, his tone firm. "We're not here to bargain. We've come too far, and time isn't on our side. Name your price and let's move forward."

Sergei chuckled, a low, rumbling sound. "I like this one," he said, nodding toward Braham. "Alright, come with me. We'll talk inside."

The group followed Sergei toward the hangar, their boots crunching against the snow. The air was thick with tension, each of them acutely aware that they were now in the hands of strangers. Inside the hangar, the warmth was a welcome relief. A small office had been set up in the corner, its walls lined with maps and equipment.

Sergei poured himself a cup of steaming tea and gestured for the group to sit. "Tell me why Moscow is so important," he said, leaning back in his chair.

Braham exchanged a glance with Eleonor and Malin before speaking. "We're not just trying to get to Moscow—we're trying to stop something. Something big. But the details are need-to-know."

Sergei narrowed his eyes, his fingers drumming on the table. "Need-to-know, huh? Fine. But you'll need more than my connections to pull this off. The roads to Moscow are crawling with checkpoints. The skies? Even worse."

Timur crossed his arms. "And that's where your expertise comes in, Sergei. You've got the contacts to get us through. You owe me, remember?"

Sergei smirked, taking a slow sip of his tea. "You're lucky I like you, Timur," he said. "Alright. I'll make some calls. But if this goes south, don't expect me to save your skins."

Braham nodded. "We'll handle the risk. Just get us the way in."

As Sergei stood to make his calls, the group exchanged quiet words of reassurance. They were one step closer to their goal, but the road ahead was far from clear.

The sunrise that had once seemed so hopeful now felt like a fleeting memory, overshadowed by the challenges that lay before them in Moscow.

Sergei returned to the small office; his expression unreadable as he leaned against the doorway. "I made the call," he said, his voice steady. "There's a Yakovlev Yak-42D that can take you to Moscow, but it's not a simple matter. Flights like these are rare—sold maybe once a week at most—and they don't come cheap."

Braham crossed his arms, his gaze unwavering. "We didn't expect it to be easy, or cheap. What's the cost?"

Sergei's lips curled into a faint smirk. "Enough to make me think you're desperate, which you clearly are. But if you're willing to pay, I'll make it happen. The flight will leave in three days. Until then, you need to stay out of sight. The authorities are more watchful here than you might think."

Timur raised an eyebrow, his arms still folded. "And where exactly do you plan on hiding them?"

"There's a small house in the northern neighbourhood," Sergei replied. "It's not luxurious, but it's safe. Close enough to the city for me to bring updates, but far enough from prying eyes. You'll stay there until the Yak is ready."

Braham nodded, glancing at the others. "We'll manage. Just make sure the flight is secure."

Sergei chuckled, lighting a cigarette as he stepped closer. "I'll do my part, but don't get too comfortable. This isn't a pleasure cruise—it's a risk, even for someone like me. You'll board that Yak with no fanfare, no questions, and no mistakes. Understand?"

Eleonor shifted uncomfortably, but her voice was steady. "We understand. What about supplies? We'll need food, water, and… discretion."

"You'll have everything you need," Sergei assured her. "I'll send someone to stock the house, but don't leave unless absolutely necessary. The fewer eyes on you, the better."

Timur let out a low grunt, clearly unimpressed by Sergei's tone but unwilling to argue. "Fine. Take us to this hideout of yours, then."

Sergei's Mercedes 200 rumbled to life, its engine coughing as it reluctantly warmed up. The car was an old Berlin model, its once-polished exterior now dulled by years of wear and neglect. The seats were cracked and the upholstery faded, but it had served Sergei well over the years. As he motioned for the group to get in, the worn leather interior creaked under their weight.

Timur climbed into the front passenger seat, while Braham, Eleonor, Malin, and Jimmy settled into the back, their bodies cramped and uncomfortable. The chill of the outside world clung to them as they buckled in.

Sergei slammed the car into gear and pulled away from the small house, steering them down narrow streets lined with faded apartment buildings and weathered storefronts. The city was alive with movement, the sound of horns honking and tires screeching cutting through the air. The streets were filled with a chaotic mix of pedestrians and vehicles—an endless sea of movement that felt like an obstacle course. Sergei navigated it with practiced ease, weaving through traffic lights and intersections as though he knew every inch of the city.

"Buckle up," Sergei muttered, his hands gripping the steering wheel. "It's going to be a bumpy ride."

Braham kept his gaze fixed out the window, watching as they passed through the heart of Novosibirsk. The city's energy was palpable— people moving in all directions, the buildings towering above them. Skyscrapers reflected the early morning sunlight, their glass facades shimmering in the pale glow. The streets were full of life, but Braham couldn't shake the feeling of unease in his chest. The closer they got to the airport, the more it felt like they were headed into the lion's den.

"Which way now?" Malin asked, his eyes darting nervously between Sergei and the streets ahead.

"Right here," Sergei said curtly, swinging the car into a narrow one-way street. The tires squealed in protest as they made the turn, the vehicle bumping along the rough asphalt.

Eleonor shifted in her seat, glancing at the others. "How much longer until we get to the airport?"

Sergei's eyes were focused ahead, his expression unreadable. "Not long. But don't think you're in the clear yet. The authorities have eyes everywhere."

The car came to a sudden stop at a red light, the brakes screeching as it slid slightly across the icy road. Sergei's fingers tapped restlessly on the steering wheel. "There are too many checkpoints in this city. If we're lucky, we won't get stopped. If we're unlucky… well, you know what happens next."

Jimmy shifted uncomfortably in his seat, his eyes flicking nervously to the rearview mirror. "How do you know we won't get caught?"

Sergei's lips twisted into a grim smile. "Because I've been doing this for a long time. I know where the eyes are, and where they're not. Just keep your heads down and don't cause any trouble."

The light turned green, and Sergei slammed his foot on the accelerator, the car jolting forward once more. The tires slid briefly on a patch of ice, but Sergei kept control, guiding them through a maze of alleyways and side streets. Every turn felt like a narrow escape, every intersection a potential trap.

They crossed over several major roads, the traffic slowing and thickening as they neared the airport. Sergei took a sharp left, ducking into a residential neighbourhood filled with small houses and snow-covered yards. The roads here were quieter, more deserted.

"Almost there," Sergei muttered, glancing at the rearview mirror once more.

Braham exhaled slowly, the tension in his shoulders beginning to ease as they neared their destination. But even as the airport came into view, he knew they were not out of the woods yet. The flight to Moscow was their only hope—but it was still a long way off, and there was no guarantee they'd make it without a hitch.

"Stay alert," Sergei warned, his voice low as they made the final turn toward the private hangar. "Once we're in the air, you're on your own."

As the car came to a stop in front of a secluded hangar, the group took a collective breath, ready to move quickly and without hesitation. Sergei popped the trunk, and they filed out, gathering their belongings in silence.

The hangar door creaked open, revealing the Yakovlev Yak-42D—a sleek and powerful aircraft that gleamed in the low morning light. It was their ticket out, but even as Braham approached it, he couldn't shake the nagging feeling that they were not yet free.

Sergei motioned toward the plane. "This is it," he said, his voice more serious now. "Get on board, and don't look back."

As they boarded the plane, the roar of the engine began to fill the air, the sound of their future taking shape. There was no turning back now.

The Yakovlev Yak-42D hummed with power as it prepared for takeoff, the cabin surprisingly comfortable for a private flight. The seats were well-cushioned, and the dim, yellowish lights cast a soft glow over the interior, making it feel like a quiet retreat rather than a high-risk escape. The flight crew, a pair of young attendants, moved about the cabin with purpose, checking equipment and ensuring everything was in order. They were alert and eager, occasionally looking over at the passengers, but it was clear that their primary concern was following orders and staying out of the way.

Braham sat near the back of the plane; his brow furrowed as he flipped through an old, weathered exercise book. It was full of scribbled notes, maps, and plans for their next move. The flight from Novosibirsk had been a necessary escape, but it wasn't the end of the road. Moscow's airport loomed large in his mind, a place where every step would be scrutinized, every action carefully monitored.

He glanced up momentarily, his eyes catching the concerned looks of his companions. They were tense, no doubt thinking about the risks they were about to face. Malin stared out the window, his face shadowed with apprehension, while Eleonor kept her hands folded tightly in her lap, clearly trying to maintain composure. Jimmy was fidgeting nervously, his eyes darting to and fro, unable to settle.

"We're almost there," Braham murmured under his breath, more to himself than anyone else. The vast expanse of Moscow's airport was far from a sanctuary—it was a maze of checkpoints, surveillance, and tight security. If they were to succeed, they needed to slip through unnoticed.

The attendants, noticing Braham's absorbed focus, approached him quietly. The younger of the two, a woman with short blonde hair and a soft voice, spoke first. "Is there anything else we can do for you, sir?"

Braham looked up, his sharp eyes meeting hers. He gave her a brief nod. "Yes. We'll need to buy tickets once we land. Make sure that it's done quickly, and without drawing attention. We can't afford any delays."

The attendant nodded eagerly, already pulling out a tablet from her pocket. "Understood, sir. I'll handle it as discreetly as possible. Just let me know when you're ready."

Braham watched her leave, then turned his attention back to the exercise book. The next steps were crucial—getting through Moscow's airport would be their first real test. His mind worked over every possibility, analysing the route, the potential checkpoints, and how to avoid them. If they were caught, everything they'd worked for would fall apart. He had to be certain that they could blend in, disappear into the crowd.



When the plane finally descended toward Moscow, the city sprawled beneath them like a massive, interconnected web of concrete and steel. The airport was an immense complex, stretching as far as the eye could see. It was a place of constant motion, filled with crowds of passengers, workers rushing from gate to gate, and the constant hum of announcements in multiple languages.

Braham's mind raced as the wheels of the Yak touched down. This was the moment that would decide everything. He glanced at Eleonor, Malin, and Jimmy, each of them carrying the same weight of anticipation. They couldn't afford any mistakes.

The Yak taxied to a small terminal at the edge of the airport—far from the main complex, where less traffic would be expected. As soon as they disembarked, Sergei's associate, a man named Alexei, met them. He was tall, with graying hair and a stern expression. His attire was nondescript—a dark jacket and hat that blended seamlessly into the crowd.

"Follow me," Alexei said, his voice low and without warmth. He led them through a back entrance of the terminal, avoiding the main corridors filled with security personnel and travellers.

Sergei's influence had stretched far enough to make this part of the plan possible—Alexei had connections, and those connections would provide the means for them to move undetected.

The group followed Alexei through a series of narrow hallways, passing through doorways that led into areas where only airport staff were allowed. They arrived at a small office, tucked away from the public eye. Inside, the walls were cluttered with maps, papers, and travel schedules.

Alexei gestured toward a desk where a man sat, typing away at a computer. He looked up briefly, giving a nod of acknowledgment to Alexei before turning his attention back to his screen.

"Tickets," Alexei said curtly. "You need to buy them, quickly, without anyone noticing."

Braham stepped forward, his mind already working through the next steps. "I'll handle it," he said. He approached the desk and stood silently, watching the man at the computer for a moment. The tickets they needed were not for a direct flight—they would have to be rerouted, diverted, with their final destination hidden under the guise of something else. It was a delicate balance.

The clerk finally looked up, his face emotionless as he waited for Braham's request.

"Two tickets for the next available flight to Saint Petersburg," Braham said, keeping his voice steady. "But we'll need them re-routed immediately to a private destination."

The clerk didn't blink. "I'll need identification," he said flatly.

Braham handed over the documents without hesitation. The man glanced at them briefly, then nodded and began typing on his keyboard. Braham felt the weight of each passing second. This was the moment that could either make or break them.

Minutes passed in tense silence, but finally, the tickets were printed—each with a discreet rerouting to an obscure, private airport in the city outskirts. The clerk handed them over, his expression unchanged.

"Your tickets," he said. "Everything is arranged."

Braham took them quickly, offering a silent nod of thanks. The group filed out of the office, their hearts racing with the knowledge that they had just narrowly avoided detection.

### The Next Move

Once outside, Braham paused, taking in the bustle of the airport around them. They were only one step closer to their goal. Moscow's web of surveillance would only grow tighter from here, and the next phase of their mission would be far from easy.

But for now, they had their tickets, their passage secured—at least for the moment. The next challenge awaited: slipping through the rest of Moscow, and into the heart of the operation they had come to disrupt.

### The Flight to Moscow: Nightfall

As the night began to settle over Moscow, the group gathered their belongings, feeling the weight of their situation more than ever. Their plan was simple—board the flight under the cover of darkness, keep their heads down, and disappear into the crowd. AirSerbia was the carrier they'd chosen, a quiet and low-profile airline that wouldn't draw any unwanted attention. The late-night flight was their best chance to slip through unnoticed.

Braham glanced over at his companions, his mind calculating their every move. Eleonor was keeping a low profile, her expression pensive as she adjusted the collar of her coat. Jimmy was nervously checking the time, while Malin's posture remained rigid—every sense alert, every move calculated.

"Let's stick together and stay calm," Braham murmured, his voice low but firm. He knew that if they faltered even for a moment, their plan could unravel. "This is the quietest time at the airport. No one will notice us."

The group nodded in agreement as they made their way toward the check-in counters. The massive Moscow airport loomed ahead—vast, cold, and impersonal. The hum of the crowd, the murmur of foreign languages, and the rhythmic clatter of luggage rolling across the floor filled the air.

### The Check-In

As they approached the AirSerbia desk, Braham couldn't help but notice the long line stretching ahead of them. It seemed to go on forever, a serpentine trail of travellers all waiting their turn. It was late, but the airport was still busy—families, business people, tourists, all heading off in different directions.

Sergei's associate, Alexei, had ensured that their tickets were in order, but getting through check-in would still be the next hurdle. They had to remain calm and methodical—no sudden movements, no raising suspicion.

"We'll have to wait," Malin muttered under his breath, shifting on his feet. "I don't like this. We're too exposed."

"We're fine," Braham replied, his eyes scanning the scene. "Just stick to the routine. Nothing's out of place."

The line moved slowly, inching forward with each passing minute. Every person seemed to be in no particular rush—there was no urgency, no reason to draw attention to themselves. The group stayed close together, their eyes scanning the area while maintaining their composure.

When their turn finally arrived, Braham stepped forward. The check-in clerk, a tired-looking woman with glasses perched on the end of her nose, didn't even look up at first. She typed something into her computer and then glanced up, giving him a brief, almost bored smile.

"Ticket?" she asked, her voice flat.

Braham handed over their boarding passes and IDs, his movements deliberate but relaxed. The woman glanced at the documents without much interest, flipping through the pages as though she had seen it all before. Her eyes lingered just a moment too long on the photo of

Eleonor, but it was only a momentary pause. She stamped the tickets with a sigh and passed them back.

"Have a pleasant flight," she said, not looking up again.

Braham nodded, and with that, they were through. No questions, no issues.

## The Security Check

Next came the security check. They had expected this part to be the most difficult, but it went smoothly. The security personnel were more focused on the stream of passengers ahead of them than on any individual traveller. It seemed that the night shift was not as vigilant as the daytime staff, and the group kept their pace steady, following the others as they moved through the checkpoints.

Each of them passed through the metal detectors without issue. Their bags were briefly checked, but nothing was flagged. The security officer barely glanced at the x-ray screen as their luggage passed through. It was as though they were invisible.

"Just stay focused," Braham whispered under his breath, his eyes scanning the security staff and the sea of travellers around them.

Once through, they were free to move into the departure area. They breathed a collective sigh of relief. Their identities had been verified, their tickets processed, and they were officially on their way—disappearing into the vast anonymity of the airport.

## The Final Step

As they made their way toward the gate, the final hurdle seemed to pass without incident. The boarding process was far less hectic than they had expected. They had already gone through the necessary procedures; now, it was just a matter of finding their seats and waiting for the plane to take off.

Braham found his seat by the window, looking out at the runway as the ground crew loaded the luggage onto the plane. The lights of the airport gleamed brightly outside, but soon they would be airborne, and they would leave all of this behind.

Lukas sat next to him, his face tense but resolute, while Eleonor and Jimmy sat a few rows behind. The plane would be relatively empty, as most flights during the night were. It was the perfect time to slip away, unnoticed by those who might be watching.

The cabin door shut with a soft thud, and the flight attendants moved quickly down the aisles, their steps purposeful. The aircraft's engines began to roar, signalling that they were preparing for takeoff.

Braham closed his eyes for a moment, leaning back in his seat. They had made it past the hardest part, but they were not yet safe. The flight to London was a brief respite, a way to regroup before continuing their journey. But for now, they were one step closer to their goal.

As the plane began to taxi down the runway, Braham allowed himself a rare moment of peace. The hum of the engines filled the cabin, and soon they would be high above the city, disappearing into the night.

# Chapter 15: The Return to the Chaotic City

The city had not changed in Eleanor's absence. The honking cars, chaotic intersections, and the buzz of hurried conversations echoed through her office's thin glass windows, much like the cacophony that had defined her life before she disappeared a year ago. But for Eleanor, the chaos felt different this time. It was distant, almost like the static of an old radio she could tune out. Her new office, perched on the seventh floor of a refurbished high-rise, was a curious mix of elegance and minimalism. The muted colours and sharp lines of the décor contrasted sharply with the vivid turbulence of the streets below.

Eleanor leaned back in her chair; her gaze fixated on a small photo frame on her desk. The picture was a remnant from her old life: her standing on a sunlit beach, her face framed by wild curls, with an unmistakable grin. That was a different Eleanor, a woman untouched by the strange sequence of events that had taken her from this city, reshaped her understanding of reality, and returned her here a stranger to the familiar.

Her desk was meticulously organized, the papers neatly stacked, her pen aligned perfectly with her leather notebook. Yet, Eleanor's mind was far from the structured appearance of her surroundings. She tapped her fingers absentmindedly on the polished wood, rehearsing the details of the dinner scheduled for later that evening.

*The Dinner: Meeting the Siberian Group*

Tonight, she would reconnect with the Siberian group: Lukas, the ever-charismatic leader with his wry humour and sharp insights; Braham, the brooding strategist whose silence often spoke louder than words; and Jimmy, the group's spark of energy, always ready with a joke or a clever plan. But tonight wasn't just about reconnecting with old allies. For the first time, Eleanor's new boyfriend, James, would meet the group. James was different from anyone she had been with before. A quiet, analytical type with a penchant for solving puzzles, he had a calming presence that Eleanor found herself drawn to. Yet, as she thought about the evening ahead, a pang of nervousness crept in. How would James, with his reserved demeanour, fit into the dynamic of the Siberian group? Would he sense the subtle undercurrents of tension and shared secrets that bound them together?

*Reflections Before the Gathering*

The late afternoon sunlight streamed through the large windows, casting long shadows across the room. Eleanor's thoughts drifted to the past year. The silence of the vast, snowy expanses she had left behind felt a world away from the relentless energy of the city. She missed the simplicity of that time, the stark clarity of purpose it had brought her. Yet, she couldn't deny the pull of the life she had returned to. There was something invigorating about the chaos, a sense of potential in its unpredictability.

Her phone buzzed on the desk, pulling her back to the present. It was a message from Lukas: **"Looking forward to tonight. Don't forget the bottle of red you promised."** She smiled, a genuine warmth spreading across her face. Some things, she thought, never changed.

*Preparing for the Evening*

By the time the sun dipped below the horizon, Eleanor had left the office and returned to her apartment. She dressed with care, choosing a simple yet elegant black dress that reflected her newfound sense of balance. As she finished applying a touch of makeup, James arrived, punctual as always. He greeted her with his signature half-smile, the kind that always seemed to reassure her.

"Ready?" he asked, holding out his arm.

Eleanor nodded, taking a deep breath. "As ready as I'll ever be."

The restaurant they had chosen was tucked away in a quiet corner of the city, a hidden gem known for its intimate ambiance and exquisite cuisine. When they arrived, Lukas, Braham, and Jimmy were already seated, their lively banter filling the small room. The sight of them brought a surge of emotions—nostalgia, relief, and a touch of apprehension.

As the evening unfolded, the conversation ebbed and flowed, punctuated by laughter and moments of reflective silence. James listened attentively, occasionally chiming in with his thoughtful observations. Eleanor watched as the dynamics shifted, the group slowly warming to his presence. By the time dessert arrived, she felt a sense of ease she hadn't anticipated.

*Closing the Evening*

As they stepped out into the cool night air, Eleanor felt a rare sense of contentment. The city still roared around them, but it felt less chaotic, more like a symphony of possibilities. James squeezed her hand gently, and she turned to him with a smile.

"What?" he asked, his tone light.

"Nothing," she replied, her voice tinged with gratitude. "Just... thank you."

For the first time in a long while, Eleanor felt at home—not in the city, not in the chaos, but in the connections, she had chosen to nurture.

For the first time in a long while, Eleanor felt at home—not in the city, not in the chaos, but in the connections, she had chosen to nurture.

Eleanor stood outside the dimly lit pub, the crisp night air wrapping around her like a newfound freedom. A cigarette burned between her fingers, the soft glow catching the curve of her lips as she smiled. James's hand was warm in hers, steady despite the adrenaline still coursing through them.

Behind them, the looming shadow of the scientific centre faded into the distance—a fortress they had both thought inescapable. Now, it was just a memory, a place that would haunt others but no longer hold them captive.

Eleanor exhaled slowly, watching the smoke curl and dance against the night sky. "We really did it," she murmured, half in disbelief, half in wonder.

James turned to her, a grin tugging at the corners of his mouth. "Yeah. We're free."

And for the first time in years, freedom didn't feel like a dream. It felt real.

*The return home*

Eleanor caught sight of a pair of men in military uniforms across the street. They seemed out of place against the backdrop of bustling city lights and rushing pedestrians. Yet, she dismissed them with a fleeting thought. Military personnel were a common enough sight in the city, especially near the government district. She turned her attention back to James, who was thoughtfully holding the door open for her as they stepped into the subway station.

The platform was alive with the usual evening crowd—a mix of tired workers, lively groups of friends, and the occasional loner absorbed in their phones. Eleanor stood close to James, his presence grounding her amidst the chaos. The fluorescent lights flickered above, casting an eerie glow on the tiles as the distant rumble of an approaching train echoed through the tunnels.

When the train arrived, they found seats in a quiet corner of the carriage. As the doors hissed shut and the train jolted forward, Eleanor's gaze drifted. Her eyes fell on the same two soldiers she had seen earlier. They stood at the far end of the carriage, their stances relaxed but their eyes scanning the crowd with an intensity that made her pulse quicken.

She leaned closer to James, lowering her voice. "Don't look now, but those two guys from outside are here. Military uniforms."

James, ever composed, didn't react immediately. Instead, he pretended to adjust his watch, stealing a subtle glance in their direction. "Interesting," he murmured. "Could be nothing, but... strange coincidence."

Eleanor nodded, trying to shake off the creeping unease. The train sped through the tunnels, the city flashing by in brief, fragmented glimpses. The rhythmic clatter of the wheels was oddly soothing, a stark contrast to the turbulence of her thoughts.

When their stop approached, Eleanor and James stood, making their way toward the doors. The soldiers didn't follow, but Eleanor couldn't shake the feeling of being watched. The cool night air greeted them as they exited the station, the familiar scent of wet pavement and distant street food stalls filling her senses.

The walk back to her apartment was calm, the streets quieter now as the city began to settle into its nocturnal rhythm. The season lent a certain charm to the night; a crisp breeze carried the faint aroma of blooming jasmine from a nearby garden. James walked beside her, ever the perfect gentleman, his hand occasionally brushing hers as they strolled.

"You seem quiet," he remarked, his voice breaking the comfortable silence.

"Just... thinking," Eleanor replied. "The city feels different tonight."

James gave her a sidelong glance, a small smile playing on his lips. "Is that a good thing or a bad thing?"

"I'm not sure yet," she admitted.

When they reached her building, James escorted her to the door. He hesitated for a moment, then leaned in, pressing a soft kiss to her cheek. "Get some rest. I'll call you tomorrow."

Eleanor smiled, the gesture warm and genuine. "Thanks, James. For everything."

As she watched him walk away, a shadow moved in the corner of her vision. She turned sharply, her heart skipping a beat. But it was just a stray cat darting across the street. She laughed softly at her own nerves, shaking her head as she entered the building.

Still, as she locked the door behind her and settled into the quiet of her apartment, the image of those soldiers lingered in her mind. Something about them didn't sit right. She resolved to keep an eye out in the days ahead. After all, in her experience, even the most innocuous details could unravel into something much bigger.

*A new starting*

Where life had once stopped, it now roared forward with an intensity Eleanor hadn't felt in years. The humdrum routines she'd long avoided now carried a strange exhilaration: the clatter of coffee cups in the morning, the flurry of conversations at work, the quiet moments spent laughing with James over dinner. It was as though the universe, sensing her reawakening, had decided to pour everything into her life at once. James was the perfect partner for this new chapter. Thoughtful, steady, and endlessly supportive, he had brought a sense of stability Eleanor had never known she needed. She found herself daydreaming of a future with him—a home, a family, perhaps even the wedding she'd once dismissed as a relic of simpler dreams. The thought brought a faint blush to her cheeks as she prepared for bed that night, her mind playing out scenes of a life she could almost touch. But even as her heart soared, a darker current rippled beneath the surface of her newfound joy. The soldiers, the strange feeling of being watched—it all lingered like a shadow at the edge of her consciousness. Eleanor wasn't the kind to ignore her instincts. She had learned, often the hard way, that when something felt off, it usually was. The next morning, as she walked to her office, the city buzzed with its usual energy. The streets were alive with people hurrying to their destinations, the air thick with the scent of roasting coffee and car exhaust. Yet, Eleanor couldn't shake the sensation of unseen eyes following her movements. At first, she told herself it was paranoia—a holdover from the strange and unsettling events of the past year. But as she rounded a corner, she spotted a man in a dark jacket leaning against a lamppost, his eyes flicking to her just as she passed. She kept walking, her pace steady, resisting the urge to look back. When she entered her building, she glanced at the mirrored walls of the elevator, catching a glimpse of the street outside. The man was gone. By the time she reached her office, her nerves were taut. She closed the door and leaned against it, taking a moment to steady herself. Her desk, as always, was impeccably organized, but even the sight of its familiar order did little to calm her racing thoughts. Eleanor grabbed her phone and dialled James. He picked up on the second ring. "Hey," he said, his voice warm and reassuring. "Everything okay?" "I don't know," she admitted, lowering her voice. "Something feels... off. I think I'm being followed. " There was a pause on the other end of the line. Then James said, "Where are you now?" "My office," she replied. "Stay there," he said firmly. "I'll come over during lunch. We'll talk about it, figure out what's going on."Eleanor nodded, even though he couldn't see her. "Okay. Thank you."

After hanging up, she sat down at her desk, her fingers tracing the edge of the photo frame that held the image of her old self. The smile in the picture seemed foreign now, like a relic of another life.

Eleanor couldn't ignore it any longer. Whatever was happening, it wasn't just her imagination. Something—or someone—was lurking in the shadows, threatening the fragile peace she had rebuilt. And this time, she wouldn't be caught off guard.

Eleanor's mind raced as she pieced together the fragments of her unease. The soldiers, the man on the street, the subtle but unmistakable sense of being monitored—it all pointed to something deliberate. Her instincts told her that this wasn't random; it was orchestrated. And if her hunch was correct, the strings were being pulled by the same shadowy organizations she had crossed paths with in the past—those who controlled capital, goods, and resources with a ruthless efficiency to ensure their dominance.

This time, Eleanor was determined to stay ahead of the game. She had spent the past year honing her ability to anticipate her adversaries' moves, learning to think like them, to predict their patterns. She wouldn't wait to react; she would act first.

One sunny afternoon, Eleanor decided to take a calculated risk. She went to pick up James from his office, ostensibly as a spontaneous gesture of affection, but her real purpose was more complex. She needed to confirm a growing suspicion.

When she arrived at his office building, she parked across the street and waited. She knew James's routine well enough to predict when he would step out, and she also knew that if someone were watching her, they'd likely be watching him too.

As the minutes ticked by, her heart pounded in her chest. Finally, she spotted James—or someone who looked exactly like him. He emerged from the building, his stride familiar, his movements calm. Yet, as Eleanor watched closely, something was off. The way he glanced around, the stiffness in his shoulders—it wasn't the relaxed demeanour she knew so well.

Eleanor's breath caught. **A lookalike.**

Her mind raced. What actions were they planning? Why would they need a double of James? To observe her more closely? To manipulate her into trusting the wrong person? Or perhaps, to lead her into a trap?

Her pulse quickened as she started the car, pulling into traffic to follow the doppelgänger at a careful distance. He didn't seem to notice her as he moved through the bustling city streets, heading toward a nondescript café tucked into a quiet corner of a busy block. Eleanor parked a few cars away and watched as he entered the café and took a seat by the window.

Moments later, a man in a dark suit joined him. The lookalike nodded in greeting, but the tension in their interaction was palpable. The man in the suit slid a folder across the table, his expression cold and unreadable. Eleanor strained to see what was inside, but the angle of the window blocked her view. She considered her options, her mind racing. Should she confront the double? Follow him? Or wait to see what he did next?

Her phone buzzed, startling her. It was a message from the real James: **"Meeting ran long. Can I see you for dinner instead?"**

Relief flooded her, but it was quickly tempered by the reality of what she had just discovered. Eleanor typed back a quick reply, keeping her tone casual. **"Sure. See you then."**

But as she put her phone down, her focus sharpened. This was no longer just about her safety or her relationship with James. It was about uncovering the truth behind the layers of deceit surrounding her. Eleanor's grip on the steering wheel tightened. If they thought she would play by their rules, they had underestimated her. This time, she wasn't just surviving—she was hunting.

Two weeks had passed, and Eleanor's world was teetering on the edge of the chaos she thought she had left behind. The unsettling sense of being watched had not subsided; if anything, it had grown stronger. Every street corner seemed to harbour shadows that shifted when she looked away, and every crowd seemed to hold eyes that lingered too long on her and James.

She had spent those weeks carefully observing, piecing together fragments of information from the lookalike's actions and the occasional slip-ups from the shadows trailing her. It was becoming clear: the same people who had once manipulated her into a situation spiralling out of control wanted her back. They didn't see her as a person—they saw her as their **project**, their **guinea pig**, an asset they believed still belonged to them.

But Eleanor wasn't the same woman they had used and discarded. She wasn't going to let them shatter her life again, and she certainly wasn't going to let them ruin her relationship with James. Sitting in the living room of her apartment, Eleanor stared at the faint glow of her laptop screen, her mind racing. James sat across from her, his brow furrowed as he reviewed the scattered notes and diagrams she had compiled over the past two weeks. "We can't keep waiting for them to make the next move," Eleanor said, breaking the silence. Her voice was steady, but the tension in her tone was unmistakable. "If we don't act, they'll keep pushing until we're cornered. We need to figure out who they are, what they want, and how to stop them. "James leaned back, his analytical mind clearly working through the problem. "Agreed," he said after a moment. "But reacting too aggressively could play into their hands. If they're this organized, they'll be ready for a fight." "I know," Eleanor replied, her gaze distant. "But this isn't just about me anymore. If they think they can use you to get to me…" She shook her head, unwilling to finish the thought. James reached across the table, taking her hand in his. "They won't. We won't let them. But we need a plan."Eleanor nodded, her resolve hardening. Over the next several hours, they worked together to outline their strategy. James's methodical nature balanced Eleanor's intuition and resourcefulness, creating a plan that felt both practical and daring.

The Plan to Defend Themselves

1. **Identify the Players**: Eleanor would use her contacts from her time away—people who owed her favors or shared a distrust of the organizations she suspected. Through them, she'd gather intelligence on the group's movements and motives.
2. **Decoy Tactics**: James suggested they use the lookalike to their advantage. If they could trick the group into believing Eleanor was somewhere she wasn't, they might gain an opportunity to act without being watched.
3. **Digital Countermeasures**: James, with his knack for solving puzzles, began setting up traps in Eleanor's online presence—false trails and dummy accounts designed to confuse anyone attempting to track her digitally.
4. **Building an Alliance**: The Siberian Group, Eleanor's old allies, were still a resource she could rely on. She reached out to Lukas,

who listened carefully before agreeing to help. "But this time," he warned, "don't expect clean hands or simple solutions."

## A Moment of Reflection

Late that night, as James worked quietly at his laptop, Eleanor stepped out onto the balcony. The city sprawled before her, a patchwork of lights and shadows. The chaos that had once overwhelmed her now felt like a challenge she was ready to face.

She wouldn't let this ruin her life. She wouldn't let it destroy the happiness she had found with James. The people who thought they could control her had no idea who they were dealing with now.

Eleanor inhaled deeply, the cool night air filling her lungs. She was no longer their experiment. She was the variable they couldn't predict, the one they couldn't control.

And this time, she was ready to fight back.

# Summary

**Disclaimer:** This book is a work of fiction inspired by historical and scientific concepts. While elements of the story draw upon real events and ideas, any resemblance to actual people, events, or organizations is purely coincidental.

www.ingramcontent.com/pod-product-compliance
Lightning Source LLC
Chambersburg PA
CBHW061440150726
47987CB00001B/279